DREAMING

OF

SHADOW

MAN

Also by Debby Meltzer Quick

McKinney Class of 1986
May I Have Your Attention Please
I Just Can't Say I Love You
Absolutely and Totally Smitten
The Stories That Must Be Told

Anomaly
Don't Say a Word
Blinding Justice

DREAMING

OF

SHADOW

MAN

Debby Meltzer Quick

ISBN: 979-8-9871874-6-3
Cover design by: Jai Design
Author photograph: Milana Gilligan Photography
Copyediting & Typesetting by: Nicole Frail Edits, LLC
Chapter head silhouettes by curut design/Canva; EdvanKun/Canva;
   formatoriginalphotos/Canva; shadow by demokoo design/Canva
Section break image by Marco Livolsi/Canva

To Laurie,
my one true Garth.

CHAPTER 1

CLARENCE KEPT HIS EYES CLOSED much longer than necessary. He had made his wish already, but the thought of opening his eyes and having his friends ask what he had wished for drove him to squeeze his eyelids together tight and make a second wish that he would have the room to himself when he opened them, or that his friends would all be rendered mute.

"That must be some wish," Jerry said. Then he chuckled. "Or more than one. You only get one wish, Clare. But I guess it's okay to make it a doozy."

Clarence opened one eye. All four of his friends were staring at him in anticipation. "I know what you wished for," Jessica said with a smirk. "But unfortunately, it's still just the four of us here. Maybe there will be a knock on the door any second now and he'll walk in like he owns the place."

"Who?" Steven asked, his brow furrowed.

Jessica shrugged. "He doesn't have a name yet. I don't think he has a name yet. Clare, does he have a name?"

Clarence sighed. "I can't tell you what I wished for or it won't come true, so I won't confirm or deny anything. But no, he doesn't have a name, or a face, for that matter. He's kind of more of an idea. Like, he's kind of blurry in my head, but he's tall. And sort of muscular, but not too muscular. And he's clean-shaven. But by the end of the day, he has that really great five o'clock shadow, the kind that feels like sandpaper on your face when he kisses you, but the soft kind of sandpaper that doesn't hurt, just bristles."

"Clare hasn't put any thought into this at all," Rachel mumbled. "So you're saying that this five o'clock shadow man wasn't your wish? He sounds a lot like your wish."

Clarence cocked his head. "I'm pretty sure I just told you that I can't reveal my wish or it won't come true."

"Is there a time limit on this wish?" Jessica asked. "I mean, like, did you ask for Shadow Man to appear in front of you instantaneously, or just sometime soon, or before your next birthday?"

Clarence looked at his friend sideways. "I might have just wished for the whole lot of you to disappear, you know. And if so, then wishes don't come true."

"I hate to be that person," Steven said, "but I think you'd better blow the candles out before the whole cake is covered with wax."

"You don't hate to be that person," Rachel said. "You just want cake, and you don't want to have to chew on wax like those weird candy lips my mother always tells me about from when she was a kid. Clare, blow out the candles. If you have enough breath. Do you think you might need some help?"

Clarence rolled his eyes. "I'm twenty-four," he protested. "It's not like I'm eighty. I think I can do it." He inhaled, and then blew hard toward the cake, thinking of all of the germs that would be dispersed on the frosting and then wondering why no one ever talked about that fact. His face reddened as he looked down to find that there was still one candle aglow. He glanced at Rachel, who looked back smugly. He took another breath and aimed for the one remaining flame. The candle extinguished, but then the flame reignited after a few seconds.

Clarence glared at Rachel. "What did you do?"

Rachel laughed. "It would be way too obvious if I made them all trick candles." She reached over and snuffed out the light with her thumb and index finger. "What fun would that be?"

Clarence picked up the giant knife on the table and began to divvy up the cake for his friends. It was chocolate, and the filling was raspberry jam, his favorite. Rachel had picked it up from Cupsnakes, Clarence's favorite bakery, specializing in reptile-themed confections. This one was just a regular two-layer round cake, but it was adorned with frosting lizards and tiny plastic dinosaurs.

"Do I get to keep these?" he asked Rachel as he extracted a T-Rex. "Or do you have to return them to the bakery?"

Rachel grinned. "They're all yours," she said. "As a matter of fact, they're your birthday present. Happy birthday, Clare. And many more." She glanced around at their friend group. "We forgot to sing."

She opened her mouth wide and out poured a foul rendition of the Happy Birthday song, accompanied by Jessica, Steve, and Jerry.

Clarence covered his ears with his hands. "That was awful," he said. "Didn't you all rehearse? It would have been the least you could do."

"It's not my fault that your birthday falls on a Thursday this year," Jerry protested. "I mean, it *is* a school night." Jerry was a high school history teacher who often brought his work home with him and stayed up very late grading essays. "As a matter of fact, we need to head out soon so I can review some more term paper proposals. I need to write my comments and get them all back by Monday."

"Well, then, I guess Clare should open his presents," Jessica said, lifting a gift bag from the floor. "I have an early day tomorrow, so I'll need to hit it, too."

"It's only eight o'clock," Clarence protested. "Guys, my birthday only comes once a year. At least stay to watch a movie or something. I'll make cocoa."

"I wish we could," Steve said.

Clarence could tell that his friends regretted not being able to stay until he was safely tucked into his full-sized bed and ready to slumber. He was the only one in the group who didn't have to work until noon. He was slightly off the linear timetable of his peers. He loved his job, but that was his one issue. He hated to get up before the sun each morning, but if that was what it meant to be aligned with the rest of the world . . .

". . . but I have to catch the five o'clock train in the morning to get to a conference in Billerica and all set up by seven," Steven continued. "That means I need to be in bed in like a half an hour. I might not fall asleep, but I need to have my eyes closed for at least seven hours. I'll be a wreck if I don't."

"You guys are like grown-ups or something," Clarence said. He lifted the bag that Jessica had put in front of him and closed his eyes. "It's heavy," he said. "It's a candle."

Jessica frowned. "That's not fair. You're supposed to look first." Then her face brightened. "But you don't know what kind of candle."

Clarence grinned. "It's that nontoxic masculinity candle that's all over the socials. The one from the hot guy who chops wood."

Jessica's head dropped. "You suck."

Clarence lifted the candle out of the bag, took off the cover, and inhaled deeply. "Wow," he said. "Smells like enlightened lumberjack."

"Gimme," Rachel said as she grabbed the candle. She sniffed it. "Oh God, my ovaries can't take it." The candle was passed around the room.

Jerry took a sniff. "I don't know what you guys are all making a fuss about," he said. "It smells just like me!"

Steve grunted. "I've smelled you, dude," he said affectionately. "You usually smell like Degree antiperspirant and Dial soap." He reached for Jerry's hand. "But don't get me wrong. I love your smell." He reached over for a kiss, then looked up. "Open ours next, Clare. We really need to go."

Soon after, Clarence walked his friends to the door to say goodbye. One by one, they hugged and said good night, wishing Clarence a happy birthday. The last one to leave was Rachel.

"Are you gonna be okay?" she asked. "I mean, do you really want to be alone on your birthday?"

Clarence waited until he heard the ding of the elevator down the hall and then pulled Rachel back inside. "I would be okay if you stayed a bit longer."

Rachel bit her lip. "I have to work in the morning, too," she said. "But it just sucks that you're alone on your birthday. It's so early."

Clarence grinned. Then he put his hands on both of Rachel's cheeks. "They're all gone now," he said softly. "So . . . you're welcome to stay."

Rachel leaned forward, and they came together in a kiss. It was a soft, friendly, affectionate kiss . . . until it wasn't.

"I thought we decided that we weren't doing this anymore," she whispered as Clarence's lips brushed against her neck. "You were just talking about the Shadow Man, and now here you are . . ."

Clarence gasped. "He's not real. He's a fantasy. But right now, you're my fantasy. Stay, Rachel. Stay the night. We can go right to sleep and you can go to work from here." He nuzzled behind her ear, and she shivered.

"But my clothes . . ."

"So your coworkers will either think you got lucky or you slept in your clothes," Clarence said. He reengaged her lips and slowly backed up toward the bedroom, pulling her along.

Rachel allowed herself to be led. "Clarence," she protested. "What even is this? Is this you being lonely on your birthday? Is this a hook up? I mean, we decided to stop because we didn't know, and it was confusing. And none of our friends even know. It feels weird, sort of a reverse being in the closet."

"I know," Clarence said as he sat down at the edge of his bed and pulled Rachel down onto his lap. "I'm sorry about that. I know it's hard. But . . . I don't know. I mean, they keep expecting me to find a boyfriend. And to be honest, Rachel, I'm pretty sure that's still what I want. But I also know that I want you."

"You want me tonight," Rachel said. "But what about tomorrow, after I leave?"

Clarence looked into her eyes. "I don't know," he admitted. "I really don't. Rachel, no matter what, we're friends. You know we're friends. I don't want to lose that. So if you want to go, I won't stop you. Or if you want to stay and just go to sleep, I'll respect that. The most important thing is that we stay friends."

Rachel dismounted from his lap and sat beside him, her breath ragged. "I-I think this ship might have sailed already tonight." She gave him a light kiss and then shrugged. "Friends with benefits, I guess."

Clarence grinned at her and then engulfed her in his arms. He moved the two of them back on the bed and came down on top of his friend.

Rachel was up first the next morning since she had to work. Clarence stayed in bed, but he was awake, listening to her sounds as she moved around his kitchen. He put his hands behind his head and closed his eyes.

It had been a good night, his birthday. He had been surrounded by friends, had received fun gifts, and had spent the night with Rachel. Rachel was uninhibited and a bit wild in bed, and she brought out the animal in him. They laughed a lot during sex, and it was hot. And she had stamina, leading him to want to pace himself to make it last. And when it didn't, she was always up for another round. And not only that, but she was his best friend.

They had met in college, Boston University, five years earlier. They were in a marketing class together and were assigned to work on a group project with two other classmates. Early on, Rachel had Clarence pegged as gay and thought he was attracted to the other male member of their team. But he had shocked her well into the semester when they were the last two left after a work session in the library and had offered to walk her home. Once they arrived at her apartment, he informed her that his father had just died, and he was really feeling the loss. She hugged him close, and the hug turned into a kiss, and then another. . . .

"I thought you were gay," she had whispered in his ear as he lay above her on her single bed.

"So did I," he'd groaned back.

It was clumsy at first, as he figured out how to work her female body and make her moan. But they practiced, and got it right pretty quickly. As the months passed by, they became closer friends, but it was clear that the sex was just an act of comfort and companionship. The friendship was just that—a friendship. And a close friendship.

"But what if I want more?" Rachel had asked at the time.

There was nothing but care in Clarence's eyes when he responded. "I don't know if I can give you more," he'd told her. "I mean, I think I love you but not in a, well, romantic way. And I know I'm attracted to you, and I love being with you, but . . ."

"But you can't see it going any further than that," Rachel stated. Clarence nodded. Rachel nodded back. "So I guess I have to decide if I'm okay with that."

At the time, she'd decided she was not. They remained friends, but they stopped fucking each other and made an effort to never be left alone in an empty bedroom. They never told their friends about what had occurred between them. Over time, their friendship deepened, her friends became his friends, and his friends became hers. He brought Jerry, and she brought Steve, and soon, they became Jerry and Steve. Jessica somehow worked her way into the equation. Shortly after, there was Timothy, and Clarence's embarrassing crush on their straight friend. Timothy graduated a year before them and moved to St. Louis. Then came Tom, and in a battle of affections, Rachel won his, and they dated all through senior year. Eventually, Tom was caught with Richard, and Rachel was left by herself. Then

Clarence and Rachel, lonely and dejected, fell back into bed together. It was like that for the next four years. They would have relationships, sometimes at the same time, sometimes not, but when they were both single and lonely, they consoled each other with their bodies.

Rachel came back into the room, showered and fully dressed, carrying a mug of coffee. "Do you mind if I take this with me?" she asked.

Clarence shook his head. "No, it's fine. I know where you live." He sat up, folding his legs in front of him, and reaching his hand out toward Rachel. "Come here," he encouraged.

Rachel walked over to the bed, put the mug down on the nightstand, and sat. She took his hand. "I have to go in a minute," she said.

Clarence nodded. "I know," he said. "I just . . . I just wanted to thank you, and apologize. I feel like I'm always apologizing to you. I-I just didn't want to be alone last night, and I didn't want to be with just anyone. But I also don't want to . . . well, hurt or confuse you."

Rachel snickered. "Clare, I'm a grown woman. I know what I'm getting myself into when I get myself into it. I was here, too, not just you, and I wanted it, too. I didn't want you to spend your birthday night alone. And I wanted it to be me that was with you."

Clarence squeezed her hand and looked down. "I'm sorry that they were talking about, you know, the Shadow Man like that. If they knew, they wouldn't do that in front of you."

Rachel shrugged, her voice controlled. "I could have a Shadow Man, too, for all they know. I mean, I'm okay, Clare. Really. I'm a big girl. We're best friends. I want the Shadow Man for you, too, if it means he makes you happy. You know, I really do think you're gay. Does that make sense? I mean, emotionally gay. Is that a thing?"

"I don't know," Clarence said. "Maybe. Probably. I think you're right. I really love your body, Ray, and I love so many things about you. It's just . . ."

"I know," Rachel said, nodding. "It's just not all connected, the way it should be. I get it." She stood. "I have a job to get to. I should be going." She reached down and kissed Clarence's cheek. "I'm glad you had a good birthday, my friend. I hope your wish comes true."

Clarence watched his friend as she walked out of his bedroom door with her mug of coffee. Moments later, he heard the front door close. He lay down and closed his eyes again, in the hopes of getting a few more hours of sleep before he himself had to get up and get ready for work. He thought back on his wish from the night before and hoped he hadn't already jinxed it.

It was his greatest wish for Rachel to find happiness, even if it meant it wasn't with him. And he was very confident that it was *not* going to be with him.

CHAPTER 2

RACHEL WALKED OUT OF THE elevator and smiled timidly at her coworkers lingering around the receptionist's desk. She was still relatively new to this agency, and she was not confident that she knew all of their names yet. Therefore, it was easier to not call anyone by name. A smile or a small wave would have to suffice. She had never been good at names. For a long time, she had Steve and Jerry confused, even though Steve had been her friend before she brought him into the group and he had met and fallen for Jerry. She had too much going on in her brain to keep matching names with faces. She did much better with books. When she read, she could keep everything straight, even the most intricate or convoluted of plots. It was her superpower. That's what made her such a great content editor. She could find the tiniest plot holes or tense errors. If only she could find the plot holes in her own life story.

It wasn't unusual for her to fall for men, or boys, that were not entirely accessible to her, like Clarence. It started in elementary school when she fell for the exotic boy who was only at her school for a year. His father had some sort of job that brought them from England only for twelve months, but it made no difference to eleven-year-old Rachel. She crushed on Liam every day of that school year, constantly giving him smiles and finding excuses to talk to him. On the last day of school, he approached her. "My family's going on holiday starting tomorrow, for a fortnight," he said. Rachel almost swooned every time Liam spoke. This time was no different. Then he said *camper* in his British accent. "My dad rented a camper, and we'll be driving to the Grand Canyon. It will be smashing, except for my little brother going mental all the time when he's knackered. The best will be that we'll be sleeping in the car park. And we can use the loo when the camper's moving."

Rachel only understood half of the words that Liam said, but she smiled and nodded as if it all made sense. It took her some time to realize that Liam had come over to say goodbye. "Oh," she said sadly. "So you're going back to England after?"

Liam nodded. "But I thought it might be nice for us to have a bit of a snog before I left, if you like. I thought maybe you would fancy a snog."

Rachel stared at him. "I have no idea what a snog is," she admitted. "Is it like a collectable bottle cap?"

Liam laughed. "You Americans are very strange. A snog is a right kiss. Maybe a little kiss?" He shrugged.

Rachel could feel her heart pounding through her training bra. "Um, I've never had a snog with anyone before," she said. "Or kissed anyone either."

"Neither have I," Liam said, kicking the floor with what he had once told her were called trainers, but were really sneakers. "But if we don't now, we won't have a chance for another go." He tilted his head down and then looked up at her through impossibly long, dark lashes. Right then she knew she would follow him anywhere. She wondered if she would be able to stow away in his family's rented camper for their . . . holiday? Maybe he had meant the Fourth of July. She wondered what it would be like to sleep in a car park, whatever that was, and use a loo.

"Okay," she said shyly. Her face felt hot. She followed him down the hall and around the corner near the teachers' lounge.

"No one will see us here," he said. "But we don't have long before Mrs. Jamison misses us."

Rachel nodded. "What do we do now?"

Liam's mouth hung open slightly. "I think I put my hands on your hips." He put his hands on her hips. Her legs went weak. "And you put your hands on my shoulders." She put her hands on his shoulders. "And then…"

Liam leaned closer, and closer, until eventually there was no space between them and it made sense for their lips to touch. They touched their lips, neither of them moving at all. Then, at the same time, they both puckered and kissed each other like they would kiss their grandmothers, but on the lips. They pulled apart quickly.

"That's alright, init?" Liam asked.

Rachel nodded quickly. They stayed there, standing, hands in place, staring at each other. Then Rachel licked her lips and leaned toward Liam again. This time, the contact lingered for a moment, and then Liam moved his lips. Rachel moved hers back. She felt the tip of Liam's tongue on her lip, but then it withdrew.

"Liam! Rachel!"

They broke apart when they heard the sound of the vice principal admonishing them. It was the last day of fifth grade, and the last day of elementary school, so they were only given a harsh verbal reprimand and sent back to class. They didn't have a chance to be alone again for the rest of the day, but whenever they made eye contact, they smiled at each other knowingly. And at the end of the day, Liam got into his father's car and was gone forever.

Rachel wondered what ever happened to Liam. She wondered if he was still in England. She wondered if she should look him up on Instagram but then realized she didn't recall his last name. She would have to look for her class picture the next time she went to visit her mother. Liam and their kiss had lingered in her mind for all of sixth grade, and she failed to notice any of the other boys in her junior high class. She was lingering with his snogging ghost.

It was sophomore year when she next allowed her heart to creak open and beat for another boy. This time it was Robby Sneider, and he was on the basketball team. Rachel went to basketball games with her group of friends, but she always brought a book. Oftentimes, the games would end and she would still be buried in an exciting chapter, her friends having to pull her out of the gym by the arms of her jacket. It was exactly this behavior that led Robby to notice her. She didn't recognize him when he approached her in the hallway outside the cafeteria one afternoon. "Hey, Rachel," he called out when he was almost in her face.

She looked up from her book. "Yeah?" she said. She had to look up even more to see his face. He was well over six feet tall.

He smiled at her. "What are you reading?"

"*A Wrinkle in Time*," she said, showing him the cover. "It's my favorite book. I've read it, like, four times."

Robby wrinkled his forehead. "But you already know how it ends," he said.

Rachel nodded. "I know."

Robby shook his head, as if to remove cobwebs. "I see you reading your books at my games all the time. Don't you like basketball?"

Rachel shrugged. "It's alright," she said. "The games are just so long, you know?"

Robby laughed. "Yeah, I know." He scratched the back of his neck, as if delaying while he thought. "Do you want to go get a Coke or something after school? We don't have practice today. They're fumigating the gym or something. I think someone saw a roach. I'd really like to hang out with you, you know, and get to know you."

"Uh," Rachel said. "I-I guess so."

Robby nodded. "Great! I'll meet you in the parking lot after school. I have the red Corolla over by the dumpsters. I leave it unlocked so you can get in if I'm not there when you get there. We can go to Tammy's Diner."

Rachel tilted her head. "But that's on the other side of town. Why don't we just go to Cookies, down the street?"

Robby shrugged. "Reasons," he said. "Listen, I have to get to history class. I'll see you after school."

The reason was that Robby had a girlfriend. He told Rachel about her right away. But he also liked Rachel. She fascinated him with her indifference to the basketball games and her love of the written word. Even though Rachel knew that Robby was taken, she fell into his arms the first time he reached out to kiss her, and she enjoyed the times when they were able to steal away to a supply closet or his car for secret make out sessions and conversations. Sometimes, she would pass Robby and his popular girlfriend Mandy in the hallway, and rather than make eye contact, or witness them holding hands, she would look at her own hands as if the secret to the universe were written on her fingers.

Robby graduated at the end of the year, and he and Mandy went off to Boston College together, both on sports scholarships. Their goodbye was as final as her snog with Liam years earlier. Robby might as well have left for the moon. The one consolation is that they'd never slept together. Robby had never pressured her, or even really asked her for that matter. He really seemed to enjoy just being with her, talking, or kissing. That made it even worse. He liked her; he wasn't just attracted to her. But she could never truly be his. Maybe she would never be anyone's. That idea got her through the next two years of high school and into college, until she met Clarence.

Speaking of never truly belonging to someone . . . Rachel did everything she could not to fall for Clarence. She . . . well, she told herself not to. She begged herself not to. She reminded herself that it would never amount to a serious relationship, marriage, a house, and three beautiful children. She looked at other men, but they never looked back. She eventually realized that she must be wearing an "I'm not available" sign across her forehead, warding them all off. She even tried to fix up Clarence with the gay men she knew so he would be off the market, decreasing her already zero percent chance of something happening between them. Sometimes it worked for short periods of time, but she wasn't a very good matchmaker. She didn't know what it was that Clarence wanted in a man; she only knew what he wanted in a woman, and in this case, it was her. And it wasn't for happily ever after. That was even more obvious at this point in their lives.

She flicked on her computer and waited for it to boot up. It took much longer than it should for modern technology. It was more likely that the agency hadn't upgraded the system for much too long. It was amazing that anything ever got done around there, but it did, and it was Rachel's job to do a lot of it. She opened the file to the manuscript she was working on and found where she left off. Then she closed out the world and honed her skills on the story, word for word, letter for letter.

It was a romance. Her agency specialized in them. There were all types of romances: enemies-to-lovers, friends-to-lovers, brother's best friend, best friend's brother, sports romances, mafia romances, romantic comedies, romantic thrillers . . . female-female, male-male, bi-awakenings . . . but not one gay friend ends up in happiness with their opposite-sex best friend. It was unheard of. Intellectually, Rachel knew why. Gay men were programmed differently than straight men. They were born that way. Maybe Rachel should write her own romance novel. The only issue was that she was not a writer; she was a reader. She was a talented reader who made books prettier and easy to read for other readers, and got paid to do it. It was as if she was born for this job. She was born to get to the end and see the happy ending.

It would just be much better if she could write a happy ending for herself.

Two minutes before noon, she surfaced again for air. It was her stomach that nudged her to look up, and when she did, she noticed that it was a beautiful day outside. She thought about going out to get lunch, remembering that she had woken up that morning in Clarence's bed and hadn't been able to pack herself a lunch. If Clarence had been her boyfriend, a boyfriend from a romance novel, he probably would have gotten up with her and made her something to bring to work. Maybe a bologna sandwich, or even peanut butter and jelly. An apple. A small bag of chips. Maybe he would have included a little love note for her to find during her break, causing her to crack a smile in the lunchroom, a secret grin between lovers, leading her coworkers to speculate its source.

She closed her eyes in an effort to refocus. She was sabotaging herself again. This type of thinking got her nowhere. She stood and stretched her taut muscles and vowed to start getting up on the hour to walk around her desk. It was supposed to be good for you. But for now, she needed food for her stomach and fresh air for her soul.

It was almost spring, and the air was getting warmer. No one had alerted the wind, though, which blew cold and lazily through the downtown streets as Rachel walked along in her sensible flat shoes, listening for some sort of light fare to call out to her. She pulled her jacket around her tighter and avoided an oblivious woman walking right toward her, staring at her phone screen. She considered a slice of pizza from a stand, but she didn't want to risk dribbling grease down the front of her already rumpled shirt, which she reminded herself she had first put on the previous morning. So she settled for a salad from the make-your-own salad place and cringed at the price when she put it on the scale at the end. She went back outside and found an empty bench, saying a prayer that some talkative local would not come and sit beside her and start to blurt out their origin story. It happened sometimes. But today, she didn't have the patience to listen, nod, smile, or show empathy at just the right moments. Today she needed quiet so she could hear the thoughts inside her own head.

But when it got too quiet, it was Clarence's voice she heard talking to her.

"We're best friends, Rachel," he said. "I don't want to lose you as a friend. But still I want you in my bed."

"But sleeping with you is messing with my head," her inner voice said back. "It's keeping me from looking for someone who might really want me. All of me."

"But no one ever has," Clarence said back. Then she realized it wasn't Clarence's voice saying those admonishing words. It was the voice of her father. She quickly shook her head. No. She wasn't going to deal with that baggage at the moment. Her father was not invited into her midday Clarence crisis. There was plenty of room for him in her nightmares.

"I'm sorry," phantom Clarence said. "I don't mean to keep you from meeting someone. I just want you to be happy."

Rachel nodded slightly. "Good," she said. "So we're on the same page. We're just friends. And I'm open for business. I'll let everyone know I'm on the market and looking."

"Great," invisible Clarence said. "I'll keep my eye open for you. And for me. We'll both find someone wonderful, and we'll all grow old together as best friends, and our kids will be best friends."

Rachel smiled. "Yes," she said. "That's exactly what I want."

"Me too," disembodied Clarence said. "But in the meantime, do you want to come over tonight to watch Netflix and Chill?"

Rachel let out an exasperated sigh. "Clarence, you know what that means, right? It's not really about watching a movie and relaxing."

She could almost see the smirk in ghost Clarence's voice. "Yeah, babe. I know."

Rachel shook her head, successfully dislodging this fruitless conversation from her mind. She focused on her salad.

When she finished her lunch, she tossed her trash in an overflowing garbage can, making sure it stayed balanced on the top. She hated littering. She walked the two blocks back to her office and rode the elevator up to the third floor. When she emerged, it appeared that all of the same coworkers were standing around the same desk, chatting.

One of the women looked up at Rachel and smiled. "Rachel, you're single, right?"

Rachel stopped in her tracks and actually took a step backward. Was it possible that Chrissy . . . no, Katie? Maybe Kaitlin had heard her imaginary conversation with Clarence over lunch? No, of course not. So she nodded.

"Yeah, I am."

Caroline? Cathy? Carlie? Whoever . . . smiled at her. "My brother just moved here a few weeks ago, and he's single. What are you, about twenty-five?"

"Yeah, about," Rachel admitted. "But I don't know . . ."

"Come on, Becca," another employee said to the sister of the new resident in town. "I don't think it's a good idea to ambush the new girl into a blind date. And with your brother? What if it doesn't work out?"

Becca? Her name was Becca? Rachel was so sure it had started with a C.

"No, it's okay," she said. "I don't mind. But I have a lot going on right now, so it's not a good time. Maybe later?"

Becca nodded, satisfied. "Sounds great! You know, he's really good looking. Everyone back home thinks so. All of my friends had a crush on him during high school. If you wait a minute, I'll get my phone and show you a picture—"

"No, that's okay," Rachel said, moving close to the hallway. "I'll hit you up to show me another time. But right now I need to finish the last five chapters of *The Duke of Swellington* before the end of the day today. Hey, if I don't see you before the end of the day, Becca, have a great weekend."

Rachel proceeded down the hall and ducked into her office. She sat down in her chair and reactivated her computer by moving her mouse back and forth on its pad. Just then, her phone buzzed in her purse. She pulled it out and looked at the text before her.

"You left your wallet here this morning," text-Clarence told her.

Rachel furrowed her brow. If she left her wallet at Clarence's place, how did she buy her lunch? Then it occurred to her that she had used her pay-by-phone app.

"Crap," she texted back. "I guess I'll have to pick it up over the weekend."

"That's okay," the instant response came back. "I can just bring it by your place tonight. Do you want me to bring some takeout? We can watch a movie or something."

Rachel dropped her head down onto her arms on the desk. She sighed. Here it was. Netflix and Chill. And she was going to say yes. "Sure," she typed. "Maybe you can bring Thai?"

 CHAPTER 3

CLARENCE ROLLED ONTO HIS BACK and sighed. "That was fun," he said, his voice a bit raspy. It was no wonder it was raspy after all of his recent, uncontrollable verbal emissions.

Rachel pulled the sheet and blanket up to her neck and nodded. "Yeah," she said wistfully, staring at the ceiling.

Clarence, catching the tone, rolled halfway toward her and put his hand on her shoulder. "What's wrong?" he asked, his forehead creasing.

"Nothing," Rachel said flatly.

Clarence was not convinced. "Ray, I've known you for five years. Intimately. I know when there's something on your mind. Spill, or I'll be forced to tickle you." He gave her a sinister grin. Rachel returned it with a weak smile.

"It's just . . ." She turned to face him. "What was it like for you, when your father died?"

Clarence fell back onto his pillow. It was not a question he was expecting, and it caught him off guard. "Well, it sucked, obviously."

Rachel sat up and looked at him. "No," she said softly. "I know it sucked. I know how hard it was for you. I guess I just mean, well, how has it been for you now, you know, dealing with it?"

Clarence sat up next to her but looked toward the door in contemplation. "I have no idea," he said. "I mean, I guess I have no choice but to deal with it. If I choose not to, nothing changes. He's still gone."

"Do you ever talk to him?" Rachel asked tentatively.

Clarence nodded, his face slack. "I do," he said. "Sometimes, I see or hear something I want to share with him, and I want to text his number, but I figure by now someone else has had it assigned to them, so I'd freak out if I got a reply."

"I hear they have these phones in Japan," Rachel said, "where you can go and call your loved one who's dead, and tell them anything you want. I guess tons of people go to do it."

"What's the point?" Clarence shrugged. "I mean, yeah, you get to say what you want, but you never know if they really . . ." He fell back down on the pillow. "What brought all of this on, anyway?"

Rachel lay down next to him, their shoulders grazing each other. "Do you ever wonder what it would have been like if you . . . if you'd had the chance to, you know, tell him—"

"You mean come out to him?" Clarence closed his eyes. "Yeah, of course. I mean, I planned to do it a lot earlier, but then he got sick, and it seemed like it could wait. I had no idea that he would, well, be gone."

"He wasn't the same person when he died," Rachel said.

Clarence nodded. "He wasn't the same person for three years before he died. Dementia has to be the worst disease in the world, especially since he was so young. It's like it took him twice. If I had come out to him . . . I have no idea how he would have reacted. And then he would forget. So it made no sense."

"What do you think he would have said," Rachel asked, "if you had told him when he was able to understand?"

Clarence sat with that for a few moments. "I think he would have had questions," he said. "Not, like, procedural questions or anything. He would just want to understand. He would want to make sure that I was sure. And then he would do what he could to support me. My dad was kind of older when he had me. And my older siblings are so, well, normal. You've met them. They'd make a very boring movie if anyone ever dared to write about them. I think the whole plot would revolve around me and my antics."

Rachel smiled. "I'd like to think that I'd be in that movie, at least in a supporting role."

Clarence took her hand lightly, and then squeezed it. "You're my best friend, Rachel," he whispered. "You'd even be in the sequel." They lay for a minute in silence, still holding hands. "What made you ask about my father?" Clarence finally asked. "It seems kind of random, especially after epic sex."

Rachel laughed. "Epic," she mimicked. Then she let go of his hand. "I guess I was just thinking about my own father."

"Oh," Clarence said. Now he understood. There was a history between Rachel and her father that he didn't quite understand. "What were you thinking about?"

Rachel stared at the ceiling, and then sighed. "I guess that sometimes I think it's like he's dead, you know," she said. "Or that it would be better if he was, because that would mean that it wasn't his choice to be, well, absent. But then I think that it wouldn't be a relief for him to be gone. It would just be a totally different kind of hurt."

Clarence stared at her. "That's very insightful," he said. "I'm really impressed. Yeah, I can see what you mean. But I bet that it's hard to have him out there, always having some sort of hope that things will change, but they never do. At least I know that when I go back to California, my father will be in the same place as I left him last time I saw him."

Rachel appeared to be trying to look horrified at this statement, but she failed and started to laugh. "Oh my God, Clare," she said. "Only you could make me laugh when talking about your deceased father. But I get what you're saying." She cozied up to his side, resting her cheek on his chest. "I just wish—" She stopped.

Clarence pulled her closer. "What do you wish?"

Rachel gave him a lopsided grin. "If I tell you my wish, it won't come true."

Clarence chuckled. "That's only for birthday candles."

"You tell me yours and I'll tell you mine."

Clarence shook his head. "I don't want to tempt fate. But you don't have to tell me your wish if you don't want to." He kissed the side of her head. "Do you want me to go home?"

Rachel stiffened. "No. I mean, well, you can if you want, but tomorrow's Saturday, so I don't have to work. You can stay if you want. Maybe we can go get breakfast, or brunch in the morning. Or you can go home if you want to. It's up to you."

Clarence felt the old, persistent feeling of guilt wash through him. He knew it was his fault. He knew what he was doing to Rachel was wrong, but he felt helpless to stop it. He was being just as unavailable to her as her father, but in this case it was worse, because he was right there beside her, taunting her. She wanted something from him that he couldn't give her. He wanted to be able to give it to her, but it just wasn't there in his heart. He loved her so much, but it was a different kind of love than what he sought. It was comfortable, familiar. He felt at home in it, as if he were wrapped up in a warm blanket in front of a fire toasting marshmallows when he was with Rachel. But the fire was always external. What he was missing was the passion, the fire inside, the burning. And to be completely honest, he missed the fact that she didn't have a dick. He was a gay man. He liked dick. There was no use denying it.

"I think maybe I should go," he said softly. He gave her one more squeeze and then let go. "I have a lot of errands tomorrow, and then I have to work on Sunday. So, yeah." He gave her a quick kiss and then got out of bed.

"Oh," Rachel said, her tone nearly breaking him. "Okay. Yeah. I mean, I have a lot to do tomorrow, too. And it's better if you're not here, because then I'd feel, like, all this pressure to actually get up in the morning and shower and get dressed and stuff."

Clarence slipped on his boxer briefs, and then his jeans, turning away so he couldn't see the look on Rachel's face while she made up excuses as to why it was okay that he was leaving when she clearly wanted him to stay.

"I had a really good time," he told her as he pulled his shirt over his head. "I enjoyed the movie. And, you know, the company. I'm glad you forgot your wallet this morning." He sat on the edge of the bed and put on his socks. "Do you want to meet for lunch this week before I go to work?"

Rachel didn't answer right away, and Clarence turned to look at her. She was sitting up again and looking at her hands. Her face was unreadable.

"I don't know," she finally answered. "I mean, maybe. I'm not sure. This woman at work, Becca. She has this brother that just moved here, and she wants to introduce me to him. I told her I'd like that, and she's gonna set it up. I don't know when that's happening, so I'll have to let you know if I'm free."

Clarence felt his blood run cold. "Oh," he said. "Yeah. That's cool. So, what, you're gonna like, show him around town or something?"

He started to put on his shoes so he didn't have to look at her face. He couldn't tell if she was telling the truth or just trying to get a reaction from him. It wasn't like Rachel to lie, or try to make him jealous. There really must be a brother for her to meet. Then why did she sound so, well, tentative?

"I'm not sure," Rachel answered in a low voice. "I think . . . maybe she wants to fix us up. I don't know. I mean, I don't mind meeting him. I can always use more friends."

Clarence felt like he had been kicked in the stomach. "Right," he said. "Friends. You can never have too many friends." Clarence and Rachel were friends, after all. Friends who fucked.

"Yeah, so I'll have to let you know about lunch," Rachel said, her voice slightly shaky. "I mean, we can work around it, I guess."

"That sounds good."

Clarence finished tying his second sneaker and stood. He approached Rachel, about to give her a kiss, but then thought better of it and gave her a peck on the cheek.

"I guess I'll just text you tomorrow to check in."

Rachel nodded. "Thanks for bringing dinner."

Clarence nodded. "Anytime."

He had a feeling that something in their relationship had just shifted, and he didn't know how or why.

"Sleep well."

He walked to the door, unlocked it, reset the lock on the knob, and stepped outside, closing it. Then he leaned up against the locked door and closed his eyes.

He knew that Rachel was at some sort of turning point. That had been clear to him when she started talking about her father and how he was never there for her. She was making connections and picking up on a pattern. Clarence had picked up on it long ago, and it caused him bouts of acid reflux when he thought about what he was doing to her. But it had been so long now, and he didn't know how to not be this way with Rachel. He didn't know how not to crave her body, how not to long to see the v-shaped birthmark on her hip, not to stare into those deep-brown puppy eyes and run his fingers through those bouncy brown curls as they kissed deeply, their bodies close.

Sex was their love language, but love was not supposed to cause pain. It was supposed to relieve it. The thought of him being the cause of her pain . . .

And then there was the thing about the coworker's brother. Was that just a ploy to make him jealous when he told her he wanted to go home? Was it a punishment? Or was she trying to protect herself by putting this between them? Or, maybe, she really was open to meeting someone, to starting an actual healthy relationship with someone who would want her, one hundred percent.

He thought back to the wish he had made on his birthday candles, just one day earlier. He had wished for Rachel to find happiness, and he knew inside that it would not be with him. But he still wasn't sure he wanted it to be with someone else. That thought led to a moment of self-loathing. He knew how selfish he was being. He knew he was holding her back every time he called her for a meet up. It was keeping her from being out there, from being available.

He would encourage her to meet this coworker's brother. It might not lead to anything, but it could. And he had absolutely no right to get in the way of her finding the right person. Anything he did to stop the natural progression would make him the sort of monster he could never live with.

He made his way to his car, got inside, and turned the ignition. He set his Bluetooth to Spotify, and put on the *Heartstopper* soundtrack. Those songs always led him to feel something, though he wasn't sure what. He didn't know if it was the key the songs were in, or the story they represented, that of two young men finding love and defying the odds. It was a sweet, refreshing tale, even if both boys had to overcome obstacles in order to be there for each other. Wasn't that what love was about? The urge to make yourself a better person, the person your partner already saw inside of you, waiting to come out into the fresh air and thrive? Clarence knew he was a better person than the one he was when he was with Rachel, and he knew she deserved better. He wanted to be better, just for knowing her. And being better meant that he had to do something, something to show her that her happiness was important to him. And not just a wish on a birthday cake.

When he arrived home fifteen minutes later, he stripped down to his underwear and went into the bathroom, brushed his teeth, and splashed water on his face. In his bedroom, he sat on the bed, his phone in hand. He opened it up to the long text chain he had going with Rachel. "I hope you sleep well," he typed. "And I hope everything goes well when you meet your coworker's brother this week. I can't wait to hear all about it." He turned down the volume on the phone and plugged it into the charger on his nightstand. Then he crawled under the covers, turned off his bedside lamp, and planted his face on his pillow. The pillow smelled of Rachel's shampoo.

On Sunday, Clarence arrived at the museum half an hour early so he could get some lunch in the cafeteria. Sunday was pesto pasta day, his favorite. Carlo scooped some steamed vegetables onto the plate next to the entrée and gave him a familiar smile. Clarence smiled back as he took his plate.

At the register, Marian gave him his thirty percent employee discount and then threw a free cookie on his tray. "You look like you could use some sugar, honey," she said affectionately.

Clarence nodded his thanks with a grin. "Thanks, Museum Mom." It was a peanut butter chocolate chunk cookie—again, his favorite. His mom still made them from a special recipe every time he visited, and Marian had heard the story.

Clarence looked around the dining area until he spotted his coworker Todd sitting by himself at a table by the window. He carried his tray across the room. "Mind if I join you?"

Todd looked up and smiled. "I figured you'd probably show up early today," he said. "I was thinking of packing a lunch, but then I thought better. It's pesto day." He motioned to the chair across from him, and Clarence sat. "You look tired. Late night?"

Clarence shrugged. "Not really," he said. "I just couldn't sleep very well. A lot on my mind."

Todd looked at him in concern. "Is everything okay?" he asked. "What's going on?"

Clarence had worked with Todd for the past two years, and he was the closest thing he had to a friend outside his college circle. "Just some stuff with my friend," he said. "I'm worried about her."

"Rachel?" Todd asked.

Clarence's eyes went wide. "Yeah. How did you know that?"

Todd shrugged. "You talk about her a lot. And when you do, you look, well, sort of defeated. Like you worry about her."

Clarence pondered that statement. "I guess," he said. "I-I worry about her being lonely. And I think she has these expectations around relationships. Like that meeting the right person will fill all of the empty holes in her life."

"I think we all feel that way," Todd said. "I mean, we all have holes left from past relationships."

"That's true," Clarence conceded. "But I don't think I've been a very supportive friend to her, and I want to help more. She . . . has a date this week, and I'm hoping it will be something good for her."

"Then why do you look like you want the date to crash and burn?"

Clarence felt his head jerk back like whiplash. "I do?" he asked. "I-I guess I didn't realize that."

"Well, she's your friend," Todd said. "I mean, it's always weird between women and men when they're friends."

Clarence raised an eyebrow. "But I'm her gay best friend," he reminded Todd. "I thought every woman wanted a GBFF."

"Maybe," Todd said. "I mean, I have Joann, and Joann's married to Peter, and I'm married to Ken, so we have that. No weird feelings between us. But you and Rachel are single, and you've been really dependent on each other for years for emotional support."

Clarence wondered if somehow Todd had worked out the true dynamics of Clarence's relationship with Rachel over the past couple of years.

"Maybe it would be better if both of us were in relationships. I mean, then the pressure would be off, you know? We wouldn't both feel like finding someone would take something away from each other."

Todd nodded. "You said she had a date coming up this week. Maybe you need to get out there, too, and find someone to distract you."

"I guess," Clarence said. "But I don't know anyone. And I'm really not into the bar scene. It's too hard with my work schedule. And I'm not really looking for just a hookup. I mean, if I'm gonna do it, I should do it right. Do you know anyone?"

"Not offhand," Todd said. "But I can call Ken over dinner break later and see if he can think of anyone. He has a much better pool of men, working at the Boston Garden. Maybe he can find you a nice, closeted member of one of the pro sports teams."

Clarence quickly shook his head. "I don't think so," he said. "I could just see that ending in some sort of tabloid scandal, with me in the middle. I can already see the headline: Big Tall Basketballer Found Balling with Archeologist. Dug Himself into a Big Hole. Or Maybe a Smaller One."

Todd laughed. "Okay, so we'll skip the pro athletes. But there's a ton of guys in the office, and there are vendors and stuff. I'll just have him keep his eyes open. Is it okay if I ask him?"

Clarence sighed. He couldn't see any reason to say no. Not because of Rachel. If he held back because of her, he was doing the same thing to himself that he was doing to her. No, he had to stop the madness. Starting now.

"Okay," he told his friend. "I'm in."

CHAPTER 4

RACHEL HAD ALMOST SPILLED IT all on Friday night.

Clarence had asked her what she'd wished. She hadn't even meant to say she had a wish. Sometimes, Clarence was just her best friend, someone she could confide in. But the one thing she couldn't share with him was the one thing she needed to talk to him about the most. She almost told him that she wanted to resolve her issues with her father so she could move on to a healthy relationship.

It must have been why she'd told him that she had a date that week even though she had turned down her coworker's offer to introduce her to her brother. She wasn't even sure if it had been a legitimate offer. Sometimes people said they wanted to set up their friends or family, but even when everyone was in agreement, it never happened. It seemed like a good idea in their head when they offered, but when the time actually came, they realized it was a bad match, or they just couldn't be bothered to make the effort. Either way, it didn't matter. Rachel wasn't going to go out with Becca's brother. She knew nothing about him. She didn't even know his name. She didn't even really know Becca. Until that conversation, she had thought her name was Charlotte. Or maybe Clair. Why was she so stuck on the letter C? So yeah, meeting with Becca's brother was just an excuse. A bad one. Because now Clarence would want to know how it went.

She spent all day Saturday in her sweatpants and a T-shirt puttering around her apartment. She halfheartedly cleaned her kitchen and tidied the table in the dining area. She meant to clean the bathroom but somehow never got around to it. As soon as the sun set, she settled herself in front of the TV and binge-watched *Gilmore Girls*, her favorite throwback guilty pleasure. It was late when her phone started to buzz that she had text messages. She rolled her eyes. It was probably Clarence with a booty text. But three nights in a row?

She forced herself to pick up her phone and hold it up in front of her so her face could unlock the screen. Her brows went up. The three quick texts weren't from Clarence. They were from their mutual friend, Jessica.

Jessica
Hey

Are you up?

what are you doing tomorrow

Rachel had to think about it for a second. Was she free tomorrow? She had planned to sleep late, then go to the coffee shop to read and drink coffee, and then maybe get lunch and sit at home. Sounded like a full day.

Rachel
Nothing

Jessica
I'm not doing anything either let's do nothing together

Rachel
Or maybe we could do something

Jessica
Like what

Rachel
Idk, what do you want to do

Jessica
Idk

This exchange went on for a while until they finally decided to sleep in and then meet at Cafe Georgie at 11:30. Rachel immediately regretted agreeing to that time. It meant she had to get up by ten to take a shower, and then do her hair, get dressed, and act human in front of people before noon. But she had made a commitment and she had to stick with it. It was ten o'clock now. She finished the current episode she was watching and got ready for bed. Then she slipped between the sheets with a plan to read for an hour and then go to sleep.

Unfortunately, her plan didn't work out. By the time she looked up, it was twelve thirty. She closed her eyes and sighed. Reading put her in a time warp. She never tired of reading, even though it was a large part of her job. She reluctantly slipped a bookmark into her book, still dying to know what happened next in the story. It would have to wait until the next night. She turned off the light and tried to sleep.

When she woke up, it seemed as if only a few hours had passed, and that might have been the case. She had laid in bed for what felt like hours just thinking about her life. She thought about her father, and what it was like growing up living in the same house as him. It was almost as if he hadn't even lived there. He was always off somewhere doing the right thing for those who needed it. He was a doctor, a surgeon to be more specific. He was well known in the community for projects that led him overseas to Africa to fix people who would otherwise not get fixed. When she was a child, she was so proud of him and told everyone she knew what a superhero he was. He helped people. He gave of himself to help them. He was selfless.

Except that none of that was true. Yes, he did go to Africa and perform surgery on people who needed it where it wasn't available. But it wasn't out of the kindness of his heart. Dr. Jeffrey Morris was a textbook narcissist. The first time Rachel had seen the definition of *narcissism*, she knew it was true. It was her mother who showed it to her, shortly after the separation. She wanted Rachel to realize that there had been nothing either of them could have done to make things different. But it was too late. The damage had already been done. Rachel saw herself as unworthy of the love of a man, and almost didn't bat an eye when someone she fell for didn't reciprocate her feelings. Almost.

She forced herself to sit up and swing her feet over the side of the bed. Then she willed herself to stand. And that's when she felt it. The first obvious signs that her period had appeared during the night. She crossed her legs and made her way to the bathroom, sat on the toilet, and hung her head in despair. Well, at least she hadn't accidently gotten pregnant with the gay man who loved to fuck her but didn't love her enough to put a ring on it. There was always that.

She took a shower and then dressed in her period underwear, loose pants, and a baggy T-shirt. She stuffed her purse with pads and tampons, put on her shoes, and headed for the door. She would most likely get to Cafe Georgie before Jessica, but the sooner she got her first infusion of caffeine, the sooner she could feel human. Halfway to the coffee shop, it started to rain. By the time she found a parking spot three blocks away, the rain was coming down in buckets. She put the car in park and reached to the floor of the passenger seat for her umbrella. Her hand came up empty.

"Shit."

She lifted her butt so she could swivel around to look in the back seat. No umbrella. The only other option was the trunk. She grabbed an old fast food bag that still smelled of French fries, held it over her head, and got out of the car.

Her hair was soaked by the time she finished the fruitless trunk search for her umbrella. She imagined that she must have left it somewhere under a chair. It was probably residing in someone else's front closet now. At this point, the rain was dripping down her neck and inside of her shirt. She didn't even bother to run. When she finally arrived at the cafe and pulled the door open, she was almost knocked down by a large, brown dog pulling a woman toward the freedom of the outdoors, and then was faced with a long line. Apparently, only one person was working behind the counter. Rachel sighed.

She was sitting on a stool at the long, bar-like table fifteen minutes later, sipping on her mocha latte, when she looked through the large, foggy window and saw Jessica's car pull up just as a car directly in front of the cafe pulled out. She got out of her car, opened a functional umbrella, and looked in the window. She located Rachel, smiled, waved, and rushed toward the door.

"Ray!" she shouted. The other customers all looked up momentarily to find the source of the outburst and then went back to their books or laptops. Jessica jumped onto the stool next to Rachel and threw her umbrella under the bar. "What happened to you? You look like a wet poodle."

Rachel reached up and attempted to fluff her mass of curls. "I got caught in a monsoon," she told her friend. "Why do you look like you just came from sunning at the beach?"

Jessica threw her head back and laughed. "Ray, you still look cute. Poodles are cute! Everyone loves poodles!" She rooted through her purse and pulled out her wallet. "Let me go order something and I'll be right back."

Jessica jumped off the stool and headed back up front. Rachel watched with interest as all the eyes in the place followed her and her energy. Within a minute, she had everyone in line laughing along with her as if all of the clouds had cleared up and the sun was blazing in on them all. Rachel took a few more sips of her latte as she waited. She felt the warmth move down through her chest and settle in her stomach. She squished her toes around in her wet sock, inside her wet shoe, and thought about just giving up.

Jessica floated back onto her stool and put her mug down in front of her. She made a face of concern at Rachel. "What's going on with you? You look like you just finished a guaranteed happily ever after book and everyone died on the last page."

Rachel couldn't help but laugh. Jessica clearly knew what made Rachel tick. "I'm fine," she insisted. "I got rained on and couldn't find my umbrella. I had to walk three blocks. I just started my period one day early. Do the math. I feel gross."

Jessica shook her head. "No, that's not it. I mean, I'm sorry for all that, but it seems to me that when you're feeling down, you attract disaster. Is that what's happening now? Are you feeling down?"

Rachel's nose twitched. She couldn't make words with her mouth. She was worried that if she did, she would say something she would regret. She did not want Jessica, or anyone else in her friend group, to know the truth about her and Clarence. It wasn't that they made an oath of secrecy; it was just that she knew what others would say. They would be against it. They would see what she could see but continued to push to the back of her brain: she was fighting a losing battle. She didn't want to hear it, because coming from someone else's mouth, especially a friend's, she wouldn't be able to ignore it. And if they did find out, it would make things awkward for all of them.

"I don't know," she finally said. "Maybe. Maybe it's the rain. Maybe it's just . . ."

"Nothing really going on in your life?" Jessica asked, nodding with confidence in her assessment. "I mean, it's been really, really long since you went out on a date. Is it that you haven't met anyone, or you're not willing to meet anyone?"

Rachel shrugged. "I don't know. I mean, it could be, but—"

"You need to let me fix you up," Jessica cut in. "I know you've never wanted me to, but that was back in college. We're in the so-called real world now, right? You don't need to be such a martyr. Let me ask around for you, and see if there are any guys who are even close to worthy of having you in their lives. I'm sure I can find someone either at work or at my gym. Come on. Let me help you."

Rachel wrinkled her nose and then shrugged. "I just don't know. I have a coworker who wants to fix me up, too, but I'm just not—"

Jessica slammed her hand down on top of Rachel's. "Is—is there someone . . . I mean, are you, like, seeing someone? Or, like, have a crush on someone? I mean, Ray, why else would you be so reluctant for a fix-up? Are you into someone? Who is it?" She gasped and put her hand over her mouth. "It's not that guy Chris from your building, is it?"

Rachel's jaw dropped. "No! You know I would never date that guy. He's the kind of guy who would send you an unsolicited dick pic and then get mad at you for not being grateful. Ew."

Jessica nodded knowingly. "But there *is* someone, isn't there? I mean, at least someone that you're interested in."

Rachel looked down and took a cleansing breath. "Well, not really. I mean, yeah, I have had someone who keeps floating in and out of my life, but nothing will ever come of it. I mean, he's just not available."

"Is he married?"

"No," Rachel said quickly. "No. I could never be with a married man. It's just that he . . . he's not at a place where he'd be able to settle down. Not just with me, but with any woman he would meet. He's got other things going on."

"Is he a workaholic?" Jessica asked.

Rachel bit her lower lip. She had to find a way to change the subject away from the only topic that she could never discuss with Jessica. "Yes," she said. "It's his work. He's very ambitious. So yeah, he could never make me his priority."

Jessica shook her head in disgust. "What does Clare think about it?"

Rachel's eyes went wide, and she almost lost her balance on her stool. "Clare? I mean, uh, well, I guess I've never really talked to Clare about this sort of stuff. I mean, it hasn't really come up. Hey, you know what? I think when I go to work tomorrow, I'll tell my coworker I'm willing to get fixed up with her brother."

Jessica's face broke out in an excited smile. She practically bounced in her seat. She grabbed Rachel's arm.

"Yes! I think that's a great idea! But you have to be really careful with fix-ups. I mean, you don't want to get yourself into an awkward situation. You need to meet him somewhere. And go somewhere public in case he's an escaped felon and needs to take you hostage when the cops arrive . . . wait. No. That's not right. I mean, so you're not in private in case he's some perv. And you need to call me immediately after. Well, only if you don't end up, well, you know."

Rachel picked up her drink, held it to her mouth, and closed her eyes as she drank it. Now she had backed herself into a corner. In order to stop her friend from asking uncomfortable questions, she had somehow committed herself to the fix-up with Camilla's brother. No, her name was Becca. Why was that so hard to remember?

She swallowed her coffee, put her mug down, and smiled at her noisy friend. Tomorrow, she would go into work and approach Cass . . . Becca, and tell her she was in. And then she would have the next in what was sure to be a long line of future panic attacks.

She barely slept that night. Her heart was pounding as she crawled into bed at ten o'clock. She picked up her book, the one that she hadn't wanted to put down the night before, and couldn't even get past the first page of the chapter she was on. She tried several times, and then put it back down. She got out of bed and paced around her apartment for half an hour and then got back into bed and did some relaxation breathing. She picked her phone up from the nightstand, and lingered her finger over the keyboard, poised to send a text to Clarence. But she couldn't think of what she would even say to him.

"Hey, Clare, what do you think I should wear on my date with this stranger

I'm going out with to distract myself from wanting you, and fool my friends that I'm ready to meet someone? And by the way, why can't you just be bisexual and love me?" No, that would never work. And her aim was not to hurt Clarence, or even make him jealous. She just wanted to move on with her life. She wanted to be happy. She had no idea if this fix-up would be her happiness elixir, but there was only one way to find out. She shut her phone off and set it back down. Then she turned out her light and closed her eyes. For what it was worth.

The next morning, she exited the elevator and walked straight up to the group of her coworkers milling around in front before going back to their desks to start their day. She rested her hand on Cathy's . . . Becca's arm. "Do you have a sec?" she asked.

A baffled Becca looked back at her and nodded. Rachel led her off to the hallway in front of the bathroom and stopped to face her.

"I think maybe I do want to take you up on your offer to meet your brother, the one who's new in town. Is he, uh, still available?"

Becca grinned the grin of the victorious. "I knew you'd come around," she cooed. "Yes, he's still available, and he's still new in town. I bet he would love for you to show him all of your favorite hot spots. I'll text him in a bit, and I'll make sure it's okay for me to give you his number."

She started to walk back to the front, but Rachel grabbed her arm to stop her. "What's your brother's name?" she asked.

She figured it might be easier to handle all of this if she knew the name of this mysterious brother.

Becca looked back and tilted her head. "Oh yeah. His name is Barry." She giggled and walked away. Rachel was left to look after her. Barry. That was sort of an old-fashioned name. She wondered how old this Barry was. And she wondered what it was that Charlene . . . Becca was giggling about. Was there something she wasn't telling her? Well, if there was, there was only one way to find out. Rachel Morris was taking a chance. She was going on a date with a total stranger. And she hoped that somehow it would lead her to some sort of happiness.

CHAPTER 5

CLARENCE STARED AT THE ROCK in his hand. He passed it to his other hand and then tossed it in the air and caught it. He tested the weight in his palm. It was granite. Just plain, common, local granite. He put it down on his desk. It would make a good paperweight. It was amazing, the objects brought to him by the regular people who roamed around Boston on a daily basis. Someone had found this stone by the side of the road and thought it might have some significance. It was about as significant as a tail feather from a pigeon. It *was* kind of pretty, though.

Clarence was not a geologist. He was an archeologist, and a new one at that. He'd received his master's degree the previous December. He was in his entry-level job, working at the Boston Museum of Archeology, now the home of the permanent "Big Dig" exhibit, among others. The Big Dig was a major undertaking, no pun intended, that had taken place between 1991 and 2006 in Eastern Massachusetts. It had been going on for years before Clarence was born until he was six years old. At age six, he didn't know a life where there was no Big Dig. While other Boston-area residents shook their heads and talked about what traffic was like before the Big Dig, Clarence and his friends stood stupidly with their mouths hanging open. But now Clarence's life was dominated by Big Dig artifacts; things that were unearthed and put aside while the city was busy working on moving major highways underground and building a new tunnel to the airport.

There were bones, both human and animal. There were objects, such as car parts, and in one case even an entire frame and an engine. There were interesting rocks and fossils. There was an antique sewing machine that actually functioned once cleaned and oiled. Clarence was sure many other objects had either been missed or smuggled home by workers who thought they were interesting or wanted to get them appraised, such as jewelry and coins.

The exhibit featured blueprints and other plans from the project that initiated in the early 1980s and television sets showing videos of before and after. Newspaper clippings with opinion pieces and cost estimates of the project, which was the most expensive project of its kind in the whole country. And then the display cases of the most interesting finds, and that was Clarence's department. This job was a young archaeologist's wet dream. And he barely even had to get his nails dirty doing it. Most of the digging had been completed before he was even born.

There was a knock on his open door, and Todd came in. "Hey, man, how's it going?" Todd threw himself into the chair next to Clarence's desk. He absentmindedly picked up the piece of granite. "Nice rock," he said. "Weighty. Significant?"

Clarence shook his head. "Common granite."

"Pretty though." Todd put it back on the desk. "So listen, I talked to Ken and told him about your dilemma."

Clarence smirked. "Which dilemma are we talking about?"

Todd smiled. "The one where a hunky, tall, skinny but muscular guy with dark hair and dreamy blue eyes can't find himself a man on his own. He agreed that it was tragic, and he wants to help."

"Oh, great," Clarence said. "So now there are two of you who think I'm pathetic."

"But good-looking," Todd corrected.

"Thanks." Clarence folded his arms in front of him. "So does Ken have any ideas?"

"He said that there's this one guy who just started working in the accounting office at the Garden. He said he's good-looking, straight dark hair, brown eyes, tall, but not taller than you, and he always dresses nice. Ken said he smells good, too."

"Well, that's a bonus," Clarence said. "I really don't want to go out with some guy who stinks. What's he like?"

"Ken doesn't really know him too well," Todd said. "He's seen him in the lunchroom and he was pleasant."

"How does he know he's gay?"

Todd laughed. "Uh, gaydar? And also they were doing this training at work about diversity and inclusion. They broke everyone into different discussion groups. This guy chose the 'self-identified as gay' group. I think that was Ken's second clue."

"And he's single?"

"Ken was in the group with him, and he said something about being single."

"Huh." Clarence couldn't think of anything else to ask. It seemed that Todd had covered all the bases. Except for the most important one. "And he's into a fix-up?"

"That, we don't know yet," Todd admitted. "Ken wanted to make sure you were okay with it before he asked."

"I . . ." Clarence let out a breath. "Yeah, I guess so. I mean, why not, right? It's not like I'm involved with anyone else." He envisioned Rachel, and his stomach shifted. "Yeah. Tell him to give this guy my number. What's his name?"

"It's Luke," Todd said. "I don't know if it's short for Lucas, or something else. But Luke is good."

"Yeah," Clarence said. "Luke is good." He picked up the granite and silently weighed it again in his hand. He put it down, stared at it, and picked it up again.

Todd took the rock from his hand. "Are you nervous about this?"

Clarence shrugged. "It just feels so forced, you know? It's not like you or Ken are friends with this Luke guy. I don't know what kinds of things he likes, or what he's into. I don't even know if he prefers to be a . . ."

Todd cleared his throat. "There are a few things you'll need to learn as you get to know each other. Things that Ken can't ask. But maybe it would feel more comfortable if we did it as, like, a group thing? I mean, Ken can invite him out with us as a friend. That way, if you hate him, the pressure's off, and you can just go home after."

Clarence poked his lower lip out and nodded slowly. "Yeah, I think that would work. It would feel more . . . I don't know. Not as staged. Yeah. I like that idea."

"Good." Todd pulled his phone out of his pocket. "I'll text Ken right now. Maybe we can set it up for Friday night. You have the day off, but we can just meet you there after I punch out at five. Wherever there is." His thumbs went into motion on his keypad. Then he stared at his phone. After a moment of silence, he smiled. "Ken said he'll ask him right now. He'll let me know. I'll tell you what: I'll go back to my office and then come back and let you know when I hear back." He started toward the door.

"Thanks, man," Clarence called after him. "Thanks for doing this. It means a lot. I mean, it's not easy to, you know, ask for this kind of help. I appreciate it."

Todd turned around and nodded. "We gotta stick together, right?" He started down the hall. A minute passed, and suddenly Todd was back in the doorway, grinning. "Ken says Luke's in! He suggested we all meet down at Frank's Grill at six on Friday. That good?"

"Uh, yeah." Clarence had already started clacking on his computer keyboard, but now he stopped. "Yeah, that will work. Do I have to, like, dress up or anything? I've never been to Frank's Grill."

Todd gave him an amused smile. "Just wear something like you have on now. You'll be fine. You're a good-looking guy, Clarence. I don't think you'll have any problem catching Luke's eye." Todd winked and left the office again.

Clarence tried to ignore the fact that that was the third time his coworker had mentioned him being attractive, just in the last half hour. He wondered if maybe Ken needed to keep a closer eye on his husband. Because his husband's eyes appeared to be fixed on Clarence. He laughed to himself at the hilarious thought of Todd having a secret crush on him and went back to work.

Despite Todd's assurances, Clarence decided he would feel better if he bought a new shirt for his, well, "date" on Friday night. So after work he drove to the mall and went to Macy's. Once in the men's department, he chose several button-downs to try on and ended up leaving with a long-sleeved, light-blue shirt that he could wear tucked into jeans with a leather belt. He took a detour to the food court before heading back to his car and left with a bag of takeout from Panda Express.

When he got home, he brought his food to the couch, turned on the TV, and settled back to stream an episode of *Young Royals*. After eating, he cleaned up, changed into pajama pants and a T-shirt, and sat back down on his couch with his phone to scroll his socials. He noticed an Insta post from Rachel, showing a picture of a book she said she stayed up late reading, and she recommended it to her book-loving friends, five stars. She mentioned something about a group called Bookstagram. Clarence had never heard of it. He clicked on Rachel's profile and started to scroll through her pictures. He stopped on one from the previous week of Rachel with an arm around his shoulders, kissing his cheek over his birthday cake. He was smiling, looking relaxed. He let out a sigh. Then he switched to his text app and started a message to Rachel.

Clarence
Hey R how was your day

Rachel
hold on

. . .

Sorry I was in the bathroom. Alls well. U?

Clarence
All good. You free on Sat? Wanna hang?

Rachel
. . .

I have plans Saturday

> *Clarence*
> What, you have a date or something lol

Rachel
...

Actually ...

> *Clarence*
> Really? OMG that's great. That guy you men-
> tioned? Your coworker's brother?

Rachel
Yeah. Having dinner. Can meet up Fri though

> *Clarence*
> I can't do Fri. Have plans.

Rachel
Oh. Date? LOL

> *Clarence*
> Well ... sort of

Rachel
Oh

> *Clarence*
> Group thing. With Todd and Ken.
> And this guy. Luke

Rachel
Luke is a good name. My guy is Barry

Clarence
Barry? Uh is he sixty?

Rachel
uh no. People are named Barry

Clarence
yeah Barry Manilow is named Barry. Are you gonna meet at the Copa?

Rachel
???

Clarence
yk the Copa Cabana . . .

Clarence
you there?

Rachel
I'm ignoring you

Clarence
you can make fun of Luke

Rachel
Luke is cool

Clarence
My name is Luke-a

Rachel
ugh

Clarence
lunch tomorrow? I'm off . . . I'll come to you

Rachel
only if we can get burritos

"Are you nervous about your date?" Clarence asked as he scooped up a blob of guacamole with a tortilla chip.

"Nervous?" Rachel asked. She dipped her burrito into the pond of salsa verde on her plate. "I mean, I guess, just because I never met the guy. But, you know, I think it will be okay." She took a bite of her lunch and wiped her mouth with her napkin.

Clarence smirked. "Do you have the notebook with you?"

Rachel looked up at him. "What notebook?"

"The one that you write possible topics of conversations in. You always do that before parties or going somewhere where you don't know anyone."

Rachel blushed. "It's at home on the dining room table," she confessed. "I had to watch the news last night to get some ideas of what was going on in the world. But the way things are now, I don't think the news will make good small talk over dinner."

"Your work is pretty interesting. And didn't I just see on Insta that you finished a book recently? You can talk about the book. You liked it, right?"

Rachel rolled her eyes. "It was a romance. I don't think Barry will be interested." She sighed. "It will be okay. I'm sure he'll keep up his end of the conversation. His sister Carmella—I mean, Becca, is really talkative and loud. Maybe it runs in the family, and I'll just have to sit and nod and smile."

"Sounds like an exciting time." Clarence cut into his burrito with his fork and knife. It was too large to fit in his mouth if he used his hands.

"What about you?" Rachel asked, setting her wrapped entree back on the table. "You nervous for your date?"

Clarence shrugged as he chewed. "I wouldn't say nervous," he said. "More like curious. I can't wait to see what guy Todd's husband thinks I would find attractive." He smiled. "I bought a new shirt."

Rachel laughed. "Wow. I guess this is serious. A new shirt. I hope it's blue to match your eyes."

Clarence felt a twinge in his chest. "It's blue," he said. He picked up his beer and took a deep gulp. He had the day off. He could splurge a bit.

Rachel smiled vacantly. "At least it's a guy and I'm not helping you win over the competition." Her eyes went wide, and she put her hand over her mouth.

Clarence furrowed his brow. "Competition? What do you mean by that?"

"Nothing," Rachel said quickly. "I was just joking."

"Rachel." Clarence reached across the table and put his hand over hers. "Are you feeling—"

"I'm not feeling anything," she interrupted. "I was just kidding. You don't date girls, Clare. You're gay. You seek out guys. And I want you to find one. It's not that I want you to not meet anyone." She paused. "I'm just gonna miss . . ." She circled her hand in front of her.

Clarence nodded. "I'll miss it, too," he said. "But maybe it's time for us to, you know, stop what we were doing. Maybe it's time for us to talk about what all of that meant."

"I don't think we have to," Rachel said. "I mean, I'm okay with it, and I know you are, too. I mean, we were both lonely, that's all. Right? And we're best friends. It was just . . . just a thing we did to distract ourselves. We both knew that. Know that. It's fine."

Clarence stared at her. Her words sounded pretty, but he'd known her long enough to know that they didn't match the sadness in her eyes. But he also wanted to honor her wish to drop the topic. "Okay," he said. "But I just wanted you to know that us becoming friends was the best thing that ever happened to me, and I wouldn't change a thing that's gone on between us. I really love you."

Rachel gave him a weak smile. "I know. I love you, too, Clare. I want everything for you."

They finished their burritos, and Clarence walked Rachel back to her office. Outside the revolving doors, he gave her a hug and a kiss on the cheek, promising to let her know how his date went the following night. Then he walked back to his car.

# CHAPTER 6

"SO YOU HAD A GOOD time?" Rachel was curling her hair with an iron in front of the bathroom mirror, her phone on speaker.

"It was fun," Clarence said. "I mean, it was hard to really get to know him in a group, but he seemed, well, pleasant enough."

Rachel laughed. "Pleasant? That's not a huge endorsement. The breeze outside my window yesterday was pleasant, but it doesn't mean I want to see it on a regular basis, or take its clothes off."

Clarence snorted. "Well, for what it's worth, he's good-looking. He has chocolate brown eyes and a dimple on his right cheek when he smiles. He was wearing a cashmere sweater. That was a nice touch. And he smells nice."

Rachel sprayed her hair lightly with hairspray. "You got close enough to smell him? That sounds more than just pleasant."

"No. It's just the way we were sitting. I was right next to him. Ken had told Todd that he smelled good, so I made a point of sniffing him. No big deal."

Rachel dropped her mascara on the floor while laughing. She retrieved it quickly and unscrewed the top. "I'm getting this visual of you sniffing him! Did he notice?"

"No," Clarence said. "But Todd did. I could tell he was biting his tongue to keep from cracking up!"

"What did he smell like?"

"It was a combination of some really nice shaving cream, and something else. Maybe his natural smell. Pheromones, maybe?"

Rachel snorted, and her mascara wand slipped onto her nose, leaving a black streak. She grabbed a washcloth and dabbed it off. "They make pheromone colognes now. Maybe he was wearing some. I think it's supposed to enhance your own pheromones. So do you think this guy is Shadow Man?"

"Shadow Man?" Clarence asked in an amused tone. "Why does that sound familiar?"

"Jessica dubbed him at your birthday party, remember?" Rachel checked her reflection in the mirror and used her finger to blend her eyeshadow a little more. "Your ideal guy. I can almost remember it word for word. He's muscular but not a bodybuilder. He's clean shaven by day, but bristly by night, just enough to give you a little rash on your cheeks. I don't think you specified which cheeks, though."

Clarence groaned. "Oh yeah, *that* Shadow Man. I almost forgot about him. It doesn't sound like a lot of criteria though. Some muscles and a baby-soft face. I'm guessing I would need to fill in a few more details, like salary and position preference."

"You like to be on top," Rachel said knowingly. "I mean, well, that's what you like with—I mean, I just assumed . . ."

Clarence chuckled. "I mean, obviously it's different with a man. And by the way, this guy has a goatee."

"Oh." Rachel thought about that. "What was his name?"

"It's Luke," Clarence said. "Biblical. At least the New Testament."

"Ironic," Rachel mused. "Does he have muscles?"

"I'm not sure. He was wearing a sweater. I can ask him if he wants to go get matching tattoos together on our next date so he can take his shirt off. What do you think I should get? An anchor? Mom in a heart? The word *pheromone* spelled out?"

Rachel rolled her eyes. "Or you could just take him home after a few drinks and take his shirt off yourself."

"Will you be drinking on your date tonight?"

Rachel felt her face grow hot. "I-I guess maybe a drink or two. But I know my limits."

"Good." There was a pause. "I wish you weren't meeting him by yourself. You know, for safety reasons."

Rachel drew in her breath. "I'm not gonna take him home, Clare. I'm gonna make sure he doesn't follow me home. And I know how to block a phone number if he text-stalks me."

"Maybe you and Barry can double with me and Luke if things progress."

"Yeah, I don't know about that," Rachel said, feeling a weird numbness in her feet. "I mean, at least not yet. Maybe when things are, you know, kind of settled. If that happens."

"Ray, you're my best friend," Clarence said. "I don't want us to have to avoid each other."

Rachel could hear a twang of regret in Clarence's voice. She sighed. "I'm not gonna avoid you, Clare. I just think . . . I think a double date needs to wait. Just until . . ."

"Yeah, I get it." Another silence. "Are you nervous?"

"A little." Rachel sat on her bed and put the phone on her lap. "I mean, just like regular nervousness like you get before meeting a blind date."

"I get that."

Rachel looked down at her shoes. She wondered if she should trade her heels for sensible shoes. "I really should get going," she told Clarence. "I need a few minutes before I head out. What are you doing tonight?"

"Just staying in," Clarence said. "Steve and Jerry asked if I wanted to hang out with them, but, you know, I didn't want to be a third wheel or anything."

Rachel stared at the phone. So Clarence would be sitting at home all night, doing nothing, maybe watching TV or reading, while she was out on her date. Would he be wondering what was going on with her and Barry? Would he be worrying? Would he be jealous? Would he . . .

"Well, I guess I'll call you tomorrow to let you know how it went." She stood up. "What time do you have to go to work?"

"I'll probably go in at eleven thirty so I can get lunch first. Maybe text me if we don't talk earlier and I'll call you when I'm free."

"Sounds good. And Clare? For the record, I hope things work out with you and Luke, if it's what you want."

"I know. And Ray? I hope Barry is truly the one for you."

"Thanks. I'll talk to you later."

After ending the call, Rachel put on her jacket and headed for the door. At the last minute, she grabbed her umbrella, just in case. It never hurt to bring protection on a date.

"Rachel!" The tall man in the black T-shirt tucked into neat jeans stood up when he saw her. Rachel smiled. He was really hot. His dark hair was neat on top with one stray wave falling across his broad forehead. His smile was carefree, and he smiled like a model. His body was . . . well, he made his T-shirt and jeans look they had been painted onto nicely refined musculature. Musculature. Rachel didn't even know how she knew that word, but it fit.

She walked over to him, and as she got closer, she noticed his eyes were a sort of hazel, just like Cindy . . . Becca's. Yes, they definitely resembled each other. When she thought about it for the fraction of a second she had to think before reaching the table, she realized that Becca was pretty attractive. It figured.

"Hi," she said. "You must be Barry."

The man stared at her for a second in confusion but then chuckled. "Yes, I'm Barry. And you're Rachel and you work with my sister Rebecca at the publishing house."

"Actually," Rachel said as she let Barry pull her chair out so she could sit, "it's not really a publishing house. We contract with publishers to do the editing and we also have self-publishing clients, and . . . wait a minute. Did you just say your sister's name is Rebecca?"

Barry looked confused again, and his mouth opened slightly. "You're the right Rachel, right? I mean, you work at the editing place, and my sister set this up? You just seem kind of—"

Rachel laughed. "No, really, I'm the right person." She privately prayed she was the right person. She wanted to touch this guy. Any place on his body. Even his ear. "No, it's just that I only know her as Becca and it never occurred to me that her name was Rebecca. I kept having the hardest time remembering her name, and I couldn't figure out why. But now I think I know why."

Barry's head cocked to the side with a look of amusement on his face. "Enlighten me?"

Rachel maintained her smile. "It's just that my parents are divorced," she started. "They split up when I was fourteen."

"Oh, I'm sorry," Barry said softly.

"Oh, no, don't be. It was a good thing. We never really saw much of my father when he was part of our family, but once they got divorced, at least we stopped expecting him to show up once and a while. But the reason the divorce finally happened is because my father had an affair. He came home from one of his savior doctor trips overseas and announced to my mother that he had fallen in love with another woman and he didn't love my mom anymore."

"That's a real dickhead move," Barry said.

"Yeah," Rachel agreed. "Dickhead is my mom's nickname for him. But the thing is, the woman that he left her for? Her name is Rebecca. I've never actually met her. As a matter of fact, I wasn't even invited to their tabloid-worthy wedding, and since the divorce I've only seen my father a handful of times, usually when he's traipsing through town and wants to score Father of the Year points. But anyway, yeah. Her name's Rebecca. And I guess I have some sort of hang-up about that."

"Wow," Barry said. "That's kind of complex."

Rachel opened her eyes wide in horror. "Oh my God, I'm so sorry. We just met, like, five minutes ago, and I just trauma dumped on you first thing! I'm so embarrassed!" She put her hands over her face and imagined what it would feel like to die so publicly of shame.

Barry laughed. "No, really, Rachel, I think it's pretty cool. I mean, I've been on a lot of dates where all we talk about is the weather and the food we're eating. This is the most real first five minutes of a date I've ever had. I already feel like I know something real about you."

Rachel winced. "Well then you have to tell me something about you that you've never told anyone on the first date so I don't feel so stupid. It's only fair."

"Okay." Barry thought for a moment. "Well, you told me about your family, so I'll tell you about mine. So Becca and I are really half-siblings. We have the same father, but different mothers. Her mother was married to my father first, but then they divorced, and he married my mom. Then they had two more kids, me and my full sister. I also have an older half-brother, who's the oldest, but he's like eight years older than me."

"So you and Becca didn't grow up in the same house?" Rachel asked.

"When I was six and she was eight, her mom died," Barry said. "So she ended up moving in with us, and she was with us until she graduated from high school. Then she came to Boston for college and stayed here. I graduated two years ago, and I just moved here last month. I'm working now, but I'm thinking about going to grad school here."

"Where are you from?"

"I'm from a small town in Michigan called Greenway. It didn't seem so small-town to me growing up, but after college, I suddenly felt really claustrophobic. I understand now why Becca left when she did. She convinced me to come to the Boston area. I stayed with her and her boyfriend for the first two weeks before I could move into my own place."

"Are you right in the city?" Rachel asked.

"I'm in Watertown," Barry said. "It seemed like a good place to settle. If I end up going to grad school in Boston, I can park and ride to the city every day. What about you?"

"Waltham," Rachel said. "Of course I commute to Cambridge for work, but it's not bad. And yeah, it's nice to have access to the commuter rail. I'm originally from Amherst, but I went to BU."

"That's supposed to be a great school," Barry said. He fidgeted with his menu. "I'm thinking of checking it out for the graduate school of psychology."

Rachel felt her face get hot. "You're gonna be a therapist?" she asked. "Okay, now I'm really embarrassed! I just spilled my guts to you! I'm sure analyzing psyches isn't your idea of a fun time on a date!"

Barry gave her a winning smile, showing straight, white teeth. "Rachel, it's fine. Really. It's no big deal, like I said. I promise, I'm not secretly texting my sister under the table asking her to come rescue me." He pointed to his phone on the table. "See?"

Rachel let herself relax. She picked up a menu. "My friend Clare and I come here all the time. I can help you decide. What kind of food do you like?"

"I prefer white or no meat, and lots of veggies," Barry said. "Stir-fry is always good."

"Maybe you could try the chicken fajitas," Rachel suggested.

Barry looked for the fajitas on the menu. "Looks good."

After dinner, Barry took out his wallet, and Rachel raised a hand. "Let's split it," she said, digging into her purse for her own wallet. "I mean, I don't think this was really officially a date. It was a meet-up. You don't have to treat. And even if this was a full-on date, you wouldn't have to pay."

Barry looked at her with curiosity. "So this wasn't a real date?"

Rachel shrugged. "I don't know. I mean, I guess it's a date, but not like we met randomly and we liked each other and you asked me out, or I asked you out. It was a fix-up."

Barry nodded thoughtfully. "Okay then. We split the check. But I want to ask you something."

"What?"

He smiled. "Would you go out with me tonight? Maybe get a drink? Like a date?"

Rachel laughed. "You're asking me out?"

"Yes," Barry said. "I met you here at the restaurant, and I liked you, and I think you liked me too, and now I'm asking you out."

"Usually when someone asks someone on a date, it's for later, like, the next weekend or something. Not after dinner."

Barry shrugged. "I'm not like most other people."

Rachel tried not to blush. "I—well, I guess . . . yes. I'll go out with you. Tonight."

Barry nodded again. "Where should we go?"

"There's this pub near here that Clare and I like to go to. They have really good mixed drinks. But I can only have one. I have to drive home after."

"Same here," Barry said. "We'll go out on our date and have one drink, and maybe some cocktail peanuts. And if our first date goes well, I might ask you on a second date. But maybe we can do that one on another day."

Rachel laughed, and Barry smiled. That was when Rachel noticed the dimple on his shaved but stubbly chin.

Rachel got home after midnight, sober and wide awake, Barry having ended the date with a hug and a kiss on her cheek. As soon as she walked in the door, she marched right to her couch, sat, and took her phone out of her purse. She opened her text app.

Rachel

Are you awake? You'll never guess what happened tonight

Rachel

Ok I guess you went to bed already. I just got back from my date and you'll never believe this. Clare, Barry's the Shadow Man!

CHAPTER 7

CLARENCE HAD BEEN AWAKE WHEN the text came in, but he didn't want to intrude on Rachel's postdate euphoria. He wanted to give her the night to process. He was fine with her text-dumping, but he didn't want to ruin anything by being part of the debriefing process. At the same time as he wanted her to be happy, he also didn't want his discomfort to take away from her excitement, and he knew she would be able to sense it if he replied.

The next day he woke up at ten and took a shower. He decided to skip breakfast in lieu of having a hearty lunch at the work cafeteria. He sat on the couch and read Rachel's texts over and over. Shadow Man. That was now the code word for Mr. Right. But it was Clarence's Mr. Right, not Rachel's. Or maybe it was hers, too. It kind of made sense. They were best friends, and best friends often shared hopes and desires. He wondered what Barry looked like, how he looked at Rachel. He thought that Barry had better look at Rachel like the goddess she was. If he didn't, or if he ever did anything to hurt her . . .

He was one to talk.

He had been hurting her for years.

Finally, he started his reply to the texts.

Clarence
Sorry I missed your text last night. I went to bed early. Sounds like it went great!

Rachel
That's okay. It was late when I got back. But yeah, he's really nice, and funny, and really hot. And interesting. I can't wait for you to meet him.

Clarence
Maybe it would be best to have a few dates under your belt before you introduce the best friend. I might freak him out

Rachel
LOL you would not. You're my best friend. He'll love you. But yeah maybe the introducing the friends thing should wait until after the second date

Clarence
So there's a second date planned then?

Rachel
He asked me out for a second date. It's a really cute story but I know you have to get ready for work

Clarence
Come meet me at the caf for lunch. I'll let he ticket office know you're coming and they can waive admission

Rachel
Cool! What's for lunch today?

Clarence
Basil tortellini

Rachel
LOL you SO have a type!

Clarence was just getting into line when he saw Rachel enter the cafeteria. When she noticed him, she smiled, waved, and made her way over. "It's been a long time since I've met you for lunch here," she said. "I miss that. I love this place. It's so . . . historic."

Clarence laughed. "That's the point," he said. "Bringing the past into the future so we can learn from it."

"What did we learn from the Big Dig?"

Clarence thought for a moment. "We learned that Boston is the best city in the country for mucking up traffic and spending money on gigantic projects, and that we love baseball so much, we're willing to name tunnels after our baseball legends."

Rachel nodded. "Sounds legit."

They reached the front of the line and placed their orders. They made small talk until they paid for their food, found a table, and sat. "So tell me more about your Shadow Man."

Rachel beamed. "He's all that and the kitchen sink," she said. "I'm just waiting to figure out what's wrong with him. He's a really good listener. You know, the kind that asks a lot of really relevant questions. And he looks right into your eyes when you answer. I don't think I've ever had anyone listen to me like that." She quickly backtracked. "I mean, you excluded, of course."

Clarence shifted in his chair. He stabbed a tortellini with his fork and put it in his mouth, giving him time to be silent. He swallowed. "We can just assume present company excepted," he said. He ate another piece of cheesy pasta. "So he just moved here?"

Rachel nodded. "He moved from a small town and he's just getting used to being so close to the big city. I guess if you're gonna make a big move like that, it's good to do it where you have family."

"Yeah," Clarence said. "I remember when I first arrived in Boston for school when I was eighteen. I didn't know anyone. I was really lucky that I met Jerry, and then you and Steve. And then Jessica showed up."

"I sometimes forget how hard that must have been for you." Rachel put her hand on top of the hand that Clarence wasn't using to stuff his face with food. "I guess we're your Boston-area family now."

Clarence smiled. "I got really lucky."

Rachel smiled back. "Me too." She went on to tell him about the date. "And I guess it was a good thing that we didn't do more than a hug and a kiss on the cheek. I mean, it was the first time we met, and we only know the first-date versions of each other so far. We were both on our best behavior."

Clarence fought through his relief that there had been no close touching. "But it sounds like he really liked you. It's really cute how he asked you on a date from your date. And you brought him to Stony's Pub for the date. That was a good choice."

"Well, they do have the best drinks." Rachel's face was slightly pink, and Clarence thought it was a good look for her. "He has sort of a messed-up family, too, but they all get along, which is good. His parents are still together, but there was a lot of drama at one point. I think when I go to work tomorrow, I'll make an effort to spend some time with Becca. When Barry talks about her, I can tell how close they are. I'm pretty sure that means she's a decent person. Maybe I can finally make a friend at work."

Clarence smiled at her warmly. "I think that's a great idea. I guess that even if things don't work out with Barry Manilow, at least you could gain a friend out of the whole thing."

Rachel furrowed her brow. "You're already talking about it like it's not gonna work. Did you sense some sort of red flag from what I told you about the date?"

Clarence froze. He hadn't even realized he'd said that. "No! No, sorry. I didn't mean that. I just meant—"

Rachel laughed. "It's okay, Clare. Really. I'm just giving you a hard time. But I think you would like Barry. He's easygoing, and he has a killer smile. I almost want to get past our first few dates just so I can bring him to some get-together with our friends. I don't want to rush things too much, but it would be really cool, you know, if this worked out for me."

Clarence nodded slowly. "It would be really cool," he echoed.

Work went by slowly that day. It started to rain in torrents outside, and the good people of the Boston metro area seemed to have uniformly decided to stay home and read a good book. Clarence spent some time wandering around the exhibit halls. He stopped in front of several displays and silently remembered how the objects came into possession of the museum. He touched the glass of one case, where a copy of *Catcher in the Rye* lay open to a center page. It was worn and eroded, and yet the words were still clear. It had been found early in the dig by a worker who kept it in a box for years before finding it while unpacking from a move and donating it to the museum. It had been cleaned and preserved and now lay in posterity for all to see. Clarence remembered reading the book in high school and always feeling some level of disdain for Holden Caulfield. It was hard to feel that way now, looking at the old, dog-eared book that managed to survive the ravages of time, including who knew how much time underground. He wondered about the person who had originally owned it. Was it some high school student who tossed it over their shoulder muttering good riddance on the last day of school? Or maybe it was a beloved belonging of some scholar or bookworm who had misplaced it and spent hours combing the city trying to find any trace. Whatever the case, here it was, in Clarence's museum, with a hidden past. Clarence lived for this shit.

After work he took the train home through the rain-darkened streets, made himself a peanut butter and banana sandwich, and took his perch on the couch with his plate. He pointed the remote at the TV and tried to decide what to watch. His mood was somewhat melancholy due to the weather, so he opted for *Fellow Travelers*, a show highlighting the closeted lives of gay men in 1950s Washington, DC. Every time he watched it, he felt a nauseating pull in his gut for the characters and a sense of relief and guilt that things were better for gay people in his own lifetime. It was hard to imagine the fear and loathing of that era. Fear and loathing still existed, but at least now it was bearable, and enough people in the world believed that gay people had a right to exist and live authentic lives. After one episode, he switched over to *Heartstopper* to cheer himself up. One look at Kit Connor's shaggy, golden retriever head always had him smiling.

He was halfway through season two when his phone buzzed. He picked it up and was only half surprised to see a text from Luke.

Luke

Hey Clarence I had a good time the other night. Do you want to maybe get drinks sometime this week?

Clarence

That would be cool, but I have to work 12-9 through Thursday. Would have to have a late night, or we could wait until Friday when I'm off

Luke

We can have a late night. What about tomorrow? We can meet at Stan's Rodeo

Clarence raised a brow. He had never been to Stan's Rodeo. It was a gay club in Wellesley that was, well, rougher than he was accustomed to.

Clarence

I guess that would be ok. Not so sure I'm into the scene though

Luke

LOL not saying I am either, but it looks like a kick. It's just for drinks though not for pickups since we'll be there together. Meet there at 9:30?

Clarence

Yeah 9:30's good. I'll be in my work outfit so don't be horrified

Luke

LOL you're cute

Work on Monday was a bit more animated, and Clarence was able to keep busy without feeling too distracted. Luckily the rain had subsided, and it was a temperate, early spring day. After work, he found his way to the T stop and headed into Wellesley. He walked five blocks to the club, and when he opened the door to face the bouncer, he was assaulted by loud, 1980s punk music. Once he was admitted, he looked around and found Luke sitting alone on a leather loveseat, halfway into his drink.

Luke stood and smiled at Clarence's approach. "Hey, you made it," he said, giving him a quick hug. "Thanks for coming on a work night. I didn't want to wait until the weekend. What do you think of this place?"

Clarence looked around. It was dark, black lights illuminating neon purple messages on the walls. A tight group of men danced, or rather slammed into each other, on the dance floor. It appeared to be a diverse crowd, some dressed in leather with bushy mustaches, bears in vests, skinny punks in black T-shirts and jeans with piercings and spikes, and some, well, normal-looking guys like himself, wearing jeans and button-downs. Luke was somewhere in the middle, wearing black jeans and a black T-shirt with black leather boots. But somehow, he still looked proper.

"It's interesting," Clarence said.

Luke laughed. "It is." He took Clarence's hand. "It's big. There's room in the back where it's not so noisy. C'mon."

He pulled him toward the back of the building and down a hallway. It was clear this wasn't Luke's first time at the Rodeo even if he'd implied it was. They went down the hall, and the further back they got, the more muffled the music became. They entered a room where there were couches with coffee tables sprawled in front of them, and couples sitting close, holding hands or on laps, talking, or in some cases, making out. Luke found a couch and they sat down, inches apart.

"It's kinda nice back here," he said. "Like a big, gay living room."

Clarence glanced over to the recliner next to them where two bulky biker dudes were practically on top of each other, hands exploring, tongues in each other's mouths. "Yeah," he said.

Luke chuckled. "I didn't take you back here to make out," he said. "Well,

I mean, it's not out of the realm of possibilities. It's just that it's nice to not have to act like we're two bros out for drinks to talk about chicks."

Clarence smiled. "Yeah, the bro thing. Been there. But Boston is pretty open to the gay scene. I don't think it would be that bad."

"I grew up in Newton," Luke told him. "It wasn't bad, but it wasn't good either. I mean, being out in high school."

Clarence nodded. "I grew up in Southern California. It was probably better than Newton, but it's not as enlightened as everyone thinks. I mean, California is pretty liberal for the most part, but that doesn't mean that everyone who lives in California is open-minded. Even Southern California. You'd be surprised how some of my friends' parents reacted when they found out they were hanging out with a gay guy. I wasn't allowed over some of their houses."

"That sucks." Luke took a swig of his beer. "So this is the first time we're alone together. I want to hear all about you. You work in a museum. Are you the guy who wanders around all day telling kids not to touch the exhibits?"

Clarence laughed. "No, not quite. I'm an archaeologist. Well, sort of. I mean, I am, but that's not exactly what I do. I examine objects that are donated to the museum and help get them carbon dated and all that. Some really boring stuff. I also give talks to, like, student groups about our exhibits. And I help with cleaning things up a bit. What I really want is to be on a real dig site. I want to be the one to discover some ancient civilization, or at least some new sort of dinosaur. It's hard to do that in the middle of Boston. The really fun digs are overseas. Man, it would have been really fun to be in on Pompeii."

"Have you ever been there?"

Clarence nodded. "We took a two-week trip in college for credit," he said. "It was amazing. I want to go back there someday. Have you been?"

"A couple of times," Luke said. "Yeah, it's pretty cool. Can you imagine being there when it all happened? But I prefer Milan, or Venice. I love the whole Italian lifestyle."

"You've spent a lot of time in Europe?"

"Pretty much every summer when I was living at home with my parents. And they're having a big thirtieth anniversary party in Tuscany next year. It should be epic."

"Sounds like fun." A waiter brought a beer on a tray and handed it to

Clarence with a wink. He smiled back and then took a large gulp. It felt icy going down his throat. "I've only ever been to Europe for that trip to Pompeii, and we didn't get a lot of time for tourism."

"Too bad." Luke looked around the room. "We could play a game of Guess the Bottoms in here." He pointed to the two tangled bikers on the chair. "Guy with the hoop earrings? Bottom vibes for sure."

Clarence laughed. "I was having this conversation with my best friend the other day, about positions. She had no idea about what gay men do. She thinks I'm automatically a top because I've always been on top with her."

Luke's eyes went wide. "You fuck your best friend? What, you're bi?"

Clarence hadn't realized what he had revealed while trying to relay that anecdote. "I—well, no, I'm not bi. I'm totally gay. It's just . . . well, we're platonic, but—"

Luke shook his head. "No, dude, if you're sleeping with women, you're bi."

"I'm not, though," Clarence insisted. "It's not like that. It's hard to explain. I feel close to Rachel, but I'm not in love with her. I can't be. I mean, she's not—"

"You're totally bi, Clarence." Luke took another drink of his beer and then nodded as if to certify his words. "You're kidding yourself if you think otherwise."

"I'm not kidding myself," Clarence said, feeling his blood start to rise to his head. "I know what I am, and that's what matters. Yeah, I've had sex with my female best friend, but I'm not interested in any other women, and I'm not interested in taking it any further than what it's been. I finally decided that I needed to stop so I could let her move on, and that's why I'm here tonight. So we can both move on."

Luke snorted. "You are *so* in denial. You're basically here on the rebound from a relationship with a woman. You're trying to distract yourself."

Clarence actually found himself laughing. "I can't believe you're sitting here trying to tell me what I am. I think I know myself much better than you do. Dude, I like guys. I like dick. I've been in love with a guy before. I've never felt romantic love for a woman. I feel close to Rachel, and we've been there for each other. My relationship with Rachel doesn't define my sexuality or my orientation, and I can't even believe I have to sit here and try to explain this to you."

"It sounds more like you're trying to convince yourself than me."

Clarence had had enough. "Listen, Luke, you seem like a nice guy, but I really don't want to be having this conversation with you right now. Okay? Maybe if we knew each other better, you'd understand my motives, and then we could have a civil conversation."

Luke shook his head, finished his beer, and stood. "Nah, you know what? I don't really want to waste my time on some guy who doesn't really know what he wants. You need to pick a side, man. Maybe get your head together, tell yourself some truth, and then give me a call." He walked away, down the hall, and out of Clarence's sight.

Clarence remained sitting, staring, his mouth agape. He had no idea what had just happened. Had his date really been trying to convince him he was bisexual? Even Rachel, who he had been screwing, knew that wasn't the case. He shook his head and looked around. All of the couples around him were now making out, some of them getting a little too handsy in public for his comfort level. He stood, grabbed his beer, and made his way back to the bar where he found an empty stool and sat down, nursing his beer.

A few minutes later, the two men to the left of him walked away. Seconds later, another man eased onto the stool beside him. "Is this seat taken?" he asked.

Clarence looked up and froze. The man sitting next to him was clearly Adonis, with his dark hair and laughing eyes. "Uh, no," he said. "Help yourself."

The man made a motion, and the bartender appeared. "A beer for me, and one for him." He pointed at Clarence and then looked him in the eye. "You look like you might need another beer."

"Thanks," Clarence said limply. "But I need to let you know, I'm not here for a pick-up. I was here on a date, and he just left. And by left, I mean for good."

"Oh." The man nodded. "Yeah, that's tough. Sorry. So it sounds like the beer is a good idea."

Clarence laughed. "Yeah, the beer is a very good idea." He held out his hand. "I'm Clarence."

The man shook his hand with a warm smile. "I'm Giacomo."

CHAPTER 8

"HOW DO YOU SPELL THAT?" Clarence asked.

"G-i-a-c-o-m-o," said the handsome man who had bought him a beer.

"Oh," Clarence said, peeling the label off his first, now empty, beer bottle. "I always thought that was pronounced Gia Como. Not Jacamo."

Giacomo laughed. "Yeah, I get that a lot. It's Italian. My mother's Italian and my father's not. She wanted to name me after my grandfather and my great-grandfather. My father agreed, but he insisted on calling me Jack. My mother calls me Trey because I'm the third. I have all sorts of nicknames, like in high school—"

"Does anyone call you Moe?" Clarence asked.

Giacomo tilted his head. "Strangely enough, no," he admitted. "Moe. Not sure about that one. It makes sense, but . . ."

"I think I'll call you Moe," Clarence said. He took a sip of his second beer. "Nice to meet you, Moe."

Moe smiled. "This is gonna sound strange and trite, but do you come here often? I mean, you don't really seem like the type."

Clarence looked Moe up and down. "Neither do you with your khakis and polo shirt. But no, my date thought this would be a good place to meet up. I work late, so I agreed. But he got all hung up on something and bolted. It was really our first date. We met on a double date last week with mutual friends. Well, not really friends, just acquaintances."

Moe nodded. "That sucks. He just stranded you in the middle of a leather bar in your work clothes."

Clarence laughed. "How did you know they were my work clothes?"

Moe winked. "You told me you came from work. Plus, I picture you comfortable in a logo T-shirt and ripped jeans. I mean, stylishly ripped jeans, not ones that are ripped from decades of hard labor."

"You got me," Clarence said. "If I could go out in pajama pants, I probably would."

"Pajama pants are in these days," Moe said. "I see people all the time on the train in pajama pants. Plus, a lot of people sleep in things that aren't pajamas, so anything goes, really."

Clarence glanced around the area. "I don't see any possessive guy looking toward us, scowling right now," he said. "Did you come in here alone?"

Moe nodded. "I just wanted to check it out. I've driven and walked by here on occasion and I was curious. Curiosity is now sated."

Clarence laughed. "I don't know if I'll come here again," he said. "It's a little too . . . flashy for me. I prefer something more, well, intimate. Some place where I don't have to yell to be heard."

Moe nodded. "To tell you the truth, I had no idea when I walked in here that it was a gay club. Maybe I should have been clued in by the Rodeo in the name, but I'm not too bright at times."

"Oh," Clarence said. "Are you not gay?"

Moe shrugged. "No, not really. But I figured I'd get a beer anyway since I was here." He looked at Clarence. "I'm sorry. I didn't mean to lead you on that I was gay. I mean, we were just talking. I'm enjoying talking to you. I hope we can keep talking."

Clarence nodded. "Yeah. Like I told you, I'm not looking for a pick up. So I guess now I know I'm safe."

Moe gave him a shit-eating smile. "I'll be your beard for the rest of the night," he said. "Everyone will leave you alone. I'm surprised you were alone when I came over, though. You're a really good-looking guy. I can see a lot of guys checking you out."

Clarence scanned the room again. Sure enough, he met some eyes and received some smiles. "It's my curse," he said. He took another sip of his beer. "So what do you do when you're not trawling gay bars?"

Moe chuckled. "I work at Stop & Shop right now. I'm between professional jobs. It actually pays okay. I'm stocking shelves, spending time thinking about my next move." He checked his watch. "Oh shit. I didn't realize how late it had gotten. Listen, sorry, but I have to go. I have to be at work at six tomorrow morning, and I need to get some sleep. Hey, Clarence, it was really nice meeting you."

Clarence nodded. "Same here, Moe. Thanks for the beer. Hey, if you ever change your mind about being gay, maybe we can talk again."

Moe laughed. "I don't know about that, but for sure we should get together again for a beer. What's your number?"

"So you exchanged numbers with the straight guy?" Rachel asked. "I mean, and you're okay with that?"

"I guess I have to be," Clarence said into the phone. "I mean, it's not like I'm cheating on anyone or anything."

"But I don't really get what happened with Luke," Rachel said. "You had a fight? It was your first real date! What could you have to fight about?"

For the moment, Clarence was fighting his impulse to tell Rachel all about the conversation with Luke, but he didn't think it was wise. "We're just a lot different when it comes to values," he said. "He's a rich kid from Newton whose parents took him to Europe every summer. Kind of pretentious. And the bar he wanted to meet me at . . . he kind of lied to me, like it was his first time going there. I could tell he knew his way around the place. I'm not really into that sort of stuff. I'm pretty sure there were some private rooms there that might have some kinky equipment."

"But you met this Moe guy there," Rachel said. "Maybe he was lying, too. Maybe he'd really been there before, but just wanted you to think that it was curiosity that brought him in. Maybe he's a regular, and maybe he uses that straight guy line to get some guy to think he can flip him."

Clarence sputtered out a laugh. "Flip him?" he asked. "You mean like a house? Rachel, where do you come up with these things?"

Clarence could almost see Rachel's blush through the phone. "I don't know. It's like gay people have their own language. Maybe you'll switch him from top to bottom. I mean, maybe I would have liked to be the top with us sometime."

Now Clarence couldn't hide his amusement. "Rachel, are you honestly telling me that you don't know what a top or bottom are in a gay hookup?"

"Well, I mean . . . Well, I've never been a guy with a guy before, so I wouldn't know, would I?" Rachel's words were either defiant or defensive, Clarence couldn't really tell.

"Oh, my dear sweet summer child," he said. "Being a top doesn't mean being on top, like a guy on a girl. Being a top is being the guy who actually penetrates the other guy during sex, like in the ass. The guy getting penetrated is called the bottom."

"Oh," Rachel said. "Yeah. Okay. But I don't get it. So one guy is the top and the other is the bottom, and then you switch off?"

Clarence closed his eyes and shook his head. "No, there's no switching. Well, for the most part, unless both guys have a lot of stamina, but it's kind of like one guy takes on the role of the top all or most of the time, and the other guy takes on the role of the bottom. It's like a personality type, what you prefer."

"Wait." Rachel paused. "I really don't understand. Why would anyone want to be the bottom all the time? It seems like the guy on top would always have the upper hand, so to speak. The guy on the bottom would be like a receptacle."

Clarence paused. "Oh," he said. "Oh, Rachel, you're not thinking like a guy right now. I mean, why would you? But no. No. The guy on the bottom really, really likes being on the bottom."

"But why?" Rachel asked. "Is it some sort of inferiority complex? He doesn't feel like he deserves to get off or something?"

Suddenly, Clarence understood Rachel's disconnect. "Sweetie, have you ever heard of a prostate?" he asked.

"Uh, yeah. I think guys have them and women don't. I'm not sure what they do, or what would be the equivalent on a woman's body. Maybe it has something to do with peeing? I've heard guys say something about going to the doctor and being told to turn their head and cough."

Clarence laughed. "Yes, Rachel, that's called a prostate check. To be honest, I'm not a hundred percent sure what the prostate's actual function is either, but I can tell you what it does to a bottom. Stimulation of the prostate can make a man want to implode. Or explode. Either way. Prostate stimulation is probably the best sensation known to mankind."

"Oh." There was a silence from Rachel's side of the phone. "Oh. Well, clearly women don't have an experience like that. I mean, we have the clit, but nothing up our ass. The one time I let a guy do that, I hated it, and I ended up with a fissure back there. But yeah, I can see the draw if that's the case. So why don't straight guys ask their girlfriends to put a dildo up there during sex?"

"I would guess some do," Clarence said. "But others might think it would be too gay to ask for that. It's a thing."

"Wow," Rachel said. "You guys are so complicated. When we were together, did you want to—"

"No," Clarence said quickly. "I had other places to go. Besides, I tend to be a bottom."

"Really?" Rachel sounded surprised. "I would think because you liked it with me . . ."

"Like I said, it's different. Plus, there's a lot of preparation you have to do."

"Like foreplay?"

Clarence rolled his eyes again. He hadn't been expecting to give his best female friend a tutorial on gay sex when he first woke up that morning. "No, foreplay is foreplay, and preparation is preparation. You have to stretch the guy out."

"Stretch?" Clarence spent the next five minutes explaining the concept to Rachel. "Wow," she said. "So you really need to be dedicated to getting off to be a gay guy. I had no idea. You guys are so complicated. So when you meet someone, you have to figure out who will be the top and who will be the bottom."

"Not to mention what type of gay they are."

He could hear Rachel sigh. "I have no idea what you're talking about."

"Like, if they're a bear, or an otter, or maybe they're into BDSM, and then if they're a twink or a daddy, or some category of daddy—"

"I've heard of bears, but otters?"

"Skinny hairy guys."

"And daddies?"

"Just what you'd imagine."

"Are they sugar daddies?"

"Sometimes but not always."

"Are you a twinkie?"

"In college, I might have been considered a twink in some circles. But now I've aged out."

"You know, this is kind of like book genres and tropes," Rachel said. "Everyone has categories they like and keep going back to. They might try some other ones, just to see what they're like, but they always end up with the comfortable, old hat in the end."

"That sounds kind of nice," Clarence said. "Cozy."

"What is Moe?" she asked.

"Straight," Clarence answered. "But if he were gay, I would peg him as a top, a masc top. He seems to have a surety about his way in the world. And he's very comfortable in his masculinity."

"Would that make you a fem?"

Clarence laughed. "No, it's okay for two mascs to be into each other. Anything goes, Rachel. We all don't fit into an exact category. Just like us having sex didn't make me bisexual."

"I never said it did," Rachel said. "Do people say things like that?"

"No," Clarence said quickly. "I mean, actually, they might, but since I've never told anyone about us, I don't know. It was just a thought."

"Okay." There was a shuffling noise on her end of the phone. "I just got a new manuscript tossed on my desk. I just finished the last one about twenty minutes ago. No rest for the weary. I hope this one doesn't suck like the last one did."

"I guess I'll just talk to you later. Are you seeing Barry again?"

"We're meeting for coffee during work on Friday," Rachel said. "Maybe we'll make plans for the weekend."

"I hope that works out," Clarence said. And he did. "I'll talk to you soon."

After he got off the phone, Clarence sat and thought back on the conversation, smiling. That had been the first time he and Rachel had ever really talked in-depth about the gay lifestyle. He had always avoided that kind of talk with her, because it would have led to the discussion about what they were doing, and why. But now, it seemed easy. Maybe they were turning some sort of corner in their friendship, talking about their dates and their preferences. He had to laugh when he thought about some of Rachel's reactions to what he was telling her. He couldn't tell if she was horrified or just surprised. He just hoped she wasn't worried that she hadn't given him what he wanted during their time together. He had chosen to be with her because he always enjoyed it. But it would be hard for Rachel to understand that. It was hard for him to understand it himself.

Todd approached him in his office that afternoon. "Ken said that Luke said that things didn't work out with the two of you." He sat down and folded his arms on Clarence's desk. "What happened? I mean, you don't have to tell me if you don't want to, but I feel kind of bad because I'm the one that offered to fix you guys up."

Clarence shook his head. "No, there's no way you could have known." He told Todd about his conversation with Luke. "I mean, he had the nerve to tell me I was lying to myself about my own sexuality. I can tell you right now, I'm not."

Todd nodded. "I think you know yourself best," he said. "I mean, it might be unusual for a gay guy to have sex with a female friend, but I don't think it's unheard of. And you're right. It's not up to him to define what you are. That's all on you." He paused. "And you're sure you're not bi?"

Clarence laughed. "I'm not bisexual. I promise you. I have no attraction to women. My attraction to Rachel is an attraction to Rachel, who is a woman, but does not represent all women. I mean, I think it's possible to have a soulmate that is not necessarily anything more than a friend. And we just found a different way to express our friendship. But now, I'm making an effort to redefine it. I have to let her go. I'm not saying she's in love with me, but I know she's confused about us. She needs to know that it's never going to be more than it is now and move on. She's already been on a date with this one guy, and she's seeing him again on Friday. And I did kind of meet this new guy the other day . . ."

Todd smiled. "Way to move on, my friend."

Clarence shook his head. "He's straight," he said. "But that's okay. He wants to be friends, and I could use some more guy friends. I mean, guy friends who are straight. I don't really have any right now. It will be an adventure."

"Is he good looking?"

"He's hot, and you should see his eyes. . . ." Clarence was looking up at the ceiling, and he looked back down. "I mean, yeah, sure, you could say he's okay looking. But that's not what this is all about."

Todd laughed. "Yeah, right. Just do me a favor. Don't get yourself into a relationship with a guy that can't be your guy, okay? It sounds a lot like what you and Rachel had going on."

Clarence shook his head. "The straight guy isn't gonna have sex with me."

"How do you know that?" Todd asked. "The gay guy had sex with a woman. Anything seems to go these days."

Clarence thought about that. "I don't know. Maybe. But I don't think I could flip a guy."

Todd laughed. "Did you just say flip a guy? Like a pancake?"

Clarence had to smile. "That's a Rachelism," he said. "Oh, and by the way, you're really the first person I've told about Rachel, including any of our friends. So if you're ever with all of us, please don't say anything. We've never told them, and I'm pretty sure none of them know."

Todd stared at them. "I find it hard to believe they don't know."

Clarence's eyes went wide. "What, you think they know?"

Todd nodded. "You've been friends with them all since college, right? I'm pretty sure they know or at least suspect. How could they not? They're your close friends."

Clarence considered this. "Do you think they hate me for it?"

Todd shrugged. "I have no idea. I don't know your friends and what they're like. But they're your friends. I would think if they thought you didn't know what you were doing, they would tell you."

"You'd think that," Clarence said. "Or maybe they just think it's none of their business. Or they're judging me silently, or to each other."

Todd smirked. "Maybe you should ask one of them. That might be the best way to find out."

# CHAPTER 9

"I'M SO BORED!" JESSICA COMPLAINED. "Go out with me!"

Rachel smiled. "I would. You know I would. But Barry and I are going out tonight."

"You went out with him last week!"

Rachel laughed. "That's called dating, Jess," she said. "It's not a one-and-done thing."

Jessica sighed. "Take me with you. Maybe he'd be into a threesome."

"I don't think so. At least not yet. Why don't you just do something with the guys tonight?"

"I texted Steve and he said that he and Jerry are getting together with Clare tonight."

Rachel shrugged to herself. "So go out with them then."

"But that's just the thing," Jessica whined. "I asked if I could join them, and he said that Clare wanted to meet with them to talk about something. He wouldn't say what it was, but he did say that it wasn't up to him to invite me. It sounds like a gay friend summit."

"But you're a gay friend," Rachel said.

"I'm talking about gay men, Ray, and I'm bi. You know that. Hence the idea of a Rachel-and-Barry sandwich with Jessica in the middle! No, I guess Clare must have something on his mind. I wonder what it could be."

Rachel's face felt cold. "Uh, I have no idea." She wondered if it could be about Moe, the straight guy he had met earlier in the week. Maybe he was more into him than he let on and needed to get some real talk from their friends. "Seriously, though, Jess, I wish we could hang out, but just not tonight. Maybe tomorrow afternoon?"

Jessica sighed. "We could go to the movies. You've wanted to see that new Timothée Chalamet movie for a while."

Rachel cringed. "That's what I'm doing with Barry tonight. I told him on our first date that I wanted to see it, and when we were at coffee yesterday, he asked me to go. He had even looked up the show times already. We're gonna get something quick to eat and head for the theater."

"Whatever." Rachel could tell that her friend's frustration was not aimed directly at her. "I guess we can just go shopping or something."

Rachel smiled. "I'd like that. And I can blabber all about my date, and you can tell me all about whatever show you binge-watched all night tonight."

"Who are you kidding, Ray? You know it will be *Community* again. Alright. Have a great time tonight, and tell Barry I said 'hey, sailor!'"

Rachel laughed. "I'm saving the threesome conversation for our ten-year anniversary, Jess. Have a good night."

"So you liked the movie?" Barry asked as they walked back through the parking lot to his car.

Rachel nodded. "It was really good. I just love Timothée Chalamet. When I was in high school, I thought for sure I would marry him someday. It was a nice dream. But now I don't think I'd want to. I like the fantasy of the book boyfriend better than the reality, and I think that goes for movies, too."

Barry laughed. "Book boyfriend?"

Rachel smiled. "Yeah. You know, it's about experiencing escapism in a book. You lose yourself in the story, and you start to feel like you're the character you relate to. And you have preferences. If you read a book and don't feel like the male main character could be your soulmate, it's kind of a waste of time."

"But what if it doesn't work out between the two characters in the end?"

Rachel chuckled. "Oh, that won't happen. I only read guaranteed HEAs."

Barry looked intrigued. "HEAs? Sounds like some sort of homeowners' association."

"No, it means happily ever after. It's kind of my thing. I mean, not only what I read, but also what I edit. It's my department at work."

"Oh cool," Barry said. He reached his car, unlocked the doors, and opened the passenger door for Rachel. He went around the car and got in the driver's seat. "Becca works on kids' books, right?"

Rachel nodded. "She's an art editor. Most children's books are picture books. I don't think I could do what she does."

Barry laughed. "That's what everyone says to me when I tell them I'm planning to go to school to be a therapist. But I think there's a reason people can't do what other people do. If they could, they would, and everyone would have to fight over the best jobs, even more than they do now. I mean, I don't think I could collect garbage, but the people who do it are good at it. Could you imagine if all of the sudden no one agreed to collect garbage? The world would be a wreck."

"I really like the way you look at things, Barry," Rachel said. "I think you'll make a great therapist. You explain things well."

Barry smiled bashfully. "Thanks. That means a lot. So do you want me to bring you home, or do you want to go get dessert or drinks or anything?"

"I'd be up for both," Rachel said.

Barry nodded as he started the car. "I know just the place." He pulled out into the parking lot, and then onto the street.

"You haven't lived here very long," Rachel said suspiciously. "How could you know just the place?"

"Becca and Jason brought me out for my birthday," Barry answered. "It's a place called Amaretto Pie. Have you heard of it?"

"No." Rachel was shocked that the new kid was going to expose her to something she had never experienced in her own backyard. "It sounds really good. Do they really have something called amaretto pie there?"

"They do. Becca had it and said it's amazing. I don't think it can make you drunk. I think all of the alcohol is cooked out. But we can get drinks, too. Do you like mixed drinks?"

Rachel nodded. "Amaretto is my favorite liqueur," she said. "I love a good amaretto sour."

"Well, then this sounds like the right place for us to end our night."

They were quiet on the ride over. Rachel thought about what Barry said about ending the night. Was that his way of saying he was going to drop her off after their date and say goodnight, or did he just mean the completion of the first part of their night? She had no way of knowing him without asking, and it didn't feel like something she would feel comfortable asking about. So that meant she just had to wait and find out in real time.

Barry parked in front of the restaurant. They went inside and sat on high-backed stools at the bar. They picked up the menus and looked at the dessert options.

"I'm totally getting the house pie," Rachel said.

Barry smiled. "Good choice. I'll tell you what. I'm gonna get the chocolate silk pie. If you like that, too, we can share."

Rachel's face started to warm. Sharing desserts was an intimate act. "Okay," she said. "I like chocolate silk, too."

They talked about the movie while they sipped on their cocktails and waited for their desserts to be delivered. When the pie arrived, Rachel took a small bite of hers and closed her eyes. "This is incredible," she said. "It's the best pie I've ever had!"

Barry took a bite of his. "I might have to fight you on this. I think mine's better."

"Ha!" Rachel replied. "I think you've challenged me. I'm up for your challenge!" She cut a bit of her pie with her fork and held it up to Barry's mouth. "Try it."

Barry accepted the spoon into his mouth and made an almost sexual sound. "Oh God," he said. "This is . . ." He pointed to her plate. "I think I lost. I think I could die right now and be happy having tasted that pie."

Rachel laughed, and then accepted the bite of Barry's pie. The chocolate cream melted in her mouth. "Oh," she moaned. "There's regular chocolate, and then there's this pie. I don't know, Barry. I might have been wrong." They looked at each other for a moment, then picked up their plates and made the switch.

They spent five minutes in silence as they devoured their desserts. When they were done, Rachel felt as if she had just had the best orgasm of her life. "We need to come back here again," she said. "But not right away. Like in a couple months, or something."

Barry smiled at her, but it wasn't the warm, welcoming smile she was getting accustomed to.

"Did I say something wrong?" she asked impulsively.

Barry looked surprised at the question. "What? No. It's just . . . well, I've kind of been in a weird place lately with moving to a new city and trying to find where I fit in. You mentioned coming here again in a few months, and I want to come here again with you in the future, but I think I just need to let you know that I'm not sure I'm really looking for a serious relationship right now. I mean, if one comes from this, that would be great, but I'm kind of in a place where I think it's a good idea to meet other people, you know? I came from a small town, and while everyone wasn't exactly the same, they were kind of the same. I want to see what it's like, being among a more diverse set of people. Does that make sense?"

Rachel considered his words, trying to take them the way they were intended rather than personally. "I mean, I think it does. It sounds like you're saying you want to date other people."

Barry's head tilted. "Yeah, I guess that's sort of what I mean. I want to meet other people. Lots of people. But I really like you, and really enjoy spending time with you, so I wanted to let you know right away, so there would be no, like, misunderstandings down the line. I guess where I come from, people date more than one person. Well, at least when they're young. But it makes sense not to tie yourself to the first person you meet. God, this doesn't sound as good out loud as it sounded in my head. I'm not saying that I want to stop seeing you. But I'm saying that I can't promise that it's going to lead to a long-term relationship. Or it might. I don't know."

Rachel forced herself to smile. "Okay," she said. "I get it. Yeah. That's fine. I mean, maybe we should aim at just being friends then. You know, so no one gets hurt." It was her weak attempt at not making herself readily available to the next guy who was not available to her. There always seemed to be the next guy.

Barry looked a bit hurt. "I-I don't know. I mean, yeah. I do want to be friends with you. But I also find you really attractive, and I want to, like, kiss you. But I just want you to know—"

"I know," Rachel interrupted. "Don't get my hopes up. I get it."

Barry sat back in his chair in defeat. "I don't think that's what I meant."

Rachel looked at her shoes quietly. "If you want to kiss me, but you're not thinking about the future—"

"I am thinking of the future, Rachel," he said. "I mean, that's all I'm thinking about. I'm thinking about hanging out with a really great woman who I just met and want to know better. But I just don't want to make any promises. If that means that you don't feel like we can hang out anymore, I guess I can be okay with that. I just didn't want to lead you on."

Rachel wished she had a hundred dollars for every guy who had said those exact words to her throughout her life. "You're not leading me on," she said firmly. "I'm a fully grown woman. I make my own decisions. And you've been honest with me. And I want to kiss you, too."

Barry's eyes lit up. He sat up. Then he leaned in closer. "Can I kiss you right now?"

Rachel considered this question. Then she nodded. "You can kiss me, but that's all. For now. Okay?"

Barry nodded. "Okay." He leaned in even closer, and their lips made contact. And his lips were soft. And warm. And skilled. And his tongue made light contact with her lower lip but went no further. Just the way Rachel liked to be kissed. They continued the kiss for several seconds, until Rachel pulled away to take a breath. "That was nice," Barry said softly.

Rachel nodded. "Nice," was the only word she could produce.

They stayed at the bar for another half hour, talking and making each other laugh. Finally, Rachel looked at her phone. "I need to go home and get some sleep," she said. "You might have figured this out about me already, but still I'll tell you, I'm a major reader, and I can't sleep unless I read in bed. So I have to go to bed an hour or so before I want to sleep. It makes for some earlier nights than other people might like."

Barry grinned. "I like that about you," he said. "You have a passion. Not everyone has a passion, but you are truly devoted to reading. It makes you more interesting."

Rachel snickered. "What are you truly devoted to, Barry?"

Barry thought about it. "My shoe collection." He laughed. "I'm kidding, but I really do enjoy my shoes. No, I guess I'm very loyal. I treasure my family and my friends. I've stayed in touch with every one of them since I moved. I have nieces and nephews back in Michigan, and I Facetime with them once a week. I don't want them to forget me."

"I don't think they would ever forget their Uncle Barry," Rachel teased.

Barry shook his head. "No. I don't think any of them would forget their

Uncle Barry." He had an amused expression on his face that Rachel couldn't read. "Do you want me to drive you home? You came on the train, right?"

"Yeah." Rachel had a moment of panic while she tried to decide if it was okay for Barry to know where she lived. Then she realized it was probably more dangerous to take the train home this late at night by herself. "Okay. That would be great. Thanks."

They talked about light topics during the fifteen-minute drive back to Rachel's apartment building. Barry pulled up into visitor parking and walked her to the entrance. She unlocked the lobby door, pushed it open, and then turned to look at Barry. "Thanks for dinner and the movie. And the pie. The pie was amazing. I guess maybe I'll see you soon?"

Barry nodded. "For sure. Let's do something next weekend, if you're up for it." He leaned in and gave her a soft, lingering kiss on the lips. When he pulled away, his eyes were closed, but he opened them quickly. "I'll text you tomorrow." And with that, Rachel went inside, and Barry went back to his car.

Rachel usually took the stairs up to the fourth floor, but tonight, she didn't have the energy. She rode up on the elevator and lumbered down the hall to her apartment. She let herself in and went straight to the couch, falling onto the cushions. She removed her phone from her purse, and opened it up directly to Clarence's contact. She started her text.

Rachel
I'm not sure what to do. Barry likes me but he thinks he wants to date around. Am I doing that thing that I do again? Am I just gonna get hurt? Help!

Clarence

Clarence

Clarence
. . .

Clarence
Oh, sweetie. I'm so sorry. I'll come over tomorrow morning before work. I'll bring ice cream.

CHAPTER 10

Earlier that night . . .

"SO WHAT WAS SO IMPORTANT that you needed to see us alone?" Jerry asked. "It's our fifth anniversary tonight."

Clarence snorted. "What anniversary is this one? The anniversary of when you first did laundry together as a couple?"

Jerry scowled. "No. This is a big one. This is the anniversary of the day I first wore an article of Steve's clothing. You know, like the morning after. I left his dorm room wearing his sweatshirt. It was a big fucking deal."

Clarence laughed. "How does one celebrate that kind of anniversary?"

Steve rolled his eyes. "Have you ever seen me wear this shirt before? It's clearly Jerry's. And he's wearing mine. Don't ask about our underwear and socks."

"Oh my God, you guys," Clarence said. "Steve, how do you keep up with all of these anniversary traditions? I wouldn't be able to keep them all straight."

"Oh, I don't have to," Steve said with a sardonic grin. "There's a calendar.

It has all of these crucially important occasions on there. Every New Year's Day, he copies them all into the new calendar for the year and hangs it up in the kitchen."

Clarence turned to Jerry. "You could do it all on your phone calendar, you know."

Jerry shook his head. "It's not the same. You have to go into it to check it, or you get an alarm on the day. With the paper calendar, it's always there for us to look at when we go to the kitchen, so there's no forgetting. And if there are gifts involved, we get a heads-up to start shopping."

"Are there gifts for the first time sharing clothes?"

Steve nodded vigorously. "Of course there are gifts, Clare. There are always gifts. For First Time Sharing Clothes Day, we buy each other an article of clothing that the other one will actually wear, that the other wouldn't mind wearing on First Time Sharing Clothes Day."

"So last year . . ."

Steve nodded. "Yeah. I got Jerry this shirt that I'm wearing tonight."

Clarence nodded. "Okay. So, happy First Time Sharing Clothes Day, guys."

"Thanks," Jerry said with a pleased smile. Then he got serious. "But really, Clare, what are we doing here tonight, besides having a beer and pretzels?"

Clarence sighed, then sat up straight. He looked back and forth at his friends. "I have to ask you guys something. It's kind of hard to do, but I have to know."

"Sounds serious," Steve said.

Clarence nodded. "It's just . . . well, I have to know. Have you guys noticed anything, like, weird, going on between me and Rachel lately?"

Jerry and Steve looked at each other with knowing expressions. "What do you mean?" Jerry asked. "You mean like tension or something?"

Clarence could tell that Jerry was being irreverent. "So there is something," he asked.

"Recently?" Steve asked, "or maybe for the last five years or so?"

Clarence nodded. "We're best friends."

Jerry nodded. "Best friends. Yeah, best friends who have a habit of getting naked and doing the bedtime jig together."

Steve turned back to him, his mouth hanging open. "The bedtime jig? How on Earth did you come up with that one? I mean, it's not wrong."

Clarence let his face fall down to his hands. "So you guys always knew."

"It was kind of cute," Steve said. "I mean, you two thought you were keeping a big secret from all of us, and it was really us keeping the secret that we knew the secret. It was like we were some sort of double agents."

Clarence felt his limbs go weak. "Does Jessica know, too?"

Steve glanced at Jerry and then back at Clarence. "Jess was the first to figure it out, and she told me. Then I told Jerry. I mean, there was no way I was keeping it from Jerry. Then I'd have to be celebrating the Day I Kept a Huge Secret from My Boyfriend Day each year. But I mean, it was too hot a secret to keep to myself."

"So what did you think was going on with us?" Clarence asked.

Jerry shrugged. "Well, mostly it's not our business, but we were a bit confused about the whole thing. It wasn't like the two of you were dating, and you kept it all a secret. We knew you were gay and not bi, but still you were doing this thing with Rachel. So yeah. We don't know. Do you even know?"

Clarene shook his head. "I have an idea about why she was doing it. I mean, it's all about her father. But me?" He shook his head again. "I think it's just that I love her and I didn't have any other way to express it as much as I wanted to. But I can't give her what she wants, and I know that she's not really what I want either, but still, when we're together . . ." He sighed. "But I'm hurting her, and I don't want to. And it has to stop. So I'm trying to make it stop." He paused. "I went out with this guy last week, but it didn't work out. Probably because I brought up the fact that I was regularly having sex with my best woman friend, and he thought that made me bi. He couldn't let it go."

"That's weird," Steve said. "I mean, sexuality is fluid, right? What business of his is it how you label yourself?" Clarence felt warmth run through his body. "I knew you guys would understand."

"So why are you asking us about you and Rachel today anyway?" Jerry asked. "I mean, it's been going on since college, right? Did something happen?"

Clarence went over his answer in his head for a moment. "I . . . I guess nothing really happened. We just went a long time without it happening, but then it started up again on the night of my birthday after you all left, and then for a little bit, and then I realized I couldn't do it anymore. I mean, I've felt that way before, too, but just kept letting it happen. But this time, I'm really committed to stopping it, and just being her friend, and I think she realizes it, because she's just started seeing this guy. I think she's not let herself get involved with anyone for a long time because she was worried about what would happen between us. She wants to protect me, and my feelings, but I feel like a total shit for letting her do that. I can't be what she wants, and I know she can't be all of it for me, too. Ugh." He put his palm to his forehead. "I think she really likes this new guy."

Jerry reached out for his hand. "And that makes you feel some kind of way, huh?"

Clarence nodded. "It does, but maybe not for the reasons you would think."

"I would think it had nothing to do with you wanting a long-term, romantic relationship with Rachel," Steve said. "I mean, maybe there's some jealousy about another man taking some space in her life, and that he can provide something to her that you can't, and that she needs. Is that it?"

Clarence smirked. "Okay, maybe it is for the reasons you think. Yeah. And I worry that if this guy hurts her in any way, I'll want to go after him and tell him off, and then go and comfort her in the way I know how to, and that's no better than what was going on before she met him."

"Maybe he won't hurt her," Jerry said. "Maybe they'll fall in love and live happily ever after."

Clarence shook his head. "That would be nice, and I'd be the first person to be happy for her. I would even give her away at her wedding if she asked me. But knowing what I know about Rachel, there must be something about this guy, something that makes him unattainable. Something that will keep her hanging on and then hurt her. Just like I was doing. I want to find some way to end the cycle, you guys, and I don't know how." His eyes started to fill with tears.

"Oh, Clare," Jerry said. He stood up and moved toward him to give him a tight hug. "I guess I didn't realize it was as deep as all this. I thought that it was just you and Rachel recreationally screwing around sometimes. But it sounds like your feelings are . . . complicated."

Clarence nodded his head against his friend's shoulder. "Yeah. It's complicated. And what's even more complicated is that I know now that I really want to find love. I mean, real love. I want to meet a guy, and fall in love, and have it all. And I'm trying, but . . ."

Jerry pulled away. "But what? What's holding you back?"

Clarence looked at the floor. "I don't know any guy I can do that with. I was hoping that Luke guy might have potential, but he had no ability to even understand me, let alone date me or even just fuck me."

"There are other guys, Clare," Steve said. "There are tons of gay guys out there who are also looking for the same thing you are. You just have to make yourself available for them. And you can't do that if you're reserving your heart for a woman who will never be all that for you."

Clarence sniffed. "There's another complicating factor."

Steve threw his hands up in the air. "Of course there is. This is not the first time we're meeting you, Clarence Steiner. What is it?"

Clarence straightened his posture on his chair and then slouched again. "There's this guy . . ."

Jerry rolled his eyes. "What's wrong with him? He has a boyfriend? He's deep in the closet? He's a mama's boy? Deep into BDSM?"

"He's straight."

"Oh Lord," Jerry said as he sat back down hard on his chair. "A straight boy? Clare, didn't we have this talk already in college?"

"How did you even meet this straight boy?" Steve asked.

"That's the thing," Clarence said. "I met him at a gay bar. The Rodeo."

"The Rodeo?" Steve asked. "What on Earth were you doing at the Rodeo? Do you even own any leather undergarments?"

"It was where Luke wanted to meet. He said he had never been there, but now I'm having the feeling he's a regular. This guy, Moe. He said he came in just to check it out. He didn't know it was a gay bar."

The couple on the other side of the table glanced at each other again. "He just wandered into a gay club out of curiosity? He didn't know it was a gay bar? Something sounds suspect here."

"No, he swears he's straight," Clarence said. "He told me. He was cool about us being friends. I gave him my number so we could hang out again."

"You gave him your number?" Steve asked, eyebrows raised. "You gave your number. To the only straight guy in the gay bar." Clarence nodded. "Do you have some sort of death wish?"

"What exactly did he say to let you know he was straight?" Jerry asked.

Clarence thought back. "Well, he told me that he didn't know that it was a gay bar. So I asked him if he wasn't gay, and he said, 'no, not really.'"

"No, not really?" Jerry asked, his voice getting higher and higher pitched as the conversation progressed. "I mean, c'mon, Clare. When in your life have you ever heard a straight guy say 'no, not really' when you ask him if he's gay? They mostly jump back, cover their dicks, and run off to find the first woman in their sight to start humping to prove how straight they are. But this guy, in a gay bar, says, 'no, not really'?" This is really sus."

Clarence thought about it. "I mean, yeah, I guess so. Or maybe he's just not an asshole straight guy."

"Or maybe he's questioning things," Steve offered. "Maybe something drew him to the Rodeo that night. Maybe it was curiosity."

"Or maybe he really just didn't know it was a gay club," Clarence said, "and I'm just a glutton for punishment, and I gave the straight guy my number, and now I haven't put my phone down in days, waiting for him to text me."

"Has he?" Jerry asked.

Clarence shook his head. "Not yet. But I mean, why would he take my number if he didn't want to contact me, right? I mean, yeah, if he's a straight guy in a gay bar, it would be weird to ask for a guy's number if you don't really want it, especially if it's for non-romantic purposes."

"It's completely unheard of for a truly straight guy to ask for a guy's number in a gay bar," Steve said. "Clare, be careful, okay? This guy sounds like he might be bi-curious. He might just be looking for someone to experiment with, to show him the ropes, to see if he likes it. I don't want to see you get hurt."

"You mean like I've been doing to my best friend for years? Maybe payback should be that harsh."

Steve sighed. "Dude, you don't know anything now. I mean, the guy might ghost you after all this. It might be a non-issue. Or you might just get a good straight friend out of it. Or he's gay, and the two of you fall in love and have a happily ever after. That would be nice. But another possibility is that you fall in love with him, and he's not able to be all that for you, just like you can't be all that for Ray."

Clarence grabbed a handful of his hair and felt product crunch between his fingers. He sat there with his friends while they all finished another drink, and then they drove him home. When he got there, he grabbed another beer from the fridge and sat down on the couch, his normal place to wallow in self-pity. He turned on the TV and flipped through the channels. He didn't have the energy to pick a show to stream and commit to watching a whole episode. He landed on a repeat of *America's Funniest Home Videos*, said a quick prayer to the memory of Bob Saget, and settled in to watch.

It was near midnight when his phone buzzed. He knew it could only be one person.

> **Rachel**
> I'm not sure what to do. Barry likes me but he thinks he wants to date around. Am I doing that thing that I do again? Am I just gonna get hurt? Help!

Clarence read the text over and over again. He had been worried that something like this would happen. He just hadn't thought it would happen so quickly. He wanted to comfort Rachel. He started to write a text: Do you want me to come over? He quickly deleted it. That would just lead them back to the old behavior he was trying to stop. Then he came up with a better plan, one that sounded like it was coming from a gay best friend:

> **Clarence**
> Oh, sweetie. I'm so sorry. I'll come over tomorrow morning before work. I'll bring ice cream.

> **Rachel**
> That would be great. Ice cream fixes everything.

> **Clarence**
> I'll get chocolate brownie.

> **Rachel**
> My favorite! BTW, how did things go with the guys tonight?

Clarence
How did you know about that?

Rachel
Jess told me. She was jealous we all had plans
tonight without her. I'm going shopping with
her tomorrow afternoon

Clarence
It was good. I'll tell you more about it later.
But I think we both should go to bed. Did you
drink?

Rachel
Just two drinks over four hours. Not even
buzzed anymore. You?

Clarence
Working on my third beer right now. I'll text
you tomorrow before I head over. Don't worry
about showering or getting dressed. It sounds
like jammies would be appropriate attire for
this event

Once he and Rachel finished their conversation, he plugged his phone into the charger next to his bed and went into the bathroom to get ready for bed. When he was done, he went back into the living room to turn off the lights. As soon as he entered his bedroom, he heard another buzz on his phone. He walked back to check it, wondering what Rachel had forgotten to tell him. He picked up the phone, and what he saw knocked him down onto his bed in a sitting position.

Unknown caller
Hey, is this Clarence?

Clarence

Clarence
. . .

Clarence
Yes

Unknown caller
Hey, it's Giacomo. Moe. You know, from that club last week?

Clarence
Oh, yeah. Hey. What's up?

Clarence added Moe to his contacts but decided to use a name that would remind him of their unique situation.

Hot Straight Guy from the Gay Bar
Sorry I didn't text sooner. I had a good time talking to you. Even for just a short time. Wanna get together again? I know a sports bar near me where we can have a beer and hang out.

Clarence

Clarence

Clarence
Okay.

Hot Straight Guy from the Gay Bar
Great. How about Thursday? Didn't you say you work late? What about after work?

Clarence
I get out at 9. .Where's the bar?

Hot Straight Guy from the Gay Bar
It's actually in Weston. It's close to the store I
work in. Is that too far from you?

Clarence
I can get on the T. If the stop's too far from the
bar, you may need to pick me up if that's ok.

Hot Straight Guy from the Gay Bar
I can do that. What are you up to tonight? Did
you go out?

Clarence chatted with Moe for a few more minutes, talking about his night with his friends. Moe told him that he had been out on a date and had a good time. He said that he was a night person and would probably be up for the next hour or so, puttering around his apartment, maybe making himself some food before going to bed. Clarence told Moe that he would be working the next day, and that someday he should stop by the museum so he could give him a personal tour. Moe said he would like that.

Clarence started to yawn, so he told Moe he had to go to bed. He promised to see him on Thursday night, and they would text each other if there were any changes in the plan. Clarence changed the contact name to Moe and put his phone back down on the nightstand. He finished turning off all his lights and got into bed. He was tired. He needed to get some sleep so he could be on his best game for work the next day. But there was no way in hell he was going straight to sleep. Not after hearing from Moe. He knew exactly what he needed to do to calm himself down enough to sleep.

CHAPTER 11

"I DON'T THINK IT'S AS bad as you think it is," Clarence told her.

Rachel shoved another overflowing spoonful of Ben & Jerry's Chocolate Fudge Brownie into her mouth. "What, you can see into the future?" she asked.

Clarence reached over and wiped a smudge of mascara off her temple. "Dude, you really need to remove your makeup before going to bed."

"I usually do," Rachel said, reaching up and rubbing her own temple with the sleeve of her pajama top. "I was just too upset last night and didn't have the energy. I'm lucky I was able to drag myself from the couch to the bed to go to sleep." She leaned her head against Clarence's shoulder. "Why do I do this to myself? Do I have some sign on my forehead that screams that I'm looking for a guy who can't focus on me, or ever make a commitment?"

Clarence patted her arm. Rachel was aware that he was avoiding touching her in an intimate way. "You're not sure that's really what's going on here, Ray," he said. "He's new in town. He wants to feel it out for a while. He wants to make friends. It makes sense. If you moved to a new place, you wouldn't want to tie yourself to one person immediately. I mean, if you ended up dumping him, he'd have no one to comfort him. He'd have to deal with a heartbreak and make new friends at the same time."

Rachel sat up and looked at him. "That actually does make a lot of sense," she said. "It's just . . . what if he's just saying all that stuff? What if he's some sort of player who wants to have a girl in every Boston suburb? What if he isn't really out for my best interest, only his own?"

"It sounds like you're talking about your father," Clarence said.

Rachel sort of hated the fact that Clarence was right. She *was* talking about her father. She and her mother had been a stop in a port when he came back to the East Coast a couple of times per year. He didn't feel committed to them. He felt committed to no one but himself. It was easy to see similarities in all of the guys she met. First, the boy who moved back to England, then the basketball player with the girlfriend. And last, the gay guy. The guy who had no capacity to love her in that way. But at least Clarence hadn't left her.

"Maybe I *am* talking about my father," she said. "But you have to admit, I tend to date my father over and over."

Clarence nodded. "I know," he said softly. "But Ray, if you really think this guy isn't gonna be able to be the guy you need, you might just need to cut him loose right now, before you get too attached. I know that's not as easy as it sounds, but if you wait, and he's never able to commit, you'll be so attached that it will be harder to walk away."

Rachel sighed. "I just don't know. I keep thinking that I need to see him a few more times and see how it goes. I mean, we've kissed a bit. Not even really made out."

Clarence grinned. "How was it, kissing him? Is he a good kisser?"

Rachel felt her face go red, but then she relaxed. This was Clarence. She smiled. "Yeah, he's a really good kisser. He has awesome lips, really soft, and he had that little bit of five o'clock shadow. It didn't scrape my face, but it bristled a little. He wasn't all tongue, which was good."

"Yeah, you don't like a lot of tongue."

Rachel laughed. "No, I don't. Remember that time I bit yours? I think you got the message pretty quickly."

Clarence absentmindedly reached his hand up to his cheek and touched it lightly. "Yeah, it bled a little. It hurt to drink orange juice for a week."

Rachel shoved him in the arm. "You're such a baby. And a revisionist. But yeah, he's a gentle kisser. I'd like to see what he's like in the heat of passion." She hung her head. "If we ever get to that point."

Clarence picked up the pint of ice cream and looked inside. "We'd better hurry before this melts." He scooped some up and fed it to Rachel. "Chocolate is a love simulation, you know that. Plus you know I love you, too. If Barry makes any dickhead moves, I'll beat the crap out of him."

"He's like six-foot-two and muscular," Rachel boasted.

"Oh. Well, maybe not beat the crap out of him then, but I'd formulate some sort of stern statement that would get him thinking about what he did."

Rachel laughed. "Yeah, I can see that."

Clarence ate some more ice cream. "I think you should keep seeing him for now, if you want my opinion. But maybe set a limit. Like, if after two more dates you're not feeling like it's going anywhere, or you can't tell if it is, talk to him about it, and see what he has to say. If you're feeling like you want more, and he's still not sure what he wants, then you might have to make some hard choices. If you decide to walk away from it, I'll help you. All of our friends will, too. I think that's the part that's been missing in your past relationships. It's like you feel that you deserve the treatment you're getting."

Rachel gave him a teasing smile. "Present company excluded?"

Clarence looked into her eyes, his expression as serious as a heart attack. "No, Rachel. Present company *in*cluded. But in our case, I think we were both to blame. Maybe me more than you, since I knew your pattern and never did anything to stop it from happening again. But yeah, I mean from the very beginning, we both knew that what we were doing wouldn't change who I am. Maybe we both hoped it would, for different reasons, but it never could have."

"We're having the talk I don't want to have," Rachel said. She was holding the pint of ice cream, but now she put it down on the night table. It was starting to wilt.

Clarence shook his head. "I know you don't want to talk about it, but I do. Rachel, even if you don't want to hear me say it, I need to say it. I've been a terrible friend, which is even worse because I knew I was being a terrible friend, and still I did nothing to change that. I hurt you. No, don't shake your head. I hurt you, over and over. Yes, you could have said no at any time, but it was up to me as your best friend to help you say no. To support you. I know all of your strengths, but I also know your weaknesses. And I took advantage of them."

Rachel's hands were shaking. She sat on them. She crossed her legs in front of her on the bed. "I'm not sure what to say, Clarence," she said. "I mean, honestly, I'm a bit upset with you for saying all of this, because it feels like you're taking away my right to have made my own choices, which I was plenty capable of doing. You act as though I didn't know what I was doing, or what was going on. Have you ever considered that the whole time, I've known exactly what I was doing, or maybe it was something that I needed to do at the time?"

Clarence's jaw was dropped. "I never intended to say that you didn't have a choice. I'm only saying that I had one, too, and I didn't choose well. I chose selfishly, and I want to apologize for that. I want to do whatever I can to make it up to you."

"You don't get to apologize," Rachel scolded. "You didn't do anything that I didn't want you to do. Okay? I mean, maybe now I'm starting to make better decisions, but I don't regret anything that you and I did. I think there was a time about two years ago when I thought I was in love with you, and yes, that hurt. But again, it was on me. You never lied to me about who you were. Who you are. So please don't start now. I think you knew that we both knew what we were doing, and we both enjoyed it. I don't think if I went back in time now, that I would do anything to change it. Clare, we've been fucking around with each other almost since we met. It's part of our relationship. It's part of why I love you. It's part of why we can be the type of friends we are. You're right; you know my strengths and my weaknesses. Everything about me. How many other people do you think know as much as you do? How many people do I share myself with in that way?" She looked at Clarence, awaiting an answer.

"None," he said quietly. "And I'll always be grateful to you for that gift. But Ray, we need to figure out how to be friends now, in a different way. We need to be able to support each other in finding people to love romantically, people we can be vulnerable with. People who will know us, and love us, and stay with us, through the good and the bad. I want to help you with Barry, and I want you to help me with Moe."

Rachel furrowed her brow. "Wait—what?"

"So have you talked to Clarence recently?" Rachel asked Jessica as she got into the passenger seat of her car.

"I mean, I guess," Jessica said. She pulled away from the curb. "Are we going to Natick Mall?"

Rachel nodded. "I mean, has he talked to you about the guy he met at the Rodeo?"

Jessica turned to look at her briefly. "Clare's been hanging out at the Rodeo? That doesn't sound like him. What would he have in common with some guy he met at the Rodeo?"

Rachel shook her head. "No, he went there with a date, and the guy ditched him. He met this other guy at the bar. A straight guy."

Jessica raised her eyebrows. "A straight guy? Oh, come on. Clare knows better than anyone else that you can't turn a straight guy. But what was he doing in a gay club? Did he take a wrong turn?"

"That's my question, too," Rachel said. "He told Clare that he was curious about the place. I have to wonder if maybe he's curious about something else, too."

"Wow." Jessica continued to watch the road as she drove. "Soooo," she said slowly. "How do you feel about all of this?"

Rachel tilted her head. "What do you mean, how do I feel? I'm worried, of course. I don't want to see Clare get hurt. And if this guy's really straight, or wanting to experiment, he's gonna get hurt."

"No," Jessica said cautiously. "I mean, how do *you* feel? You know, about Clare meeting someone. About him getting into, you know, this kind of situation."

Rachel's stomach turned queasy. "What do you mean? Like, am I worried about my best friend? I just told you I am."

Jessica veered the car to the right and stopped at the curb. She turned to look at Rachel. "Cut the crap, Rachel. The jig is up, and it appears that everyone knows that now except for you."

Rachel's eyes went wide. "What . . ."

"Everyone knows that you and Clare have been fucking since college," Jessica said plainly.

All of the air left Rachel's lungs. "Everyone . . ."

Jessica nodded. "Me, Jerry, and Steve. And we've known since college. And now Clare knows that we know."

"He—you—what?"

"Rachel, you might have thought we were all stupid, but we're not. In college, you and Clare were always the last to leave every time we got together. You had breakfast with him almost every weekend, and sometimes, you were wearing the same clothes you wore the day before. You guys touched a lot. You still do. And you have a secret language—"

"A what?"

Jessica nodded. "You don't even realize it, do you? Sometimes, you just have to look at each other a certain way. We can all tell that you're communicating with your eyes. Only people who have been intimate can understand each other the way the two of you do. And clearly you hooked up again on Clare's birthday."

Rachel leaned forward and put her head in her hands. She tangled her fingers in her hair. "Oh my God oh my God."

Jessica reached over and put a hand on her shoulder. "It's not that bad, Ray," she said. "I mean, we don't all sit around and talk about it or anything. I think we made a silent pact years ago to just accept that it was happening and not say a word. We never judged you. I mean, we might have had thoughts, but we never talked about them. You both had the right to have your secrets. We let you think you still had them."

Rachel looked up. "How long has Clare known?"

"Not long. Since last night. He got together with Jerry and Steve and sort of confronted them. I'm not sure how he figured it out."

Rachel shook her head. "He didn't tell me. But . . ."

"But what?"

"All of the sudden, he wants to talk about it." Rachel slicked her hair back from her face. "He wants to apologize, and move forward. I thought maybe it had something to do with this guy he met."

"And?"

"And now I'm wondering if it's not about that guy. Maybe . . . it's about me."

Jessica laughed. "Of course it's about you. Ray, Clare would do anything for you. He'd want to fix what was broken, and if it was him that was breaking you, he would want to fix that, too. Why do you think he asked Todd at work to fix him up with that Luke guy?"

"He asked his coworker to fix him up? I thought it was offered to him."

Jessica shook her head. "He heard you were going on a date, and he saw it as a chance to, well, I guess, support you. He wanted you to be able to move on, and I guess, he decided to move on, too."

Rachel felt a tear roll down her cheek. "He wants to learn how to be my friend. My friend who can be there for me. I-I was crying to him about my guy issues, and he listened, and gave me advice. Maybe he doesn't have to try to be my supportive friend. Maybe he already is."

Jessica put the car back in drive and headed toward Route 9. "I think we need some serious retail therapy about now, don't you?"

Rachel nodded vigorously. "I need some throw pillows for my bedroom. A lot of throw pillows."

Rachel got home at six o'clock feeling emotionally drained. She kicked off her shoes at the door and shook her aching feet. She lugged two giant bags filled with fashion pillows into her bedroom, removed them from the bag, and placed them lovingly at the head of her bed. She stood, hands on her hips, and smiled at the effect. It was true; shopping did make her feel better. The pillows gave the room a little touch of color that it needed and made it look more inviting. At least for herself, each night, when she came into her room to go to bed. Alone.

She had started toward her bathroom when she heard the distinctive sound of a text arriving on her phone. She walked back to the bed and removed the phone from her purse. She clicked on her texts and found a new message from Barry.

Barry
Hey R how's it going?

Rachel
Hi, I just got back from the mall
with my friend Jessica

Barry
Did you get anything good?

Rachel
Pillows

Barry
I like pillows

Rachel
LOL I think everyone has feelings for pillows

Barry
I own one myself

Rachel
LOL

Barry
I'm imagining you laughing out loud right now

Rachel
I AM LOL'ing. I wouldn't say I was if I wasn't

Barry
I like your laugh

Rachel
I like to laugh. Do you know any jokes?

Barry
I know a few. Maybe we can get together
and I can tell them to you

Rachel
. . .

Rachel

Rachel
...

Rachel
Okay

Barry
Are you free on Friday? Maybe we can get dinner?

Rachel
Have you had a homecooked meal since you moved here?

Barry
Does ramen count?

Rachel
That's it. I'm making you dinner

Barry
I like food

Rachel
LOL. You like white meat or no meat and veggies. Do you like eggplant? I make a killer eggplant parm sandwich

Barry
Does red wine go with eggplant sandwiches?

Rachel
Of course

Barry
I'm looking forward to seeing your new pillows

CHAPTER 12

WORK TOOK FOREVER ON THURSDAY. Clarence gave a tour to a group of fifth graders from Dudley, who appeared to get their jollies by giggling behind his back and asking stupid questions, making the tour drag on for an extra fifteen minutes. Clarence could tell that the teacher was getting annoyed, too, as she kept looking at the time and rolling her eyes. Finally, she whistled loudly, and all of the kids shut up.

"The bus won't wait forever," she called out. "If we're not out there in five minutes, they'll leave and we'll all have to sleep here." Some of the boys cheered. The teacher rolled her eyes again. Finally, she corralled them all into the hallway and out the door and everything was quiet again.

Clarence spent the rest of his shift completing paperwork and conversing with his coworkers.

Nine o'clock finally arrived, and Clarence practically sprinted out of the museum to the T stop. The train wasn't too crowded this late on a Thursday night, and Clarence had almost a whole car to himself. He scrolled through his social media, keeping one eye open for his stop. He didn't let his eyes settle on any particular post; it was mostly just a distraction, trying to keep his stomach from doing somersaults as he thought about seeing Moe again.

He couldn't remember the last time he felt that way about seeing anyone. He was hoping that he hadn't remembered Moe's face, and body, incorrectly. If he had it right, Moe had short dark hair, cut stylishly, with a few strands that swung free over his handsome forehead. He hadn't caught the color of his eyes, but that didn't matter. They were still beautiful, deep set and almond shaped. He knew he could easily get lost in them. He had a slender waist and broad shoulders. He wondered if he had a six pack, but he couldn't tell through his shirt. He closed his eyes and imagined running his fingers over Moe's abs and feeling the hardness . . . hardness was something Clarence was starting to feel now. He thought of how it would feel to touch Moe's chin, his cheek, his lips, his . . .

The train pulled to a stop at Clarence's station, and he stood up, adjusting his pants. He looked around the street, and his eyes fell on Moe, leaning against the driver's door of a blue Honda Civic, grinning like an idiot with his hands in the front pockets of his jeans.

Clarence smiled back as he approached him. "Sensible car for the city," he said. He walked around to the passenger side, and they both got in. "So we're going to a sports bar. Is there any sports-ing going on tonight?"

Moe laughed. "I don't really know. I'm guessing there's some sort of soccer game happening somewhere in the world. It's also the end of spring training."

"I like baseball," Clarence said. "When I was living in California, I was a Giants fan, but now that I'm living in Massachusetts, I can't help but be a Red Sox fan, even though they kind of suck."

Moe laughed again. "I'm a Blue Jays fan. I'll have to figure out a way to deal with that, living in Boston. But the one thing we all have in common is contempt for the Yankees."

Clarence was feeling proud of himself for bringing up his interest in baseball, but if the conversation continued, he was going to have to let Moe know that his knowledge wasn't that deep. There were a couple of baseballs dug up in the Big Dig. Maybe that would interest him. But for now, he needed a change of subject. "How did you end up being a Blue Jays fan?"

Moe smiled. "I was actually born in Toronto. I have dual citizenship. I ended up going to college in Toronto. The University of Toronto. It was nice because my grandparents and aunt and uncle live there, and I got to see them a lot. Luckily, it wasn't too far from home, either, so I got to visit my parents and siblings a lot. Do you get to see your family much?"

Clarence shrugged. "Not much. Maybe once every year or two."

Moe glanced at him. "That's not much. I can kinda tell that there's more to it than you just being really busy." He pulled the car into a crowded parking lot and drove around looking for a space. Someone magically pulled their car out at just that moment, leaving a prime spot right in front. He parked and turned off the ignition. Then he turned to Clarence. "Do you want to talk about it?"

Clarence stared at this wonder of a man. "I . . . maybe. Maybe after I get some beer in my system." He opened his door and stepped out onto the gravel lot. "This place looks festive."

Moe laughed as he walked up beside him, hands now in jacket pockets. "Festive. That's one word for neon signage. But they have some good local beers on tap. And good service."

Clarence nodded. Then he waited as Moe opened the door and held it for him. He walked past him with a healthy dose of discomfort. This felt like a date, but it wasn't one. It was two rough-and-tumble guys getting together after work for a beer and some sports viewing. At least he figured that's what people did at sports bars.

When he walked inside, he was assaulted by the sound of classic rock music and jovial voices. Most of the regular clientele had probably arrived hours earlier and were well into their cups. Several TVs hung over the bar, mounted from the ceiling. Something must have happened, as one of the groups of men and women on one side of the establishment suddenly cheered. On the other side of the room, there were boos and grumbles. Clarence had to smile at the scene. He imagined this place buried under a thousand years of dirt and rocks and discovering it on a dig in the future. What would he make of the metal bottle openers and darts? It might resemble a warzone.

"Where should we sit?" he asked.

Moe looked around and then pointed to a dimly lit booth. "There," he said. "You go ahead. I'll get us some beer. What's your preference?"

"Hazy IPA," Clarence said, "but if they don't have that, just regular IPA."

"Got it," Moe said, and he turned and headed to the bar. Clarence walked over to claim the booth. It was situated in such a way that guests on either side would have a view of a television at all times. He looked up and saw that Spain was playing Portugal in a soccer match, and the score was tied at zero.

He tried to follow along, but he really didn't understand the sport. He was raised on American football, the Forty-Niners being his home team.

Soon, Moe arrived and placed a frosty glass in front of him. Then he sat down. "They didn't have anything hazy, but this is a Trillium. I've been told it's really good."

Clarence smirked. "Really? Who told you that?"

Moe grinned back. "The guy at the bar. Have you had it before?"

Clarence nodded. "Yeah, and it's really good. Not too bitter. Just right."

"Good." Moe took a sip of his own beer. "You were telling me about your family."

Clarence felt his shoulders tighten slightly. "You don't want to hear about my family. It's not really a conversation conducive of a good time."

"No," Moe said gently. "No, really. I'm curious. Are you an only child?"

Clarence shook his head. "I have two sisters. They're back in the Bay Area. Jill is married and has two little kids, Mickey and—"

"Donald?" Moe interjected with a smile.

Clarence laughed. "No. Her name is Daniella. And my other sister's Tara. We're closer in age and she's not married. She has a boyfriend. I hope this one lasts."

"Are you close with them?"

"I was, more so when I lived back there. But since I moved out here for college . . ." He looked down at his beer.

Moe furrowed his brow. "What happened?"

Clarence took a deep breath and then blew it out. Moe wanted to hear about it, so Moe was getting the full story.

"My father was diagnosed with early onset Alzheimer's when I was fifteen. He was only fifty-six, so it was a huge surprise. At first, the doctor thought he'd had a stroke, but then the symptoms got clearer. He was still working as an accountant, but after the first year, he wasn't able to do his work anymore. He was making too many mistakes, and often he would just stop in the middle of calculations. By the time I was eighteen, he was starting to forget some other things, and he would get lost if he went outside by himself. It was moving faster than we expected, but the early onset often does."

Moe wrapped both hands around his glass and shook his head. "God, that must have been tough for you and your family."

Clarence nodded. "It was. And what made it tougher was when I decided to go to Boston for college. I basically packed up my stuff and hit the road. My sisters were mad because they thought I should have gone to USF so I could be closer, so I could help them and Mom with Dad, but I had my heart set on the East Coast. I wanted to explore the city, and then summer on Cape Cod, maybe in Provincetown. I was coming from the San Francisco area, so a gay community wasn't unreachable for me, but still, I wanted to make a change. I didn't want to sit by and watch while my father's brain wasted away."

Moe nodded. "So there was a lot of resentment from your sisters," he conjectured.

"Yeah." Clarence took another swig from his glass. "And my mom . . . well, when I talked to her on the phone, I could tell she wanted me back home, but she never asked. She and my sisters would tell me all about what was going on with Dad, but I didn't see it. I just remembered him like he was when I was there. And then when I came home to visit over summer break, I saw it for myself."

"Was it really bad?"

Clarence nodded. "I couldn't have prepared myself for how bad it was. He . . . at first he recognized me, and asked me how I was doing, but then later, I walked into the living room where he was sitting, and he looked up at me and basically said 'I'm sorry, but can you tell me who you are again?'" Clarence sniffed. "I thought I would throw up. My sisters and my mom had been right. He was getting bad. So when I went back to Boston for my sophomore year, I made the decision that it was too painful to keep going back, no matter how much they wanted me there. I mean, I planned to visit. I even bought tickets for spring break, just to go back for, like, four days.

"But right in the middle of midterms, I got the call. My dad was living in a facility by that time, and they had called my mother to let her know that he wasn't eating, and he was nonresponsive. She called me and asked me to move my ticket up a few days so I could see him before it was too late. I told her I couldn't, because I still had to get through some exams. So she told me to call the next day and have one of the caregivers put the phone up to his ear so I could talk to him, I guess to say goodbye. So the next day I called . . ."

He closed his eyes, sighed, and reopened them.

"I couldn't get through to the front desk. I'm not sure what was going on. Maybe they were really busy and just couldn't answer the phone. But I decided to call back later, and then I went to the library to study for my last exam. While I was sitting there in a study carrel, my phone buzzed. It was my mom."

Moe closed his eyes. "He had passed away?" he asked gently.

Clarence nodded. "He was sleeping, and he just drifted off. I-I never got to say goodbye. I ended up keeping my same ticket, and made it home for the funeral. But it didn't take very long for me to realize that something had shifted in my family. They had changed. They had watched him as he slowly slipped away from them over the years, and I hadn't been there. They had these horrible memories of him that I could never share. I could still close my eyes and see my father sitting in the audience of one of my band concerts in high school, smiling and waving when he caught my eye. I could see him offering to help me with my math homework, and even earlier in my life, quizzing me on the multiplication table. My memories were sweet."

"Were you able to talk to your sisters while you were there?" Moe asked.

Clarence shook his head. "They didn't want to. They kept really busy and doted on Mom. They did so much, it left nothing much for me to do except watch them, which made them even more angry. We just got more and more distant. When I finally came back to Boston, it was like they were relieved to see me go. Not my mom though. She wanted me to stay. I think she wanted all of her kids in the same place, around her. But I couldn't do it. I-I needed to be in my own place, doing my own thing. I had developed a really tight friend group by that time. Jerry, Steve, Ray, and Jessica. They were my chosen family. And to be honest, when I got back to Boston, it was Ray I really turned to for comfort. Sometimes, you just need a certain kind of comfort, you know?"

Moe nodded slowly. "I get it," he said. "I'm so sorry for how things went with your family, but I'm glad you had such a great friend group to come back to. Do you still talk to them?"

Clarence laughed. "Only every day," he said. "They all still live around here. Jerry and Steve are engaged, to each other. Ray's always up for doing something fun, and Jess, well, Jess is Jess. I can't really pin down a way to describe her. But yeah, we're all still really tight."

"I wish I had something like that," Moe said. "I'm pretty close to my family, but they're all so busy. I have three siblings, and they're all over the place. I do talk to my parents once a week, though. I think they're waiting for me to call them up in tears saying I want to come home, but that's not gonna happen. I like it here."

Clarence smiled. "I'm glad," he said. "It's a great place to live. I just can't believe you didn't know about the Rodeo before you came in to check it out. It has a certain reputation."

Moe cleared his throat roughly. "Well, maybe I knew more about it than I let on. But I was being honest about just coming in to check it out. I was curious what it was like."

"And what was your diagnosis?

Moe snorted out a laugh. "It's . . . raunchy? Is that still a word? Yeah, not really my type of place."

"What *is* your type of place?" Clarence asked. "A sports bar? I haven't even seen you look up at a TV the entire time we've been here."

Moe shifted in his seat. "I don't know. I guess I just figured it might be, well, a safe place to meet, you know? Like, neutral or something."

Clarence was baffled. "Neutral? What do you mean?"

Moe shrugged. "I mean, I didn't really want to meet at another gay bar. But I also don't really hang around at bars much. And you know . . . I don't really know."

Clarence nodded. "You weren't sure where to hang around alone with a gay guy."

Moe looked horrified. "I mean—I don't know. I mean, I'm not, like, embarrassed or anything. It's just—"

Clarence held up his hand in a stop position. "Can I ask you something?"

Moe almost looked grateful, making Clarence guilty for what he was about to ask. "Go ahead," Moe said.

Now Clarence squirmed a bit. "Is it possible . . . is it possible you wanted to go into the Rodeo because you knew what it was, and yes, you were curious, but it was more than just curious about the scene?"

Moe stared at him intensely, lines developing around the corners of his eyes. He held on to his beer glass like a lifeline. "I-I don't know."

Clarence's face softened. "You came into a gay bar that you're now telling me you knew was a gay bar. You came up to the bar and sat next to a gay guy. Granted, a safe-looking gay guy in the Rodeo, for what it's worth. You talked to him for a few minutes, and then . . . well, you asked him for his number so you could see him again. I mean, doesn't that—"

"I really don't know," Moe said again, interrupting.

"It's okay," Clarence said. "No matter what it is, it's okay. I mean, if you're curious, it's alright. If you're not, that's fine, too. I won't judge you either way. But . . . but it would be good for me to know, because, you know, I need to know what I'm up against here. If you recall, I told you last week that if you changed your mind about being gay, I'd want you to call me. And that offer's still on the table."

The blood appeared to drain out of Moe's face, but he remained quiet. A waitress came over and asked if they wanted another beer, and Clarence waved her off with a smile. Moe looked at the remains of his beer in his glass. "I . . . can we not talk about this anymore?" he said, looking up. "I mean, like, not now? Maybe another time? Right now, I just want to finish my beer. And then maybe go out and get some air."

Clarence nodded. "Do you want to get air by yourself, or do you want me to come with you?"

Moe looked into his eyes. He looked as if his guard had come down. "I would be okay if you came with me. And then I'll drive you home."

Clarence nodded and finished the last bit of his beer. He realized three things at that moment. First, Moe had not committed himself to not being curious about being with a man. He was obviously confused, and he wanted to think about it more. Second, Moe liked spending time with him and hadn't run away screaming when he asked him what was going on. That was a good sign. At least they could still be friends, if nothing more. And third, and most important, Moe had the most beautiful blue-green eyes he had ever seen.

CHAPTER 13

"I CAN'T REALLY TALK. I'M prepping to cook. What's up?" Rachel had wedged the phone between her ear and shoulder and now didn't have any hands free to put it on the counter and push the speaker button.

"I think Moe might be gay," Clarence said. "Or more likely bi."

Rachel dropped the phone from her head onto the counter. She put down the knife and picked the phone back up. "What? Are you kidding me? What happened last night?"

A sigh came through the phone. "Nothing, really. But I questioned him about going to the Rodeo, and asking for my number, and if it meant anything besides just being curious and making a new friend, and he said he didn't know. But he did admit he knew the Rodeo was a gay club before he went in."

"He doesn't know?" Rachel asked. She pulled a chair out from her kitchen table and sat down. "So he's, what, questioning? Isn't that one of the Qs in LGBTQ?"

"It used to be," Clarence said. "I think there's only one Qs now, and it can be whatever you want it to be. But yeah, I think he *is* questioning. I think he went into the Rodeo to see if he really found guys attractive, and it's a safe place to look at guys for long periods of time. But I'm not sure he even realizes what he's doing. I think he's so confused that he doesn't even know what he's confused about."

"That's intense," Rachel said. "But if he was checking out gay guys and he ended up approaching you, that means that he might like you. At least he finds you attractive."

"I think he does," Clarence admitted. "Although, I don't really want to get my hopes up. I mean, I think for someone like him, the first person you find attractive might be more of a catalyst, you know? A launching pad to help you figure yourself out."

"So you're a launching pad?" Rachel teased. "That sounds oddly sexual."

Clarence laughed. "I wish. Ray, he's so incredibly hot. And he's a really nice, caring guy. He got me telling him my family story five minutes into our date. I mean, our . . . I don't know what to call it. It wasn't a date."

"Wow. Your family? That's heavy stuff for a first date. What happened when you asked him all the tough questions?"

"We talked a bit, and then he said he needed air, so we went outside and walked around the quiet streets of Weston. It was a nice walk."

"What did you talk about?"

"Not much, really." Clarence paused. "It was actually really pleasant. The weather was good, it was just us, and we walked in silence for a long time. I think I overwhelmed him with that line of conversation, but he still wanted to, like, hang out with me."

Rachel felt a tug at her heart. "Clare, you're not gonna get hurt here, are you? I mean, like you said already, he might just need a gay friend to help him figure out some stuff."

"I'm the one who's supposed to tell you not to get hurt," Clarence said. "You're having Barry over for dinner tonight. How do you think that's gonna end for you?"

"He said he wants to see my throw pillows," Rachel said vaguely.

Clarence laughed. "Is that something the kids are saying these days? 'Can I come over to your place and check out your throw pillows?'"

Rachel laughed. "No. I actually bought some new throw pillows for my bedroom. I'll show you next time you're here. I have no idea what will happen. I wasn't really thinking about sex when I invited him to dinner. I really just wanted him to have a homecooked meal. I mean, he's new to the area. He eats out or takes out every night. It just seemed like the right thing to do."

"But if he wants to check out your throw pillows, you wouldn't throw him out of your bedroom?"

Rachel closed her eyes. "I don't know yet," she said. "I mean, sleeping with him would be a big thing for me. But I don't want to have sex with a guy who's sleeping with a ton of other people. It's not safe, and it's not who I am. So if it does come down to it, I'll let him know how I feel. And if he's not okay with that, then he's really not the one for me."

"That's very mature of you," Clarence said. "Are you making your eggplant sandwiches?"

"I am."

"He'll for sure want to see your throw pillows then."

Rachel snickered. "I have to go. I have to cut up egg and bread the eggplant so I can broil it. I need my full concentration for this. I'll call you tomorrow."

"Have a good time, Ray," Clarence said. "I love you."

"I love you too, Clare."

Thirty minutes later, Rachel was showered, blow-dried, made up, and dressed, and the oven was preheated. Barry was due to arrive in ten minutes. She set the table with matching plates, forks, and knives, and folded paper towels down to napkin size. She debated putting a candle in the center of the table but instead decided to light a couple of votives and placed them on her breakfast bar. When she was done, her phone started to buzz and she picked it up.

"I'm at the door," Barry's voice came through.

"I'll buzz you in," Rachel said. She hit the pound key and hung up. Her heart fluttered and sped up. She closed her eyes and took a few breaths.

The knock came sooner than she expected, causing her to jump. She walked quietly to the door, waited a few seconds, took a few more breaths, and then opened it wide.

"Hi!" She smiled.

Barry smiled back. He reached out a hand gripping a bouquet of spring flowers. "I hope it wasn't corny to bring these," he said. "My mom always told me not to go to dinner at someone's house with empty hands." He drew out his other hand, revealing a bottle of Merlot. "I took her literally."

Rachel laughed and reached for the flowers. "They're really pretty. I love tulips. I'll put them in water and then set them up in the middle of the table. I was gonna put a candle there, but now I'm glad I didn't. Why don't you go ahead and open the wine? The bottle opener's on the bar, and I put two glasses there, too."

"Great," Barry said. He followed Rachel into the apartment and glanced at the table. "This is really nice," he said. "I've really missed having home-cooked meals. I'm hoping someday to have a real, permanent home so I can have them all the time. My kitchen is really small, and I haven't really gotten around to stocking it yet. I like to cook, so I miss it."

Rachel placed the vase of flowers on the table. "Want to help me in the kitchen? You can make a salad if you want."

Barry smiled. "Yeah." He handed her a glass of wine and then held his out to make a toast. "To new friends in a new place." He clinked his glass with Rachel's.

"To being adults and providing sustenance for ourselves on a regular basis!" Rachel said. They both laughed and clinked their glasses again. Wine in hand, Rachel led him to the kitchen.

Barry looked around. "This looks like a well-stocked kitchen," he said. "You even have a blender. Do you actually blend things with it?"

Rachel nodded as she lifted the tray of breaded eggplant and took it to the oven. "I like to make smoothies. I keep frozen fruit in my freezer. I can make one for you for dessert if you want."

"I'd love that," Barry said. "Should I just get veggies out of the fridge?"

"Help yourself," Rachel said. "There's a cutting board in the drainer, and a knife in the drawer under the cupboards. The salad bowl is under the sink."

Barry went around the room gathering what he needed. "Do you like raw onions in your salad?"

Rachel gave him a sly grin. "That depends on the kissing situation," she said. "If there's kissing later, then we both have to eat the onions during dinner, or neither of us. Deal?"

Barry grinned. "We'll both eat the onions then. There will certainly be kissing later."

Rachel made a show of opening the oven to check on the eggplant and to hide her reddening cheeks. "They need another ten minutes," she told Barry. "Do you want lots of cheese or a normal amount of cheese?"

"Isn't a lot of cheese normal?" Barry asked. He chuckled. "I could live on cheese alone. I've thought of becoming a vegetarian before, and I figured that cheese would be my main staple if I did. Cheese on eggs, cheese on toast, cheese on potatoes . . ."

"Cheese on cheese?" Rachel asked. She placed four bun halves on a baking tray.

Barry thought for a moment and then nodded. "I put parm on top of cheese pizza," he said. "So yes, cheese on cheese." He sliced a red pepper into strips and threw them over the romaine in the bowl. "Cheese on the salad then?" He looked up through long, dark eyelashes.

Rachel almost melted on the spot. "Of course," she said, forcing lighthearted cheer into her voice. In reality, she wanted to shove all the food off the counter, jump up on it in front of Barry, and devour his smug smile. She wanted to taste his tongue, kiss behind his ear, and then strip him naked and ravage his body.

Her pulse throbbed through her body as she forced herself to open a fresh jar of marinara. She retrieved the tray from the oven, taste-tested one of the eggplant circles to make sure it was fully roasted, and then added the marinara and heaps of cheese. "Another ten minutes in the oven."

Barry went back to the fridge and removed a bottle of ranch dressing. "Okay, now I feel at home," he said. "Only ranch. I mean, why buy anything else? Ranch is the only way to go. You can use it for anything, right? Chicken nuggets, veggies, potatoes. It's kind of like the cheese of salad dressing."

Rachel started to laugh, one of those laughs that felt like it could get out of control. "Okay, okay. We need to stop talking about cheese. I think I pulled a muscle in my stomach from laughing."

Barry smiled, and it was definitely a smile of victory. He picked up the bowl and carried it out to the table. When he returned, he stood beside her. She looked at him, and he looked back. Then he turned to face her and put his hands on her hips. He looked down at her.

"Hi," he said softly.

Rachel smiled up at him. "Hi," she said, a rasp in her voice.

Barry stared into her eyes for a moment and then leaned down toward her. He hovered an inch from her ready and waiting lips. "Can I kiss you now?" he asked. "Even though we haven't had our onions yet?"

In lieu of an answer, Rachel reached up, grabbed the hair on the back of his head, and pulled him to her. Their lips collided, causing the inside of Rachel's mouth to crash into her teeth. She ignored the pain and surrendered herself to the kiss. Barry's hands went around her back and pulled her to his body. The kiss continued as Rachel started to feel her body heat up, sweat breaking out on her forehead. It was then she realized that the kitchen was growing overheated. She broke away from the kiss and looked at the oven.

"Oh shit, I didn't close it all the way," she said. She moved quickly to the oven and pushed the door shut. Then she opened the window over the sink, allowing cool spring air to stream in from the outside. "I'm so sorry."

Barry chuckled. "I didn't even realize the oven was open," he said. "I just thought . . ." He laughed. "I really like being with you, Rachel. You make me laugh."

Rachel smiled. "The feeling's mutual." She tried to push the thought that Barry might be dating other women out of her mind. She just had to stay in the moment, at least for *this* moment. She stood in front of Barry and put her hands on his shoulders. "Now where were we?"

They kissed, their hands in motion on each other's upper bodies, for next ten minutes, when Rachel finally pulled away. "Wow," she said. "You're, um . . . well, you have a lot of . . ."

Barry grinned. "I like to kiss you," he said gruffly. "Your lips are like sugar."

Rachel laughed. "You stole lyrics from an eighties song."

Barry shrugged. "But it's true. I could get cavities from kissing you."

Rachel's smile faded. "I enjoyed it. It's just . . ."

Barry took both of her hands in his. "What?"

Rachel sighed. "Are you seeing anyone else?"

Barry stared at her for several seconds. Then he looked down. "I'm meeting people," he said. "I won't lie to you."

"Are you kissing any of them?" Rachel asked.

Barry quickly shook his head. "I haven't kissed anyone but you."

Rachel felt a slight sense of relief. "But you haven't ruled it out yet."

Barry looked down. "I . . ."

Rachel exhaled hard through her nose. "You don't have to say anything else." The timer went off on the oven. "The eggplant's done. I need to take it out." She pulled her hands out of his and grabbed oven mitts.

Dinner was enjoyable, and they found a lot to talk about. Barry talked about his siblings and their crazy antics growing up. He talked about Becca, and how hard it was when she left home. He talked about his parents, and their desire to keep their children near them, but also to support them in their endeavors. They were planning to come to Boston to visit him and Becca in the summer.

"We had a pretty happy childhood," he said. "It was really hard for Becca when her mother died. Our other brother, Lyle, was fifteen at the time. He talked our dad into letting him stay with a friend until the end of high school so he wouldn't have to change schools. I know that was hard for Becca. She adored him. But my mom really loves Becca. It doesn't feel like she's a half-sister, you know?"

Rachel nodded. "I don't have any siblings, but I can imagine. She was lucky to have all of you. I wish I had an older brother. Or a younger sister. It was hard after the divorce. Mom was so angry at Dad for the shame of the affair. He flaunted his new wife all over the place."

"Rebecca," Barry recalled.

Rachel nodded. "It was ugly. She didn't date at all after that. She has friends, but she's not interested in men. Dad ruined men for her. He did a number on me, too. I . . . I have a tendency to pick men who aren't available. I mean, men who want me, but can't keep me for one reason or another. Makes sense, huh? I mean, you could probably do a case study on me when you go to grad school."

Barry's face fell. "Oh my God," he said softly. "I-I'm doing the same thing, aren't I? I didn't intend it to be that way, Rachel. I mean, I just wanted to be honest with you about my intentions. I didn't mean to lead you into thinking—"

Rachel shook her head. "I'm gonna tell you the same thing I recently told my best friend Clare. I'm a big girl, Barry. I can make my own decisions. You were honest with me from the start. If I decide to keep seeing you, it's because I'm getting something out of it. But I do have to tell you . . ." She reached over and touched his hand. "You're not gonna get to see my throw pillows tonight."

Barry looked at her in confusion. Then he broke out in a smile and started to laugh. "Fair enough," he said. "No throw pillows tonight. And you lead the way. Whatever you're comfortable with. I just like spending time with you. I'm okay with keeping pillows out of it. At least for now."

Rachel nodded. "Good." She stood up. "So what do you want in your smoothie? I have frozen bananas, raspberries, strawberries, blueberries, and peaches."

CHAPTER 14

CLARENCE COULDN'T STOP THINKING ABOUT the hug. He still felt Moe's arms around his back, his chest pressed tight against his own. Moe's chin resting on his shoulder. He lay in bed, his eyes closed, reliving the moment. Then he relived his conversation with Rachel the day before, and the fact that he had not told her about the hug.

There were a lot of things that Clarence hadn't shared with Rachel about Moe. He'd told her the basics, about what they did when they went out, and what he looked like. He'd told her about Moe's confusion. But he hadn't shared anything he had learned about Moe. He hadn't told her about his family, about his dreams. He hadn't told her about his work, and his college friends. Those were the things he wanted to keep to himself. And he didn't want Rachel to know it all, not yet. Because it might not work out. Moe was confused. Moe didn't know what he wanted. Clarence hoped that Moe wanted him, but he had no idea if Moe would have him. Moe had a lot of work to do on his own discovery, and Clarence was willing to be by his side while he went through it. He hadn't been sure before. But ever since the hug, he knew.

They had walked the streets of Weston, up and down and past all the ornate houses with landscaped yards. They had walked in silence, hearing only the sounds of cars in the distance and the early spring crickets. They'd walked for over an hour, very few words exchanged between them. Eventually they found their way back to Moe's car. They stopped. They somehow intuited to stand side by side against the passenger side of the car. Both of them put their hands in their pockets to ward off the chill of the spring night.

Then Moe had turned to look at him. "Thanks," he said simply.

Clarence shrugged. "It's nothing."

Moe closed his eyes for several seconds, his face solemn. Then he opened them. "No, it's not nothing. It's a lot. I mean, I-I don't know. I really don't. But you're still here. That means everything."

He'd turned his body, extended his arms, and pulled Clarence into the hug. Clarence had stood stone still at first but then settled into the hug. He lifted his arms and encircled Moe's torso. He held on tight as Moe held him. The hug continued, well past the normal expectations of a friendship hug. Clarence held his breath. Eventually, Moe pulled away. He stood close to Clarence, waiting for a beat. Then he stepped back.

"I'll take you home now." They got in the car, and Moe started to drive. They listened to music from Moe's Spotify playlist and made small talk. When Moe pulled in front of Clarence's apartment, he had turned to look at him. "I'll text you," he said.

Clarence had nodded. "Please do. Any time." He got out and walked to the door of his building. He looked back and saw that Moe was waiting for him to get inside safely. He waved and let himself in.

When he got into the elevator, he'd let the door close, but he didn't push any buttons. Instead, he'd slid down the wall until he was sitting on the floor and remained there until someone else came into the lobby, called the elevator, and the door opened. He'd stood then, pushed the button for his floor, and finally went to his apartment.

It was Saturday now, and Clarence didn't know what to do with himself. So he stayed in bed. Eventually his phone buzzed. He picked it up off the night stand. There was a text from Steve.

Steve
Jerry's doing something with a work friend today. What are you up to?

Clarence
Wallowing in self-pity

Steve
: :

Steve
My boss asked me to go out and check on some properties in Eastboro today. You wanna come?

Clarence
What does that entail?

Steve
Driving 40 min to go see an apartment and a rental house, and then hanging out and maybe getting something to eat

Clarence
Is there anything good to see in Eastboro?

Steve
Carson Lake is nice. Nice houses. Nice view.

Clarence
IDK. Maybe.

Steve
I'll swing by to pick you up in 30

Clarence
ugggggh

Steve
Wait for me outside. It's nice out. And bring snacks for the car.

Clarence pried himself out of bed. He was acting put out, but in reality, he was glad for the distraction. He could have called Rachel and planned to get together, but he wasn't in the mood to hear how great her date with Barry went. Of course he would be there for her. He always was. But for this moment, he wanted to linger in his own feelings and not have to think about his best friend.

He got into the shower and did a quick shampoo, conditioner, and wash off, only stopping for a few moments to exfoliate. Then he got out, checked his face to see if he could get away without shaving, and decided he could. He dressed and then raided his kitchen, found a few Clif bars and a couple of pieces of fruit, and packed them in a refrigerated lunch bag. Then he took two cans of SanPellegrino from the door of his fridge and wedged them beside the snacks. He glanced at the clock on his oven and headed for the door. At the last minute, he grabbed his lightweight bomber jacket, throwing it over his arm as he headed for the elevator.

Steve wasn't there when he stepped toward the curb, so he took the time to check his socials. Rachel had posted a picture of two perfect eggplant parm sandwiches with the caption, "Cheese makes everything better." Clarence shook his head. He'd have to ask her about that later.

Steve pulled up within five minutes. Clarence got into the passenger seat. "Did Jerry clean out the car for you again?" he said as he fastened his seatbelt.

Steve nodded as he waited for Clarence to settle in. "It was his gift to me on National Goof-off Day. He let me lounge on the couch while he cleaned my car. He even took it to the car wash."

"What did you do for him?"

Steve laughed. "I ordered out for dinner and I let him bottom, just the one time. Oh, actually, two times. Well, maybe it was him letting me top for once. Or twice."

Clarence snorted. "Oh my God," he said. "Jerry and his holidays!"

"There were a few good food-related holidays this month. Peanut butter, frozen food, potato chips, chips and dip, and chocolate-covered raisins. We were busy on spinach day so we didn't celebrate this year. Did you know that there's a 'something on a stick' day? We had corndogs."

Clarence shook his head. "Is there a beer day?" he asked.

"It's actually next week," Steve said. "April seventh. We should all get together. Maybe you could invite Moe, and Rachel could invite her new guy. What's his name?"

"Barry," Clarence said. He scratched the top of his left foot with the bottom of his right shoe. "But I don't know if that's a good idea. They're not, like, exclusive or anything."

Steve glanced at him out of the corner of his eye as he drove. "They're dating other people?"

"He said he wanted to be able to," Clarence explained. "I don't know if he is or not, but he wasn't ready to tie himself down to just one woman. He's new to the area and wants to explore, I guess. But Ray's not seeing anyone else."

Steve shook his head. "Why does she do this to herself?"

Clarence considered this. "She doesn't, really, though, does she? I mean, this was a fix-up through her coworker. She must have thought they'd get along, and Ray really likes him. She had no way of knowing he would be like this. And I do think he likes her. I think after some time, he'll realize that she's the real deal, and he'll focus just on her."

"But if he doesn't, do you think she'll back out gracefully?"

Clarence shrugged. "I have no idea. I think she'll want to, but if history has anything to say about it . . ."

"But she has you to help her this time," Steve said. "And all of us. We'll help her to deal with it. We'll help her get over the hump."

Clarence sighed. "I hope it doesn't come to that, but it might." He looked out his window, watching the car speed by a group of industrial buildings on the Mass Pike. Then they entered a corridor of pine trees. "I just want her to be happy."

"Maybe she will be," Steve said. He reached for the volume on his car stereo. The song was "Too Sweet" by Hozier, and Steve started to sing. Clarence closed his eyes and just listened.

He either dozed off or spaced out, because before he knew it, Steve had stopped the car and had given Clarence's arm a shove. "We're at the first place," Steve was saying. "This part of town is informally called East Firehouse. We're going up to see an apartment over a pizza place."

Clarence shook the cobwebs out of his brain. "Over a pizza place? Sounds . . . creative."

Steve smiled. "You'd be surprised. These places don't go cheap. This neighborhood used to be where people would start out, like right out of school. But it's been really gentrified. Some of the dinkiest studios have been turned into prime real estate. Condos. The old firehouse is pretty exclusive now. My boss said his grandparents rented here when they first arrived from Ireland early in the twentieth century, and they lived in a three-decker house. Those were three-family homes. Now they've been broken up into twelve condos, and they're not accessible to first-time buyers. It's kind of embarrassing. I'm counting the days until I finish my master's degree and can quit this job." He opened his door. "Let's go take a look."

They explored the entirety of the apartment, including the closet that contained the water heater and the crawlspace in the bedroom. Steve took notes on his phone silently as he inspected the windows. Clarence looked out the windows onto the streets of Eastboro, wondering what it would be like to live in a neighborhood like this—quiet but full of privilege and high commerce.

Finally, Steve found him in the second bedroom and motioned to the door. "Let's go."

"What's the verdict?" Clarence said as they got back in the car.

Steve shrugged. "Overpriced, needs a lot of work, but likely to make my boss a lot of money in the long run." He started the car. "Now off to see a house rental near Aries Corp."

"That's on the lake, right?" Clarence asked.

Steve nodded. "There are several neighborhoods over there that house most of the Aries Corps' employees. So some houses are considered mini-mansions, and some are starter houses. If I lived in Eastboro, I think I would choose that neighborhood. Good schools, too."

They drove through some suburban streets, past a large two-story high school, a park, and a mini mall with an Italian restaurant before starting to circle the giant lake. "People actually have boats out here," Clarence noticed.

"Yeah," Steve said. "And there are beaches and paths, too. We'll look at the house and then take a nature walk."

Forty-five minutes later, Steve was leading Clarence down a path toward the water. Once they reached a set of benches, he sat down. Clarence sat next to him. He pointed. "Those must be where the executives live," he said, motioning toward some large houses.

"Yeah," Steve said. He looked to his right and pointed to another home. "That one belongs to Trent Billings."

"Who's that?"

Steve smiled. "That's the same thing I asked when I was told he lived there. He played football in the eighties and nineties and was on the Patriots at the end of his career. He and his wife are from Eastboro so they settled here. Trent is one of the coaches for the Patriots now. I hear they're actually really nice people."

"Huh." Clarence looked around the lake. "You're right about there being all kinds of houses here. Even smaller ones right on the water. They must still cost a fortune."

Steve shrugged. "Not all of them. I mean, it's a big lake." He stood up and started down a path that led around the water. "People ice-skate here in the winter."

The California boy inside of Clarence became excited. Ice-skating outdoors. He knew people did that at Rockefeller Center in New York, but not on a lake in the middle of a city. "It would be really nice to live here," he said.

Steve nodded. "It's nice. And the cost of living is much lower than what we have close to the city."

Clarence checked out the trees they passed and listened to the sounds of children playing in the nearby neighborhoods. He smiled as he imagined himself sending his child off to school from one of the houses nearby. He closed his eyes and saw himself handing a lunch bag to a little girl who then hugged him goodbye and headed for the car. In his mind, he looked up at who was escorting the little girl to school and was shocked to see that it was Moe, who turned around, smiled, waved, and then blew him a kiss before getting into the car with their child. Clarence caught his breath. He opened his eyes and shook his head. He was in a world of trouble.

The afternoon with Steve had been a lot of fun, and it had distracted Clarence from remembering that two days had gone by and Moe still hadn't texted. He had no idea if Moe would ever text him again, and he worried that maybe he had pushed too hard with his questions and had scared him away. He tried to imagine what it must feel like to be in Moe's position, an adult suddenly questioning everything he thought he knew about himself, trying to figure it out and possibly even accept that he's not who he thought he was. It had to be scary. He knew it was scary. The world still wasn't a safe place for a man to be gay, even with the changes that had come over the decades due to the gay men who had fought and endangered their own lives for the freedoms they now had. He wanted to hug Moe again, and comfort him, and tell him that everything would be okay. But he couldn't. He had to leave contact up to Moe. Texting him now would be unfair. He had to sit with his thoughts and work them out.

His phone buzzed. His heart skipped a beat. He took it out of his back pocket and sat down on the couch. It was a text from Moe.

Moe
Hey

Clarence
Hi

Moe
How are you

Clarence
Good.

Clarence
How are you?

Moe
Ok. Sorry for the radio silence. Got a lot on my mind.

Clarence
It's all good.

Moe
Can we have lunch on Tuesday? I want to talk more. About what we talked about last time. If that's ok.

Clarence
Yeah. Sure. I work at 12:30. Do you want to meet me at the museum?

Moe
How about somewhere more private? Do you know Lynette's Bakery?

Clarence
I love that place. Sure. 11:30?

Moe
Sounds good. Sorry, gotta go. I'll see you Tuesday.

After Moe signed off, Clarence opened his text thread with Rachel to send her a text. He had talked to Steve during their walk at the lake about the situation with Moe, but now he wanted to talk to his best friend. The last text she'd sent him said that she was going to see a movie with Barry that night. Clarence cursed to himself. He didn't want to interrupt her date if she had already left. She needed this time with Barry to try to figure out what was going on in her own situationship.

He put down his phone and picked up the remote. It seemed like it would be another night of marathon Netflix watching. This time, he opened season 1, episode 1 of *Young Royals* and settled back on the couch for a long night of teenage angst and first love, dubbed in Swedish-accented English.

# CHAPTER 15

"I DON'T KNOW HOW YOU can put all of that fake butter into your body," Rachel said as she lifted the first kernel of her popcorn to her mouth. "It's so bad for you!"

Barry laughed and then licked some butter off his finger. "It's nostalgic," he said. "Movie theater popcorn is the flavor of my youth! Otherwise, you're just eating salted corn!"

Rachel looked down at her canister. "I got mine without salt, remember?"

Barry rolled his eyes. "I know you told me about your childhood, but something must have really broken you for you to have to torture yourself with naked popcorn at the theater!" He gave her a sly smile as he took her hand and started to lead her toward their assigned theater.

"Jake!" The call came from behind them, and Barry stopped in his tracks. He turned around and smiled at the man standing behind him.

"Hey, Riley," he said. "How are you?"

The man named Riley nodded. "Good. Hey, I haven't seen you in a while. You're never home."

Barry—Barry? Jake?—nodded. "Yeah, life's kind of crazy right now." He turned to Rachel. "Rachel, this is my neighbor, Riley. He lives across the hall from me. Riley, this is Rachel."

Riley smiled as he shook Rachel's hand. "Yeah, crazy right now," he teased, giving Barry the side-eye.

"Riley, come on!"

Riley turned to a group of men who were walking toward one of the theater doors. "I have to go. But Jake, stop by sometime this week for a beer. We really need to catch up." He glanced at Rachel. "It was nice to meet you, Rachel."

"You, too," Rachel said. Riley walked away, and Rachel turned to Barry with a scowl. "Who the hell is Jake?"

Barry looked at her, then started to laugh. "I'm Jake."

"But you're Barry!" Rachel protested.

"Well, I'm Barry, too," he said. "I mean, sometimes I'm Barry. Rarely. But to Becca, I'm Barry."

"Why?"

"Because my last name is Barrett."

Rachel's eyes went wide. It was at that moment she realized that she hadn't ever heard Barry say his last name. She closed her eyes. "Oh," she said. "Oh. That explains it. That explains why when Becca told me your name, she giggled, and when we met up and I called you Barry, you looked confused. But I don't understand. Why didn't you correct me?"

Barry gave her a warm smile. "Because I liked it when you called me Barry. I especially liked it when you called me Uncle Barry that one time. It was funny, though, since my nieces and nephews have the same last name as me."

"So what should I do?" Rachel asked, feeling silly. "Do you want me to call you Jake now? It would be so weird!"

Barry shook his head. "No. You can call me Barry. It's okay."

Rachel smiled. Then a thought occurred to her. "Oh. Becca's last name is Williams. I guess I assumed you were Barry Williams. I thought you had the same father?"

"We do," Barry said. "But her mother kept her last name when she married my father and hyphenated Becca's name. When Becca moved to Boston, she decided to drop the Barrett to make things easier. She chose Williams to honor her mother."

Rachel felt warmth fill her body. She had been meaning to approach Becca to chat, but she hadn't had the chance yet. The woman appeared to have layers to her that weren't evident to the naked eye. Rachel reached out and took Barry's hand again. "I'm learning so much about you," she said. "I mean, I feel really dumb that I didn't know your full name until now, but I get why. But it's nice to get to know you like this."

Barry squeezed her hand. "We're gonna miss the previews," he said softly. "You know that's the best part of any movie."

"Becca," Rachel called out as the other woman walked past her office on Monday.

Becca stopped in her tracks and turned in the doorway of Rachel's office. She smiled. "Hey, Rachel. What's up?"

"I was wondering," Rachel said slowly and cautiously, "if you might want to go get coffee with me later?"

Becca's brows rose. "Oh! Um, yeah. That would be nice. I have a meeting until ten. Are you free then?"

Rachel smiled. "Just in time for my third cup. Great. I'll see you at ten."

Becca gave her one more look, nodded, waved, and walked away.

Rachel spent the next hour making notes on the manuscript she was working on. She had been trying to make sense of a sex scene, but it was all over the place, both literally and figuratively. If she had to see the word "precum" one more time, she would barf. She made a note of that. She had to admit the story was good, but there were tense errors and a lot of boring repetition. It was fixable, at least. She wondered sometimes if some of the manuscripts she read might be even stronger and more enjoyable if they didn't include so much explicit sex. She knew there was a market for it, and she knew these books were porn for women, so she got it. She just enjoyed the romance, and sometimes she felt like the sex got in the way.

Or maybe it was just that she wasn't getting any, and she was jealous of anyone that was, even if they were fictional characters. She was feeling horny as hell, but the furthest she had gotten with Barry was second base, if second base was the one where they did a lot of over-the-clothes touching above the waist. They hadn't even gone back to either of their apartments. After the movie on Saturday night, they had made out in the car for some time in front of her building before Barry finally pulled away, breathless, and said he had to go. He was respecting her wishes. If he was going to see other people, he was not going to see her naked. But God, that bulge in his jeans was so tempting, she had almost reached out—

"Rachel? Are you ready?"

Rachel snapped out of her revery. Becca was standing in her doorway, purse in hand.

"Oh, yeah, sorry. I was in the zone."

Becca's mouth opened slightly. "If this is a bad time—"

"Oh, no. This is a good time. I was just in my head a bit." Rachel smiled at her as she stood.

Becca grinned. "Thinking about my brother?" She winked.

Rachel bit her lip and grabbed her purse. "Maybe."

They left the building and walked the two blocks to Meyer's Beans, where they ordered their drinks and found a table near the back.

"I love the coffee here," Becca said. "I used to come here with Sasha before she moved to Nebraska. Now I just go to Starbucks with the others because they use the app. I had to get the app, too. I prefer to talk to people, not apps."

Rachel laughed. "Me too. Which is weird, because I'm an introvert. But I do like to have meaningful contact with real people."

Becca looked at her with curiosity. "I think you're a good person for my brother."

Rachel gave her a sly smile. "Your brother Barry?"

Becca's face reddened. "Oh, yeah. That. Sorry. I couldn't help myself. How long did it take you to figure that out?"

Now Rachel blushed. "Um, until last night?"

Becca stared, and then burst out laughing. "Are you kidding me? Oh God. That's hysterical!" She calmed down and then took a sip of her coffee. Her face mellowed. "I wasn't kidding when I said I think you're good for my brother. I worry about him sometimes"

Rachel tilted her head. "Why?"

Becca shrugged. "I don't think things were easy for him back home. I think leaving was good for him."

"Why was it so hard?"

"He had this girlfriend—"

Rachel raised a hand. "Maybe I should let him tell me about this."

Becca shook her head. "No, I think it's okay. He wouldn't mind. Anyway, they dated for a long time. Maybe two years? And she . . . well, she wasn't really nice. None of us liked her. Mom hated her." She leaned closer. "You can always tell if a woman is right for a man by the way she gets along with his mother."

Rachel recalled that Barry's mother was Becca's stepmom, and it made her happy to hear her call her Mom.

"What was wrong with her?"

"She cut into him all the time," Becca explained. "She criticized him, put him down, and then had all of these expectations of him. Like, he wants to be a therapist. I'm guessing he told you that. But she wanted him to go into investing and even got her father to give him an entry-level position at his firm after college. He hated it, but he did it anyway, and he made good money. But then." She paused. "Then she cheated on him. And then dumped him for this other guy."

"Oh my God," Rachel murmured. "That's horrible!"

Becca nodded. "It broke him. He had rearranged his life for her, and she had pretty much convinced him that no one else would want him because of his faults. Luckily, he had his friends to support him. She tried to push them away, but they wouldn't be pushed. Especially his best friend, Jayden. He was really there for him. I think it was hard for Jayden when Barry decided to leave, since they had been friends since middle school, but everyone understood that Barry had to start over."

"So this wasn't that long before I met him?" Rachel asked.

Becca nodded. "A few months, I think. But I thought it would be good for him to meet you. You just have this calm energy about you. Caring."

Rachel almost fell out of her seat. "Are you kidding me? Calm? I'm, like, the most uptight person I know!"

Becca laughed. "You don't come across that way. I guess you have a calm aura or something."

Rachel held her coffee cup in both hands, soaking up the warmth. "But it feels like he's not ready for something serious," she said. "He wants to see other people."

Becca's eyes went wide and her mouth dropped open. "What? He told you that?"

Rachel nodded. "I mean, I guess it makes sense if he just got out of a toxic relationship. He doesn't want to take any chances of getting back into something like that again. But it's kind of discouraging."

Becca shook her head. "That's weird," she said. "Barry talks about you. And not just because I ask about you. He brings things up spontaneously. But he's never mentioned seeing anyone else."

"He hasn't?" Rachel's heart sped up.

"No. Not at all. And he's really not the type to date more than one woman at a time. I-I don't understand why he'd say that to you."

"Maybe he's seeing someone else and he doesn't want you to know because you fixed us up."

Becca shrugged. "Maybe." She looked down at her coffee. "We were apart for a bit when all of that stuff happened with his ex. Maybe . . ." She looked up. "Maybe I underestimated the effect that woman had on him. I mean, he comes across as so wise and emotionally intelligent, you know? It's that inborn therapist in him."

Rachel nodded. "Yeah, I know." She took a sip of her cooling coffee. Then she shook her head. "You know what, enough about this. I didn't ask you to coffee just to talk about me and your brother. I want to know more about you. Tell me about your boyfriend, and how you guys ended up moving here."

Becca looked at her in surprise but then smiled. "How much time do you have? This might take a while."

It took forever for the frozen lasagna to bake in the oven. Rachel could have put it in the microwave, but it wouldn't have been the same. She liked the top noodles to be crisp, not soggy. While she waited, she sipped on a glass of red wine and scrolled through her phone. She checked her bank account and felt relief that she wasn't going to be overdrawn by the time she got paid on Friday. She opened her Instagram app and started to peruse. She read the updates on the influencer couples she followed, skipping the posts that were paid partnerships. Those always ruined it for her. She stopped at a post from Clarence.

It was a photo of a perfectly preserved bird skeleton under a glass case. Under the picture was the caption, "work just flying by today." A snort burst out of Rachel's gut. She typed out a comment: "Getting by on a wing and a prayer." She added two bird emojis.

Only thirty seconds had passed when her phone buzzed and a message notice from Clarence popped up. "Can you talk?"

Rachel immediately hit the phone icon on the top of the screen, and Clarence answered after the first ring. "Thanks for encouraging my punny behavior," he said by way of a greeting.

Rachel laughed. "Glad to see you're in a good mood. How's your day going?"

"It's okay," Clarence replied. Rachel could picture him shrugging absent-mindedly. "Work's been good. We had a bunch of tours. I love tours, especially when the people are interested. We had a group from a senior living community. They had a lot of technical questions about the dig. I didn't know all the answers, but at least I knew where they could find them if they wanted. How's your day?"

"I had coffee with Barry's sister," Rachel said. "She's really great. I should have tried to get to know her sooner. I guess I was just kind of shut off when I started working there. It makes me wonder if maybe I should try to go out with the group sometime. They always invite me, and I always say no."

"I don't know if that would be a good time for you," Clarence said. "I mean, you're an introvert. It might make you uncomfortable to go in a group."

"Maybe you could come with me," Rachel suggested. "If I have you there, it will be easier, since I can talk to you if I don't feel comfortable talking to a bunch of people at once."

"Or I'll end up talking to all of them and leaving you alone, like I do sometimes." He exhaled. "You could ask Barry to come with you."

Rachel closed her eyes. "I'm really confused about Barry," she said. "His sister told me some stuff about him today that makes a lot of sense, but then there's other stuff that doesn't even make sense to her. I have to feel him out a bit longer. But I know for sure that I don't want to wait for too long. I need to start living, not just waiting."

There was a pause on the other side of the phone. Then Clarence spoke. "If I was the one that held you back for so long—"

"Cut it out, Clare," Rachel demanded. "Remember. We talked about this. I'm the one who's responsible for all of my own misery. And it's my job to get myself out of it."

"Ray," Clarence said softly. "I know we've talked about this before, but have you considered talking to someone about all of this? I mean, you've been through a lot in your life, with your dad and everything. For God's sake, you were sleeping with a gay guy. That's got to make you an interesting case to some therapist."

Rachel bit her lip. This was not a new topic between them. Or between her and her other friends. They brought it up because they cared about her.

"I hear you, Clare. I really do. And maybe I'll look into it. But for now, I want to just try to deal with this on my own, okay?"

"Okay," Clarence said reluctantly. "But just know that you're not on your own, alright? You have me and Jerry and Steve and Jess. We're all here for you. No matter what happens. You can always count on us. We won't judge you. Just like I know you wouldn't judge me if I came to you with my stuff. Speaking of my stuff, I'm meeting Moe for lunch tomorrow. And he sounds like he wants to talk about something."

Rachel sighed. "Oh, Clare," she said. "I'll make sure to say a little prayer for you tonight at bedtime. It's not often that I wish for someone to be gay, but this one time, I'll make an exception."

CHAPTER 16

CLARENCE TOOK MORE CARE IN dressing that morning than usual, and he usually took great care. He made a habit of hanging up his work shirts immediately after taking them out of the dryer, but this time, he took out the iron and removed every last wrinkle. He ironed his khakis for good measure. He stopped short at his underwear. Boxer briefs withstood the laundry well. He used his best skin care and hair products after his shower and sprayed on a small amount of after shave.

He looked in the mirror and checked out the final product when he was finished. He figured he'd find himself attractive if he were a questioning straight man. He had been told he was good-looking, and not only by his mother and his friends. He had caught the eye of potential hookups in bars, and he'd even had people approach him on the streets to comment on the clear blue of his eyes. He knew his cheekbones looked sculpted, and his six-foot-tall body was strong and fluid. Now it was just a matter of making Moe see all of that, and in Rachel's words, try to "flip" him. He knew that some-one could not be flipped if they didn't want to be, but he figured he'd use all of the tools at his disposal, just in case.

He arrived at Lynette's Bakery fifteen minutes early and scoped out the situation. A couple of women got up from a table near the window, and Clarence headed directly there and sat to wait. He didn't have to wait long, as Moe arrived ten minutes early, his eyes going wide when he spotted Clarence already there. He headed to the table and sat across from him.

"You're early," he said, his voice clipped.

Clarence nodded. "So are you." He looked into Moe's eyes and could see how nervous he was. "Do you . . . want to get something to eat?"

Moe nodded. He hung his zip-up hoodie on the back of his chair to mark that it was occupied, and the two men headed for the counter. They came back five minutes later, Moe carrying a number to place on the table. "How are things going?"

Clarence cleared his throat. "Pretty good," he said. He fidgeted with the napkin on his lap. "How are you? You look like you have something on your mind."

Moe bit his top lip and then looked around the bakery. The lunch crowd had just started to filter in. He leaned closer to Clarence and spoke softly. "I . . . I wanted to talk to you, but I didn't want to, you know, go out somewhere that we would be drinking. I-I . . ."

Clarence reached across the table and touched his hand. "It's okay, Moe," he said gently. "I told you before. Nothing you say to me leaves this table, and I won't judge you, no matter what you say."

As soon as the words left his mouth, he realized they weren't entirely true. If Moe told him that he had determined that he was one-hundred-percent straight and didn't want to see him anymore, he would judge him harshly, but not to his face. His friends would get an earful, though.

Moe took a deep inhale, then blew it out. "Thanks," he said. "That means a lot. Really. It's just—" He paused, then stared at a bud vase on the side of the table. "I haven't been able to talk about it because it terrifies me. I . . . every time I think about it, my anxiety gets so high, and I get lightheaded, and I can't function. But that doesn't mean that nothing's happening." He looked at Clarence. "Something happened already. A few months ago."

Clarence's eyes widened in astonishment. "Oh."

Moe shook his head. "I didn't do anything. It was someone else. A . . . friend. But—but I didn't stop him. And it left me . . . confused."

"Because you liked it," Clarence conjectured.

Moe hesitated, then nodded. "I mean, it's hard not to like a blowjob, no matter who's giving it. It feels good, right? But the fact is, after, I couldn't stop thinking about it, and . . . and who did it. I-I'm not in love with him. I don't even think I'm that attracted to him. But—but it kind of opened . . . something inside of me. Something I didn't know was there."

"Was there alcohol involved?" Clarence guessed.

"Just a little," Moe admitted. "Not enough to not know what I was doing, but enough to lower my inhibitions."

Clarence nodded. "And now you have some stuff to figure out."

"Yeah." Moe poked at the pads of his fingers with the tines of his fork. "I love women. I've always loved women. I love their bodies, their smiles. Everything about them. But maybe I also . . ." He stopped and put the fork down as the server delivered their sandwiches to the table. Moe looked up and gave her a grateful smile. When she left, he continued. "I mean, I guess I could be bi. But then why—"

"Why didn't you know before? Maybe because there was never anyone who caught your eye."

Moe's face paled. "But no one caught my eye a few months ago. I mean, I don't think . . ." He shook his head. "That's not true. I've always been aware that there were beautiful men. I just thought that it was normal to look at men aesthetically, like women look at other women and find them beautiful."

"Most likely," Clarence said with a shrug. "But most men don't let their male friends go down on them, even when they've had a drink or two."

Moe hung his head. "I guess I was . . . curious?" He shook his head. "That word comes up a lot, doesn't it? But I guess it's true. I'm curious. But it's more than curious. It's like a curious *need*. It's not just like, what's behind the curtain? It's more like, if I like what's back there, will I want to keep going back there?"

Clarence snickered. "That's one way to put it."

Moe licked his dry lips. "But I guess everyone gets curious?" He looked at Clarence pleadingly.

Clarence collected his thoughts. "Did you know your friend was gay? The one that gave you head?"

Moe's eyes narrowed. "Yeah? I mean, we're close friends, so of course."

"And you drank with him, and somehow ended up alone. How did that happen?"

"Uh," Moe started. He grabbed his thumb with his other hand. "I was having a bad day. I texted him, and he came over with a couple of bottles of wine."

Clarence nodded. "So you knowingly invited your gay friend to your place to drink some wine together, with no one else there. Did you have any idea—"

Moe sighed hard. "I don't know. Maybe."

"You asked if everyone else gets curious. I don't really have an answer for you. But my guess would be that yes, everyone, or almost everyone, has some sort of curiosity sometime in their life about things that they otherwise wouldn't consider. But they don't necessarily create a situation to make it a reality. They might watch some porn about it and never mention it to their friends. But you took it to the next step."

Moe picked up his turkey sandwich and held it halfway to his mouth. Then he stared at it. He had yet to take a bite. "So what you're saying is that I crossed the line from curiosity to experimentation."

Clarence nodded. "And you liked it."

Moe's face blanched, and he put his sandwich down. "I . . ." He blinked slowly. "I don't think I've accepted the fact that I enjoyed it. I think that ever since it happened, I've been running away from it, both mentally and physically. I haven't talked to my friend since that night. I texted him, but he hasn't texted back. I feel like a total loser to have used him like that."

Clarence reached out and touched the back of his hand again. "I'm sure your friend has to understand that you're going through something. I mean, if he's your gay friend, he's probably known about you for much longer than you have."

Moe stared into Clarence's eyes with his own blue-green ones. "Do you think so? Oh my God. So basically, the only two gay guys I know figured it out long before I did." He withdrew his hand from Clarence's.

Clarence drew his hand back and made it busy by picking up and eating a potato chip. "And then you went to a gay club."

Moe nodded. "I thought my heart would explode when I walked through that door. And the first people I saw looked at me like I was a fresh slab of meat for their consumption. I walked around for a bit, just checking things out. Then I accidentally walked into this one room . . ." He shuddered. "I pretty much turned around and headed back to the door, but then I saw you, sitting at the bar, and you looked so normal, and so . . ."

Clarence fought the tremors in his stomach. "So what?"

Moe hesitated but then appeared to give in. "So . . . beautiful. Clarence, you're a beautiful man, and that didn't get past me. I felt I had to . . ." He lowered his head. "I couldn't help myself. It was as if there was an empty stool next to you for a reason. I felt compelled to sit down."

Clarence's heart was pounding now. "You were attracted to me."

Moe nodded slowly. "I had to—I had to know you. I don't know why. I just did. And then when I realized I had to leave, I knew I couldn't go without knowing I would see you again. But I didn't know if I wanted—"

"You told me you were straight," Clarence said. "You were afraid."

Moe nodded again. "Terrified. But even more terrified of letting you go without . . ." He waved his hand in front of him. "Well. Here we are"

Clarence felt like he was running out of words. He took a bite of his sandwich just to have something to do. After he swallowed it, he took a sip of his iced tea.

"I'm attracted to you, too," he finally said. "Like, really, really attracted to you. But I don't want to be someone's experiment. But I do want to be your friend. So if you decide you want to pursue something with me, take some time first to get all of the experimentation out of your system, okay? Because I want more than that. Moe, I think about you all the time. I think about your eyes, your—"

"I know," Moe interrupted. "I think about you, too. I just . . . I don't know if I'm ready to stop . . ." He paused. "I'm dating women right now. One in particular. I like her. I'm not sure I want to stop seeing her, but I also don't want to lead her into thinking that I'm something that I'm not. And I also know there's a part of me that does want to explore these feelings further, even though being bi doesn't mean I have to give up women. Does that make sense?"

Clarence laughed. "It really does. I mean, it's not the same thing, but I've been having sex with a straight woman for years. Well, until recently."

Moe actually gasped. "Are you kidding me? You? You're bi? I never would have guessed!"

Clarence rolled his eyes. "I wish everyone could understand that there aren't just straight, gay, and bi people. There's a spectrum. And to be honest, I'm the closest to gay that someone could be. I'm not bi. I don't like women, as a rule. I tested myself a few times. I don't find straight porn to be enticing, and lesbian porn makes no sense to me whatsoever. It was this particular woman that led to it happening. It was a comfort thing, just like for you. I needed it, she provided it, and it was never more than friendship and sex. No romantic feelings, no planning for the future. But like you said, we both needed to get beyond that, to find out what we really want. So we had to let go of the sexual part of our relationship, and it was hard, but we're pulling it off. She's seeing someone now, and she really likes him, so that's good. He can give her something I can't, I hope. And then there's me, doing exactly what she did. Falling for the inaccessible." He took another sip of his drink.

"I-I don't know if I'm inaccessible," Moe said softly. "I mean, maybe right at this second. I just need a little time."

"Do you have anyone else to talk to about this?" Clarence asked.

Moe shook his head quickly. "No. No one. You're the first person I've even mentioned this out loud to. And I have my own motives for doing that."

"Could you talk to your family?"

"Not yet," Moe said. "I mean, it's not like they'd disown me if I told them I think I'm bi, but they might have questions, and it might change things. I don't know. I'm not ready for that."

"That's fair," Clarence said. "I came out to my mother when I was fifteen, not long after my father was diagnosed. I never came out to him, because it wouldn't have really mattered. But I have friends that had to come out much later to their families. Some of them were shocked, and others had already figured it out. I guess we were all lucky that in the end we were accepted. I know of people who weren't, and it was hard. But in any case, I'm willing to be your friend, Moe. As long as it takes to figure things out."

Moe stared at him, some of the anxiety having melted from his face. "You really are a beautiful man, Clarence Steiner," he said. He looked at his sandwich. "I guess I should really eat this, huh? I have to work at one. But you know, working at a grocery store, I'm never lacking in access to food, so . . ." He picked up his sandwich and took a bite.

Clarence smiled at him. "You, too, are a beautiful man, Giacomo." He picked up his own sandwich and took a bite.

Rachel
How did the lunch go? Are the two of you an item now?

Clarence
It was good, but alas, no. He has some really big work to do on himself.

Rachel
Did he admit he likes you?

Clarence
He actually did. And I admitted I like him. But don't get too excited yet. He has a girlfriend. Well, I think he does. He's seeing someone.

Rachel
Is it serious?

Clarence
Serious enough for him to not want to just walk away from it. But I think it's pretty clear he's bi.

Rachel
Do you want me to call you?

Clarence
Todd's hanging out in my office right now, but maybe we can talk tomorrow. I'm really not too sure what to even talk about anyway. He likes me, he's figuring it out, and I'm gonna be his friend. I want to kiss his face, and other parts of him too, but that will have to wait. I can do this.

Rachel
I'm sorry you have to do this.

Clarence
Me too.

Rachel
You have to be prepared for the worst.

Clarence
I know. What do you think is the worst?

Rachel
He's bi, so he decides to put guys on the back-burner and stay with the girl. It's easier in the long run.

Clarence
Yeah, that is the worst-case scenario, isn't it? But I can't fault him. I mean, I guess it's just easier to be a straight couple in the world.

Rachel
But is it? It sounds like he's struggling. And being with you might make it better.

Clarence
Better for me at least.

Rachel
LOL. God, we can pick them, huh? I mean, I'm having a great time with Barry, but maybe that's just all it's gonna be. I just want to wake up one day and have some guy knock on my door and tell me he's been dreaming about me all his life and now he wants to be with me forever.

Clarence
As long as he meets your criteria.

Rachel
yeah there's that. But maybe it will be Barry.
That would be nice.

Clarence
I hope that for you, Ray. I want
you to be happy.

Rachel
You keep saying that. You know I want that
for you, too, right?

Clarence
I do. And I'm happy being your friend.
Maybe that's enough for me.

Rachel
You're sweet, but it's not. And it's not enough
for me, either. Sorry.

Clarence
Yeah. I get it.

Clarence
We need to get on a Zoom meeting. I'll text
you later when things quiet down. Love you.

Rachel
Love you too.

CHAPTER 17

"I'D NEVER EVEN HEARD OF Bristol," Rachel said as they got out of Barry's car. "I mean, you're new to the area, and you've already found it. Just like that pie place with the amaretto pie."

Barry smiled and then shrugged. "You've heard of Google, haven't you? I did a search for a place to go to see tulips, and this place popped up. I figured it was a nice enough day to go someplace outdoors, and the tulip season is limited."

"What made you think to look for a tulip place?" Rachel shoved her hands into the pockets of her spring jacket. Yes, it was a nice, sunny day, but it was early, and the sun hadn't warmed up the early April air enough yet to go without a jacket.

"When I had dinner at your place a couple weeks ago, I brought you flowers and you mentioned that you liked tulips." Barry swerved to avoid walking through a large puddle in the parking lot. "I pay attention."

Rachel grinned. "You remember more about me than I remember about myself."

They approached the main gate of the tulip farm. Barry paid the admission, shooing away Rachel's money. "My idea, my treat," he said. "But you can buy the hot chocolate if you want."

There was a gift shop attached to the farmhouse, and inside hot chocolate and plain coffee was for sale. Barry and Rachel both opted for hot chocolate, and Rachel paid. Then they made their way down to the tulip fields.

"It's so amazing," Rachel marveled. "I've never seen so many blooms
together in one place. And so many colors!" She did a theatrical twirl. "I
sometimes forget how nice it is to be in the open air with all of this space. I
spend so much time indoors at work, and then hanging out at my apartment.
It was different in Amherst. Lots of room. Room to breathe. And to twirl!"

Barry laughed at her antics. "I like Outside Rachel. Very animated. Go
stand in the red tulips so I can take a picture of you."

Rachel complied. She knelt between two rows of the flowers. "Hold on a
sec." She took out her own phone and put it in selfie mode, using the camera
as a mirror and fluffing her spiral curls. She stuck her phone back in her
purse. "Okay, I'm ready." Barry took several shots and had her pose in different positions. "I need to get some of you," she said.

"Do you want me to get some of the two of you together?" a voice said
behind her.

Rachel spun around and found a woman of about forty standing behind
her, wearing a visor with a nametag pinned on her lapel proclaiming her
name was Kathy. She nodded. "That would be great," she said. Barry came
over to join her, and they both handed their phones to Kathy.

"Say *tulips*," she said, taking several shots.

"I want to say *cheese*," Barry said. Rachel laughed.

Kathy gave them back their phones and they thanked her before checking their photo apps. They scrolled through the pictures, making comments
on each one. Barry stopped on one particular picture of himself with his
arm around Rachel's shoulders, both of them smiling. "See, we were saying
cheese in this one. This is the all-American photo. We could win a prize."

Rachel laughed. "It's definitely a hashtag-couple's goals photo."

Barry's smile fell away slowly. Rachel felt a sudden tightness in her chest.

"Did I say something wrong?" she asked.

Barry's eyes met hers. "What? Oh, no. I was just thinking we should
keep walking. We can go over there to the purple ones." He pointed to the
other side of the field and took Rachel's hand. Rachel hesitantly went along
as Barry started their trek.

The rest of the tour of the garden was fun, and they joked and laughed

a lot, but Rachel couldn't shake the feeling that something had changed
between them, had become more superficial. It had all started when she
used the word *couple*. She knew that Barry was open to seeing other women,
and maybe he even was, even though she couldn't imagine where he could
find the time. But what she had said was so benign, so innocent. It was basically a popular hashtag. But for whatever reason, it had caused Barry to act
differently. They both maintained the air of fun, and Rachel really was having a good time. But not as good of a time as she *had* been.

When they started to get tired, they headed back to the farmhouse. "I
could use a snack," Barry said. "Do you want to check out the snack bar?"

Rachel nodded her assent, and they entered the building. There weren't
too many options for food, so they chose two giant soft pretzels and Cokes
and headed outside to sit at a picnic table.

"That was really cool," Barry said, looking back toward the tulip fields.
"When I was in high school, I played soccer, and if I had ever mentioned to
my teammates that I wanted to go visit a field filled with tulips, I would have
been laughed right off the field. They probably would have said something
like I had to turn in my man card! But it's not like that. Anyone can enjoy
something beautiful like this."

"You don't have to convince me," Rachel said. "I think the whole 'divid-
ing activities by gender' thing is so wrong. I have a lot of gay friends, and
some of them like to go to flower shows, and others like to go to football
games. It has nothing to do with your sexual preference or masculinity. I'm
glad you're not influenced by that kind of thinking."

Barry looked up from his pretzel and at her, his face expressionless. "Uh,
yeah."

Rachel watched him look back down at his food. She felt her brow furrow.
What was that about? That was not the response she had expected. She had
expected him to be more curious about her friends, or to just nod and smile
in agreement. She had a moment of horror: Could Barry be homophobic?

It had never occurred to her. If she had been thinking clearly, she would
have asked him all of the questions she needed answers to right from the
start. What did he think about abortion? Was he for or against gay people
marrying each other and having children together? Did he feel like people
of different races and colors deserved the same treatment as white people?
Did he accept that a trans person was the gender they identified with? There

were so many others, but she had been drawn into Barry's gravitational pull so quickly that she had never considered that they might have very different value systems. It didn't seem likely, but she couldn't just make assumptions. If Barry was homophobic, it was a no-brainer for her. She would not see him again. No matter how much she liked kissing him.

They sat quietly for a few minutes, resting and finishing their snacks. Finally, Barry looked up, his face impassive. "Rachel, I think we need to talk."

Rachel felt a burning in her gut. Had Barry also been having similar thoughts? Was he realizing that he couldn't be with someone who wasn't into strict gender roles and befriended gay people? She inhaled deeply and let the air leave her lungs slowly.

"Okay," she said. She had never had someone tell her that they had to talk without the talk ending badly for her. "What is it?"

Barry licked his lips and then cleared his throat. "I . . . it's really hard to have this conversation, but I'm wondering if maybe . . . maybe I've let our relationship go further than I intended. I'm concerned that maybe we've taken it too far, and that's not a place I'm able to go right now. I told you from the start that I wasn't ready to look toward a long-term relationship, and I guess now it's feeling like it's going that way anyway, and I have to consider putting on the brakes."

"Oh," Rachel said. She felt as if the rest of the air had been squeezed out of her lungs. "I-I don't know what to say. I don't think I've done anything that—"

Barry put his hand over hers, shaking his head. "No," he said. His expression was one of distress. "No, Rachel. You haven't done anything wrong. You've been nothing but great. I promise. I think I just let myself start to feel comfortable with you. Too comfortable, and I'm pretty sure I've given you the wrong message. I really love being with you, and kissing you. I'm definitely attracted to you. But there are things . . . things that happened to me. Things I went through that I haven't talked to you about yet."

Rachel nodded. "I hope it's okay to tell you that Becca told me about your ex-girlfriend back in Michigan."

Barry's eyes went wide. "She did?" His head fell forward. "I had no idea she told you. I kind of wish she had let me know, just so I could . . ." He shook his head. "I'm sorry that I didn't fill you in about it before now. It was a really bad time in my life. She told you how she gaslighted me?"

Rachel nodded. Barry chuckled.

"You'd think as a guy with a degree in psych I would have seen through her, but it's different when it happens to you. She had me believing that I was the luckiest guy in the world to have her love, not just because she was so great, but because I really wasn't. And for some reason I bought every word." He shrugged. "I mean, I've done some really big thinking about it since, and I'm starting to realize my role in the whole thing, but even so, when she finally left me, I was totally lost. I felt like death. I even thought about death sometimes. I . . . I did anything I could to try to find my way, a lot of it I'm not proud of. I moved to Boston not just for a new start after the breakup, but also for a clean start for myself. I had to relocate and figure out who I was. I had to be free of all of my old ties. I mean, all of them except for Becca, of course."

Rachel nodded slowly. "So you not wanting to get into a relationship. That had less to do with wanting to date lots of women, and more to do with you trying to find yourself, to be okay with yourself again, without having any ties."

Barry sat silently. He closed his eyes for several seconds. "I don't think I'm quite there yet, Rachel. I think this journey is gonna take me some time. And I know one thing for sure: I can't be doing what I'm doing with you. I can't give you what you want, and I know that means that I'm doing to you what all the other guys have done before, leading you along and not making any promises. And before you tell me that you're an adult, and you make your own decisions, I need to tell you something. I don't think I can let you make this one. I think this one is on me."

Rachel tried to swallow, but her throat was too dry. Barry was breaking up with her. She couldn't believe this was happening. Rachel had never been broken up with before. She had been strung along by guys who were not available, and eventually those relationships faded away due to time or distance, but no one had ever said these types of words to her. She wasn't sure whether to be hurt or grateful that this was happening. She decided that she could be both at the same time.

"I-I don't know what to say," she croaked out. "I didn't think something like this was gonna happen today. I mean, we were just going on a nice drive to a tulip farm to see some flowers. We even took pictures. I mean, that's just things, I know. But still. I-I need to try to wrap my brain around what's happening here."

"I'm so sorry, Rachel." Barry tried to grasp her hand, but she pulled away without thinking. Barry grimaced. "I was worried right from the start that I might end up hurting you, and that's the last thing I wanted, but now I don't think that there's any other way to do this. I can't see into the future. I can't tell you that anything's gonna change. I have a lot of work to do. I need to be able to do it, on my own. And that's not fair to you."

Rachel realized she was breathing in gasps. Then she noticed the wetness on her cheeks. She hadn't even realized she had been crying. She didn't want to cry. She wasn't wearing waterproof mascara, and tears would make a mess. She didn't want to be a mess. She didn't want anyone to be able to make her a mess. She dabbed at her face with a napkin.

"How nice of you to figure out what's fair and what isn't," she said, trying not to sound as bitter as she felt. "Maybe it would have been fair to not let your sister fix us up in the first place. Or to not kiss me, or come to my house and make out with me in my kitchen." She paused, trying to catch her breath. "And for you to not be such a nice guy, and make me feel so damn heard all the time. You listened to me. You made me feel like my thoughts are important, and that they have value."

"They *do* have value," Barry said softly. "Rachel, you're an incredible person, and you deserve—"

"Don't say it," she commanded. "Don't you dare say that I deserve someone who can give me so much more than you can. Don't think I haven't heard words just like that before. Don't think that I don't think I deserve the things that you made me feel when we were together, and even when we weren't. Don't say it, Barry." She sniffed. "Or Jake Barrett. Or whatever your real name is. Maybe that should have been my first clue, that I didn't even know your name until, like, three dates in. Maybe there are other things you haven't told me." She looked up at him, her eyes wet with tears. "Are you homophobic?"

Barry's eyes went wide. "What? Rachel, no. Of course not! Where did that even come from?"

Rachel shook her head slowly. "We never talked about it. Maybe that's not fair of me." She stood up, grabbed the trash from her snack, and started toward the garbage cans. When she came back, she tried to gather whatever was left of her dignity. "I think I want to go home now."

Barry nodded, stood, and started to follow Rachel back to the car. They rode back to Waltham almost in silence, the radio the only sound between them. Rachel kept thinking of things she wanted to say to Barry about how unfair it all was, but she held her tongue. It wouldn't make a difference anyway. Barry had already made up his mind. He had told her straight out that he wasn't available for her the way she wanted, and she had to just grow up and deal with it. She had to be kind to herself. She had to let herself walk away with dignity and not beg to stay with someone who was not available. No matter how much it hurt, it would be her victory. Her first real victory.

After forty minutes, Barry pulled up in front of Rachel's building. "Do you want me to walk you up?"

Rachel shook her head. "No, I'll be okay," she said. She reached for the door handle.

"Rachel." Barry grabbed her arm lightly, and she stopped. She didn't look at him. "I'm so sorry. For what it's worth, I really like you, and I really hate that I didn't meet you at basically any other time in my life except this one. I wanted it. . . . I would have liked for something to come of this. You're such a great person. I wish we could be friends, but I understand—"

Rachel turned to look at him. She did everything she could to make her scowl disappear. She nodded.

"I know," she said softly. "Thanks. And for what it's worth, thanks for not being a dickhead and not stringing me along, even though I wish you had done this before I . . ." She wanted to say more, but she couldn't. She felt the sobs fighting to escape from her chest. "Goodbye, Barry."

She got out of the car, closed the door, and entered her building without looking back.

She was able to hold out until she got back to her apartment before losing control. She felt her way back to her bedroom and threw herself on the bed. She sobbed on her new throw pillows, still rife with the aroma of Macy's. She cried until she felt she couldn't cry anymore. Then she went to the bathroom, peed, and drank some water. Rehydrated, she started to sob again.

Eventually she could tell the sun was setting behind her shades, and she sat up on the bed. She reached into her purse and found her cell phone. First, she went to her photos. She looked at the pictures that were taken just that day of her and Barry at the tulip farm. Shaking her head, she deleted them all. Then she opened her text app to her friend group text thread.

Rachel
Barry dumped me.

Jessica
Oh my God. Hang on. I'm on my way over right now.

Jerry
I'm so sorry Ray. Can I do anything for you? Do we need to hurt this guy?

Steve
I'm with Jerry. Do you want us to hunt this shit-head down and kick his ass?

Clarence

Clarence

Clarence
. . .

Clarence
Fuck.

# CHAPTER 18

MOE CALLED AND ASKED IF they could meet that night, but Clarence told him it wasn't a good time. He told him his friend was having a hard time and he needed to be there for them. Moe said he understood. Clarence hated to say no to Moe. He wanted to see him more than anything, but Rachel came first. Rachel had to come first. He told Moe that he would play things by ear the next day and let him know if they could get together.

Then he called in sick. He needed to make himself available to his best friend. He couldn't get up from her couch and excuse himself at noon for the rest of the day if she was distraught. He texted Todd to let him know, and Todd told him not to worry about it. He had his back.

Rachel didn't want him to come over that night. Jessica would be with her, spending the night. Rachel said she needed a girls' night. But as soon as Jessica fell asleep, Rachel called him.

"I'm such an idiot," she said. She wasn't crying, but he could tell she had been, a lot. "I can't believe I let myself start to fall for another guy who just couldn't see it in himself to fall for me."

"I'm so sorry, Ray," Clarence said softly. "But I mean, from what you said, it sounds like the problem was that he *could* see himself falling for you, and that scared him. He wasn't ready. It sounds like he did you a favor. And I'm not saying he's not a dickhead for hurting you. I hate him for that. But it would be worse if he had stayed and you fell in love with him." He paused. "You're *not* in love with him, are you?"

Rachel sniffed. "No," she said. "I mean, I was on track to love him. But I can't realistically say I loved him. Not yet. I really liked him, though. I really liked being with him. I liked who I was when I was with him. He made me feel happy."

Rachel's comments made Clarence sad. He wished that he could have made her feel happy. Damn, he even used his one and only birthday wish on her. Finally someone had been able to bring her joy, only to turn it around and hurt her, just like he had. If he ever ran into this Barry guy, he would give him a giant piece of his mind. And maybe the steel tips of his cowboy boots. Once he bought cowboy boots.

"It's hard to know what to say," he told Rachel honestly. "I mean, I'm glad it didn't go further than it did. So that's good. But yeah, I think in any relationship, we get our hopes up that it's gonna be the one. And when it isn't, it feels so fucking bad. And it feels like a huge waste of time."

Rachel's sigh came through the phone. "Yeah." She was silent for a moment. "I had no idea . . . no, that's not true. He told me. He warned me, from the beginning. On our second date. He told me that he wasn't promising me anything but a casual good time. But Clare, I think I felt him feeling it, too. I could feel it when he kissed me. You can't fake a kiss."

Clarence wasn't sure that this was true. There was passion, and there was lust. It could be hard sometimes to differentiate the two. But it *had* sounded like Barry liked Rachel, from what she told him. He realized she hadn't told him much. She talked about their dates, and what they did, and the way he made her feel. But he had no idea where Barry lived, or what he did for a living. He knew Barry was new in town but not where he had come from. The only thing he knew about him was that he was six-foot-two with brown hair and hazel eyes. Clarence wasn't even sure he knew what hazel looked like.

"What can I do to help you?" he asked.

"I don't know," Rachel admitted.

"I'm coming over tomorrow to take you to breakfast," he said. "And you can't say no. We can go to Millie's Flapjacks if you want."

Clarence heard a release of breath coming from Rachel's nose that sounded like a chuckle. A sad chuckle. "I'll let you take me out to breakfast," she said, "but only if you don't judge me if I get a mimosa. Or two."

"No judgment," Clarence promised. They stayed on the phone for another half hour, talking about nothing, sending each other funny memes and sharing TikTok and Instagram reels that they thought were amusing

Finally, Rachel yawned. "I think maybe I can sleep now. I'm gonna at least try. Jess is snoring in my bed. I was gonna just sleep in here with her, but I might go sleep on the couch instead."

Clarence smiled. "Stay in your bed," he said. "Roll her over on her right side. She'll stop."

Rachel gasped. "You haven't been sleeping with Jess, too, have you?"

Clarence laughed. "Oh, hell no," he said. "But I have slept *near* Jess. One night in college we hung out and she drank a little too much. I had to let her crash with me. I learned how to stop the snoring with trial and error. Learn from my experience. Also, if you wake up with her hand under your shirt, don't be offended. I think she kind of sleep gropes."

"Oh Lord." Rachel laughed. "I love you, Clarence. I'll see you at, like, eleven?"

"Eleven it is," Clarence replied. "I love you, too."

Millie's Flapjacks was busy at 11:15 on a Sunday morning. But the day was unseasonably warm for early April, so they stood outside to wait for their table to be ready. Rachel pulled off her hoodie and draped it over her arm. Underneath, she was wearing a Nirvana T-shirt.

"Vintage or new?" Clarence asked her.

She looked down. "Not sure," she said. "I got it at a vintage shop, but it could be new vintage. But I'm not cheating. I actually had a Nirvana CD when I was younger, and I know their songs. Did you know the baby from the *Nevermind* album cover is, like, thirty-four now?"

Clarence shrugged. "I guess that means the album's about thirty-four now, too." He looked out into the street, watching cars drive by as they waited. He felt Rachel staring at him and looked back at her. He smiled. "What?"

Rachel smirked. "You're thinking about him, aren't you?"

Clarence feigned confusion. "Who?"

Rachel smacked him in the arm. "Moe, you transparent idiot!

Clarence felt his face get warm. "Maybe. I was wondering what he's doing this morning."

"You should text him and find out," Rachel suggested. "Maybe he could come meet us for breakfast."

"I don't think so," Clarence said quickly. "I mean, I think I need to wait longer, at least until we can define what's going on with us, before bringing our friends into the whole thing. It might confuse things, both for us and for everyone else. And I'm pretty sure either Jerry or Jess would say something humiliating if we were all together!"

Rachel laughed. "I think you're just embarrassed by all of us," she said. Her face softened. "You could go do something with him, you know. You don't have to babysit me."

Clarence took Rachel's hand and then covered it with his other hand. "You're acting like I'm with you because of obligation. I can assure you that's not true. The thing I like most in my life is being able to fulfill the terms of my best friend contract. One of the terms is the 'cheer up' term. There's also the 'trash the ex' term, and under that is the 'revenge' clause. Don't underestimate the entertainment value of our contract."

A middle-aged woman in an apron opened the front door of the restaurant. "Rachel," she called out. Two groups stepped forward. Everyone laughed. The woman shook her head. "Rachel Morris?" The other group fell back, and Rachel and Clarence entered the building.

"It kind of sucks to have such a common name sometimes," Rachel said.

"It's better than having a name no one has anymore," Clarence said as he followed her to their table. "As a kid, I could never find anything with my name on it, and people always say it makes me sound like an old man. And I'm pretty sure my parents branded me as a future gay man when they named me. You don't see a lot of straight twenty-five-year-old guys named Clarence."

Rachel smiled and handed him a menu. "Shut up and pick some pancakes."

Clarence went back to Rachel's apartment with her, and they curled up on the couch to watch a movie. At one, Jerry and Steve came by. They opened a bottle of wine, and Rachel chugged down two glasses. After another bottle and another movie, she fell asleep leaning on Steve's arm. Clarence carefully lifted her in his arms and carried her to her bed. He pulled back her sheets and laid her under the covers. He put a glass of water on her night stand and kissed her on the forehead. Then he went back to the living room and sat on the couch next to his friends.

"She'll be out for a while," he said. "She had three glasses of wine on top of two mimosas. I think it mellowed her out, so I hope she doesn't wake up with a hangover." He grabbed the TV remote. "Let's see what's on."

Jerry put his hand over Clarence's, stopping him. "It's our shift now," he said. "You've been with her all day, and I'm guessing you were on the phone with her most of the night. Why don't you go home and get some rest? Or just chill out. You have the day off. Enjoy it."

Clarence considered what Jerry said. "But I took the day off to take care of her," he protested.

Steve gave him a warm smile. "You did what you needed to do," he said. "These things go better when we all trade off. We'll make a support schedule for the week, and you'll get lots of other chances."

"Why don't you see if Moe wants to get together?" Jerry asked innocently.

Clarence laughed. "So this is less about tag-teaming and more about you guys wanting me to go spend time with my gorgeous maybe-not-so-straight guy? You know, if you push me into this and it doesn't work out in my favor, you'll all be tag-teaming over at my place soon."

"I don't think so," Steve said. "I have a good feeling about Moe. I've even worked out a couple names for you. Morence. Or maybe Claremo."

Clarence rolled his eyes. "Moe hasn't even come out to himself yet," he said. "Maybe table the couple names for now." But he did take his phone out of his back pocket and opened his text app.

Clarence
My friends can spare me for a while. You still want to meet up?

It only took a minute before the return text arrived.

Moe
Yeah, if you're up for it.

Clarence
Where should we meet? My place?

Moe

Moe
Maybe somewhere else. Like a restaurant or
something? Maybe we can go to Bay Leaf?

Clarence
That place is always busy.
We'll need a reservation.

Moe
I'll take care of that. Do you want to meet at
five thirty? Maybe we can catch a movie or
some music after?

Clarence
Sounds great, I'll see you there at five thirty.

Clarence went home, showered, shaved, and put on clean clothes. He
spent way too much time making his hair look just right. He hoped it didn't
rain and ruin all the work he had done. He wanted to look perfect. Moe
brought that out in him. Though, he imagined that Moe was going to be very
disillusioned if they ended up in a relationship and he found out Clarence
didn't wake up looking like this.

It was nearly impossible to wait until five to get on the T to go to Bay
Leaf. He checked his hair in the reflection of the train's window before he
came to the stop. After a one-block walk, he found himself in the lobby, but
Moe hadn't arrived yet. He sat in a waiting area next to a well-dressed older
couple and glanced up at the clock above the hostess stand. It was just five

thirty. Two minutes later, Moe walked in. He smiled when he saw Clarence and made his way over to him. Clarence stood up, and to his surprise, Moe hugged him. It was a brief hug, but substantial.

"It's good to see you," he said.

"Yeah, you too," Clarence said. Now that Moe was standing beside him, he could see that the other man looked tired. He had dark circles under his eyes. "Are you okay? You look like you haven't slept in a while."

Moe's eyebrows rose. "Do I? I guess I didn't realize it. Yeah. It's been kind of a rough weekend. But I'm trying to turn it around. That's why I asked you to get together. I always feel better when I'm with you."

Clarence gave him a sympathetic look. "I'm sorry it's been rough for you. I hope I can cheer you up." He snickered. "I guess that's my main job this weekend. Cheering people up. Good thing I'm good at it."

Moe smiled at him gratefully. "Let's go check in and see if our table's ready." He grabbed Clarence's forearm and pulled him along with him to the host stand. "We have a reservation," he told the hostess.

The woman looked up, and when she saw the two young, handsome, well-dressed men in front of her, she smiled brightly. "What's the name?"

Moe smiled back at her. "It's under Jake Barrett."

Clarence turned to Moe as the hostess grabbed two menus. "Jake Barrett?" he asked. "Who the hell is Jake Barrett?"

Moe laughed. "Hey, I told you I have a lot of nicknames," he said. "Almost everyone calls me Jake. Short for Giacomo. I was about to tell you that when I met you, and then you interrupted and dubbed me Moe. I liked it when you called me Moe, so I just went with it. I didn't see any reason to correct you."

Clarence laughed. "You're just full of little surprises, aren't you? I can't wait to see what you come up with next."

They both followed the hostess back to the dining room to be seated at their table.

CHAPTER 19

WHILE THEY EXAMINED THEIR MENUS, Clarence couldn't stop peeking over his to look at Moe. Moe was dressed in khakis and a green polo shirt, which made his eyes look more green than blue, with little brown flecks throughout.

Moe looked up and caught him staring. He smiled. "Do I have something on my face?" he teased.

Clarence grinned. "No. I was just thinking that you look really great tonight. I'm glad you called to get together, Moe." He laughed. "Or Jake. Man, I still can't believe that all of your friends back home call you Jake."

"My coworkers, too," Moe said. "If you ever came in to see me at work, you'd see that I wear a nametag proclaiming my name is Jake. Jake B. We have to use initials since there are a few Jakes at my store."

Clarence nodded. "I had the same problem with my friend at breakfast this morning. Is that why you gave your last name in the reservation?"

Moe nodded. "I'd hate it if any old Jake on the street got our table." He looked around. "It's a good table, too. Kind of secluded. I like that." His eyes sparkled from the light of the tea candle in the center of the table as he made tight eye contact with Clarence. Then he looked back down at the menu.

"It's cool how everything here is vegetarian. I keep thinking about giving up meat. I'm not that far from it. I just have to shake chicken and fish."

"I don't eat chicken, but I do eat fish sometimes," Clarence said. "I really don't miss the meat. Do you like tofu? The sesame tofu here is amazing. I'll probably get that."

"I think I'll get something with noodles, but maybe I can try yours?"

Clarence felt pins and needles in his hands. Was Moe flirting with him? He wasn't sure. Maybe he was just curious about the sesame tofu. Or maybe he was curious about flirting with a gay man. "That would be fine. As long as I can get a taste of yours."

The waiter appeared, and they gave their wine and appetizer orders. Clarence took a sip of his water. "You said you had kind of a rough weekend," he said. "What's been going on? Or is it okay to ask?"

Moe shrugged. "I don't have a lot of friends in the area," he said, his face looking pained. "And I kind of, well, had a misunderstanding with one of them. A big one, and it was my fault. I feel really bad. I mean, it's hard sometimes, with new friends."

Clarence nodded. "It must be hard. I know that my friend recently met someone who was new in town, too, and it was hard for him to make new friends. Do you stay in touch with your friends from home much?" As the words came out of his mouth, he regretted them. He remembered Moe's story about his gay friend, the one who had pleasured him when he was in a bad place. "Oh," he said quickly. "I'm sorry. I wasn't thinking, you know, about the friend you told me about."

Moe shook his head. "No. It's okay, really. It's probably a good idea for me to talk about it, seeing as you're really the only person I can talk to about these things. Yeah, every now and then I send a text message to Jayden, but I never hear back. I don't know if he's embarrassed, or angry, or what."

Clarence used his index finger to draw a line in the condensation of his water glass. "Do you think that maybe he might have, well, been attracted to you?"

Moe looked down at the table. Then he nodded. "I know he was attracted to me. He might have even been sort of in love with me. That's the worst part. I totally took advantage of our friendship. And I used my personal pain as an excuse. But it's no excuse. I knew how he felt about me, and I knew I didn't feel the same way. He probably blocked me on his phone."

Clarence let the silence sit for a few moments. "Can I ask what the bad thing was that happened to you? Before the thing with Jayden? What caused your personal pain?"

Moe's face paled. "It's kind of hard to talk about," he said softly. "But maybe it can help you understand my state of mind. I had this girlfriend for two years. Her name was Karina. We met senior year in college, just a couple months before graduation. We ended up staying together for two years. It was a wild time, graduating from college, deciding what we were gonna do with our lives. We hadn't been together for too long, but she decided that she wanted to be close to me, so she got an apartment in my hometown, Greenway. I thought it was too soon, but I went along with it anyway. I don't know how it was for you, but the time after graduation was hard for me. After spending four years with all people my own age, suddenly I was going back home, to my family, and having to make decisions I didn't feel I was nearly ready to make. So partly out of loneliness, I agreed to the plan. Three months in, Karina decided we should move in together. So I gave up my apartment. She also decided that I should give up a lot of my belongings, because she had everything we needed already and there wasn't much room. That should have been the first sign."

Clarence inhaled. "This isn't going to be a love story with a happy ending, is it?" He knew this wouldn't be a book that Rachel would want to read.

Moe shook his head. "It started with the belongings. Then my clothes. She bought me clothes, and got me to donate my old stuff. She found new friends, and insisted that we hang around with them. We went to concerts she liked, ate the food she enjoyed, and before I knew it, I had lost myself in the sphere of Karina. I didn't even realize how lost I was until my friends started to tell me. And then Karina started to do things to try to sabotage the relationships I'd had before I met her. Sneaky things. But I was lucky. My friends and family could see what was going on, and they weren't pushed away so easily."

"Moe," Clarence said gently. "I'm kind of surprised by all of this. You seem so sure of yourself. You don't seem like the kind of guy that would put up with that kind of behavior. What was going on there? The loneliness?"

Moe took a hitching inhale. The waiter arrived with their drinks and appetizers. They gave their dinner orders, and as soon as the waiter left, Moe took a large swig of his wine.

"She was verbally abusive, is what happened. It started off so small, I barely noticed, but by the end, she had me believing that she was doing me a favor by even putting up with me. She was gaslighting me. I didn't really know the concept then, but I've done research since, and it's pretty clear. She would turn all of her faults around and somehow make them my fault. When that happens long enough, you start to believe it. You start to doubt your own instincts."

"How did you finally get away from her?" Clarence felt pain in his heart for this beautiful man sitting before him, thinking of him being bullied and worn down by someone who was supposed to love him.

"She cheated on me," Moe responded. "She had an affair. Right under my nose, but whenever I noticed clues, she would berate me and say I was crazy. Until the day when she finally admitted it. The day she kicked me out to move him in. And guess what? She told me it was all my fault. She told me she couldn't stand the sight of me. And she told me no one would ever want a pathetic little fag like me. Those were her exact words. Pathetic little fag."

All the energy drained out of Moe, and his shoulders slumped.

Clarence's mouth hung open. In that moment, he wanted to hunt this evil woman down and choke the life out of her. Instead he reached out for Moe's hand. "I'm so sorry," he said. "She had no right. She was crazy. You know that none of that stuff is true, right?"

Moe looked up with pure gratitude in his misty eyes. "I know. In retrospect I get it. I had to do a lot of thinking about how I let myself get drawn into the whole thing. I guess I was in a vulnerable place, and she picked that up quickly. But at the time, I wasn't thinking clearly. And by the time I had pulled up to my parents' house to eat crow, what she said about my sexuality had gone to my head. I never had any inclination toward men, as far as I knew, but something nagged inside of me about her last barb. I sat with it for a few days in my old bedroom, barely eating, sleeping, or hearing the consolation my friends and family were giving me. Finally, I got up, took a shower, and drove to Jayden's house. I had something to prove. I needed to know, for my own sake, that I was a straight man. That I loved women. That everything that Karina had said about me was not true. If I didn't have any reaction to being with a man, then everything else she ever said about me was false, too. It was a strange way to try to prove things to myself, but it was all I had. So I brought wine, under the pretense that I needed comfort from my close friend. But I had ulterior motives. I don't know if he knew I had planned it, but after a few glasses of red, it came way too easily. I guess you could say, I came way too easily. And it didn't make things better. It made things worse. In addition to feeling my original angst, I was feeling guilty for what I had done to Jayden, and I had the knowledge that I had been turned on by sex with a man. It wasn't long after that I decided to leave Greenway."

"And why Boston?" Clarence asked.

"I have a sister here," Moe said. "But I didn't know anyone else. It was easier for me, so I could make a new start. And to explore my feelings. But it wasn't as easy as I thought it would be. I didn't know what I wanted. And I didn't know how to figure it out. So I ended up falling back to women, out of habit. But it wasn't right. I . . . that's why I went to the Rodeo that night. I knew how to find women, but I didn't know how to find men. Any men." He paused and looked directly at Clarence. "And that's when I found you. And the moment I saw you, I knew it was true. I knew I could easily be into a guy. At least one particular guy."

Clarence felt a stirring in his stomach. "But you were dating when we met. Dating women. Are you still dating women?"

Moe shook his head. "I can't honestly date a woman, or anyone else right now—"

"Oh," Clarence interrupted, looking down at the untouched appetizers.

Moe chuckled softly. "You didn't let me finish. You do that a lot. I was gonna say that I couldn't date anyone else right now knowing that Clarence Steiner existed in the world. But I don't think I'm ready to even contemplate a relationship with a man—I mean, I have no idea what to do. I'll be honest. I'm scared, nervous, and really uncomfortable. The only reason I feel safe telling you all this is because you told me that you were interested in me. And when you told me that . . ." He exhaled. "The first night we met, when you told me if I ever decided that I was gay that you wanted me to call you, I, well, I got . . . excited, to say the least."

Clarence felt his cheeks turn pink, and he noticed that Moe's were doing the same. He cleared his throat. "So now? What are you feeling now? Do you feel like you want to—"

"I know one thing," Moe interrupted, his voice raspy. He reached over and took Clarence's hand in his. "I know that I can't stop thinking about kissing you. I think about it when we're together. I think about it at work, and when I'm at home, and in bed. . . ."

"Are—are you thinking about it now?" Clarence asked.

The distress melted from Moe's face. He squeezed Clarence's hand. "I just told you. I think about it all the time."

Clarence felt his pants get tight, and he readjusted his body in his chair. "You can't tell me this right now," he said. "We're sitting at a table in the middle of a restaurant, with food in front of us. We're expected to eat the food, and then eat the other food that they give us after. If you keep telling me things that you want to do with me, I don't think I'll be able to eat any of the food."

Clarence witnessed Moe's pupils dilating.

"So you're saying that if I kissed you after dinner, you'd kiss me back?" Moe asked.

Clarence laughed. "Are you fucking kidding me? I've been wanting to kiss you since you first sat down on that stool next to me at the bar. I've been a total basket case. When you texted me the first time to get together at the sports bar? I almost hired a skywriter to announce it to the whole city! Moe, I've been waiting for you to give me some kind of sign this whole time."

Moe's face lit up. "Wow," he said. He shook his head. "This weekend started out pretty dismal, but things suddenly seem to be getting better." He picked up a salad roll. "We'd better start eating this stuff. The sooner we finish—"

"The sooner you'll bring me back to my apartment and walk me to my door?"

Moe shoved the salad roll into his mouth and started to chew quickly. "Do I have to wait until I get you to your door?"

They fumbled to the door, their hands moving, one of Clarence's in Moe's hair, the other on his back, pushing him closer. Moe had one hand on Clarence's shoulder, and the other on his lower back. The kissing had started in the car as soon as they left Bay Leaf. It continued as soon as they pulled up at Clarence's building, and in the elevator, and in the hall. Clarence reached into his pocket, groping for his door key. He tried to pull away from Moe's mouth, but a hand came up and pulled his head closer. Clarence laughed into Moe's mouth. "I just need to get the key so we can go inside. And go to the couch."

Moe pulled his face away, his eyes wide and his hands still all over Clarence. "Oh, yeah. The key." He waited for Clarence to remove his keychain and then drew him back into the frantic kiss.

Clarence reached behind him and unlocked the door, using his fingers to find the keyhole. The door sprung open, and he and Moe fell into the entryway of the apartment.

"So this is your place," Moe said. He kissed Clarence's neck, then his Adam's apple. "Where is this couch you promised?"

There was no grand tour offered. They didn't break apart from each other for even a moment as they moved toward the couch. They fell onto the cushions together, their lips connecting once more as the rest of their bodies followed suit.

"This is so much better than I even imagined," Clarence mumbled. He cupped Moe's face and looked into his eyes. "What do you call the color of your eyes?"

Moe smiled as he looked at Clarence. "Hazel," he said. "Kind of green-brown. And yours are a steely blue. They're the kind of eyes you never forget once you've looked into them." He leaned toward Clarence and kissed each of his eye lids. "Everything about you is beautiful. Your eyes, your lips, your neck . . ." He reached down. "Your chest. It's so different. It's so flat, and so strong." He leaned down and pressed his cheek into Clarence's shirt. "Can—can I touch it?"

Clarence felt he might melt in his spot. "Oh God yes," he said.

He watched as Moe's hand lowered toward his waist, and then slowly rose up under his shirt. He felt his soft fingertips exploring his abs, and then moving up to his pecs, and his nipples. He felt the moan before he heard it come out of his mouth.

"That . . . that feels so good. Can I . . . do you mind if I take off my shirt?" He looked at Moe and saw pure longing and passion in his eyes. Moe nodded.

Clarence was just reaching down to lift up the hem of his shirt when there was a knock at his door, making him stop in his tracks. His eyes met Moe's.

"Who the hell could that be?" he asked. He reached into his back pocket to get his phone so he could check the time. "Shit. I don't have my phone. Did I leave it at the restaurant?"

Moe shrugged. "I don't remember seeing you take it out at the restaurant. Maybe it fell out in my car?"

Clarence stood up as another knock came at the door. He adjusted his pants and smoothed out his shirt. "I'd better get that. Shit. I don't even know if anyone was trying to reach me. Hold on. Don't move."

He started toward the door, running his fingers through his hair to neaten it quickly. When he faced the door, he inhaled deeply, then blew it out. He had to get his heart rate down quickly. He felt a bit dizzy and light-headed. He took one more breath and turned the knob.

"Ray," he said, finding his best friend at the threshold. "What are you doing here?"

Rachel's cheeks were red, her makeup-free eyes taking in his appearance. She squinted at him. "Jerry and Steve had to go," she said. "I tried to text you to see if you could come back over, but then I heard your phone dinging under my couch cushion. You left it at my apartment. I had no other way to get in touch with you, and I figured you'd be going nuts trying to find it."

Clarence stared at her. "Oh. Oh my God. Yeah, I just noticed a few minutes ago that it was missing. Thanks. Thanks so much for bringing it over."

Rachel studied his face. "Your cheeks are pink," she said. "Your lips are red. You look like . . ." She glanced at the floor. "Are those . . . Clare, there are two pairs of shoes by your door. Is someone here?" She started to smile slowly. "Oh my God! Have you been *kissing* someone? Clare, who's here? Is it Moe? Can I meet him? Please?"

Clarence's face flushed. "He *is* here," he said softly. "He finally admitted that he wants to be with me. I don't know if it would be such a good idea—"

"Oh, come on," Rachel said. "You *have* to introduce us! I've been hearing about him for so long, and now he's like twenty feet away from me! He has to want to meet your best friend!"

Clarence sighed. "Okay," he said. "I'll introduce you. But then you have to go, okay? I mean, if you need me to come over, I will, but—"

Rachel laughed. "Oh my God, Clare. I can see you tomorrow. I am *not* going to be accused of cock blocking you. I'm so happy for you!" She hugged him, and Clarence relaxed into her embrace. "Now come on, introduce us." She took Clarence's hand.

Clarence smiled and pulled her through the kitchen and into the living room. "Moe, I want you to meet my best friend. This is—"

"Rachel?" Moe stood up.

Clarence stared at Moe in confusion. "You know Rachel?" He looked at his best friend. Her face was a mask of horror. "Ray, what's wrong? What's going on?"

Rachel's lip was quivering. "*Barry*?" she said in disbelief. "What the hell are you doing here?"

Moe took a step closer. "Me? What are *you* doing here?"

Rachel shook her head. "I . . . Clarence . . . he's my best friend!"

Moe shook his head. "You told me about your best friend. She's a woman. Her name is . . ." Moe fell back on the couch, his hand going to his face. "Clare."

Clarence's head turned frantically from Moe to Rachel and back. "Barry?" he asked. "What the hell? Ray, what's going on?"

"Wait," Moe said, looking up at Clarence. "Ray. You've told me about Ray. I just—I figured Ray was a guy. I had no idea your best friend was . . ."

Rachel looked like she was going to vomit. "Clare . . ."

Clarence grasped her arm and then turned back to Moe. "The friend, the one you had the misunderstanding with . . ."

Moe looked up at him. "The friend you needed to comfort . . ."

Clarence felt like his head would explode. "And how is your name Barry? Do you just give random names out to everyone you meet?"

Moe shrugged, his eyes wild. "Barrett," he said. "My last name's Barrett. My sister calls me Barry, and she—"

"How?" Rachel asked. She had her hands folded over her chest, and tears were falling down her face. "I don't understand! Barry, you told me you wanted to date other women. You wanted to keep your options open—"

"Yes," Moe said, emotion pouring into his voice. "I didn't lie to you, Rachel. I-I just didn't specify . . . I just let you believe . . ."

"Oh God." Rachel slowly sank to the floor, sitting cross-legged on the carpet. She lowered her head toward her lap. "All this time, you were Clare's Moe. I was giving him advice! I was literally praying for him that his relationship with *Moe* would work out! What the hell! What kind of sick world is this?"

"Ray," Clarence said, bending over to touch her shoulder. She shrugged his hand away.

"No," she said. "No. Don't touch me. I-I don't know what to do. I don't know what to say. This . . . this all just seems like too much not to be deliberate."

Moe stood again. "It's not," he said desperately. "Rachel, you have to believe me. I don't think any of us knew. . . . I never wanted to hurt you, but I was so confused. I had to figure things out, and I never should have let Becca fix us up. I just didn't want her to know. I wasn't ready to tell her. . . ."

Rachel stared at him. "I have to go," she whispered. She stood up. "I don't have words right now. I have to think about this."

"Ray—" Clarence started.

Rachel shook her head. "I have to go," she repeated. "I-I'll talk to you later. I think the two of you have some stuff to talk about. I-I just can't be part of this right now. Clarence . . . I'll text you. Later." She rushed to the door, and then out of the apartment.

Clarence turned to Moe. "How?" he asked. "How did we never know? How is that possible?"

"I don't know," Moe said, shaking his head. "But this doesn't have to spoil things for us, Clarence. We can work this out with Rachel. We only went on a few dates. I really liked her, but it's not like it is with you. With you, I feel passion. I feel . . . I feel so much. We can make this work."

Clarence looked into Moe's eyes, Moe's beautiful hazel eyes, and slowly shook his head. "You don't understand," he said. "There's no way you could know, and I don't think Rachel would have told you. If she had, you would have figured it all out, I'm sure of it. As it is, I'm thinking that she didn't tell you much about me."

Moe looked at him, confusion evident on his face. "What is it I don't understand?"

Clarence took a deep breath and then exhaled hard. "We'd better sit down. I have a lot to tell you. And it's complicated."

CHAPTER 20

RACHEL WASN'T SURE HOW SHE got home. Had she somehow walked there? She didn't recall being on the light rail, and her hair was wet from the spitting drizzle that was dampening the streets of Waltham. But she was in her lobby when she came back into her brain and out of autopilot. She worked her way to the elevator and pressed the up button. When the doors opened, she stepped inside, but nothing looked right.

Clarence was her best friend. He was also her ex-lover. How could it be that he had done this to her? She had finally made the decision to move on, to find someone who was there for her, who could love her the way she needed to be loved, and instead, she had found another gay man, and that gay man was in love with her gay best friend. She could tell just by looking at the two of them, both of them with their faces flushed from kissing someone with a five o'clock shadow.

Shadow.

Shadow Man.

Barry was supposed to be *her* Shadow Man.

She wasn't sure who to be angry at. Should it be Clarence, or Barry? Or maybe herself? It was impossible to know, but everything inside of her was telling her that this wasn't her fault. She was just an innocent bystander. She didn't know what she was going to do about Clarence. How could she even look at him again after this? How could he hurt her like this? She felt like she would throw up. She knew the difference between literal and figurative, but at this moment, things became very real. She bolted to her bathroom and heaved. And she didn't feel better when she was done.

She didn't know what she wanted to do. She had no idea what would make things better. She thought about texting Jessica, or maybe Steve and Jerry. She thought about a group text, but then remembered that Clarence was in the group chat, so she threw her phone on the couch and ran into her bedroom. She considered throwing herself on the bed and sobbing, but it didn't feel like tears would come. She felt drained, empty. And when she felt bad, she turned to Clarence. And he made it all better.

She had to do something. She picked up the book on her bedside table and started to read. She had to escape for a bit, let her brain rest and her imagination take over. She knew her brain would still be working on her problem in the background, but she didn't want to be present while this was going on. She read one page, and then the next, and before she knew what was happening, two hours had passed.

She went to the living room and retrieved her phone from the couch. She checked her texts. There were no new messages. She turned on the TV and scrolled through Netflix. She needed a comfort movie. She usually turned to *Red, White, and Royal Blue*, but the idea of watching two hunky men fall for each other and love win in the end made her stomach feel like retching again. She settled for *Notting Hill*, her mother's favorite feel-good movie, and she settled back to watch. There was nothing wrong with a little hetero romance now and then.

When the movie ended, she knew she had to eat. She hadn't eaten in hours. In the kitchen, she found some crackers and cheese. She took peanut butter out of the cupboard and a spoon out of the drawer. She sat at the table and alternated between crackers and cheese and crackers smeared with peanut butter. Her stomach had finally settled, and the food went down easily. She went back to the fridge to search for a bottle of wine, but then thought better of it. Wine made her cry, and she didn't want to cry. She wanted to be angry. She *was* angry.

She grabbed her phone and was about to text Jessica when a thought occurred to her:

It was no one's fault.

She gasped.

No, it had to be *someone's* fault, most likely Barry's since he was the new guy. Barry had done something wrong, but Rachel couldn't place exactly what it was. Damn, her brain had really done its work while she was checked out reading.

Was it possible that all of this was just one of those things that happened, and no one was at fault? But if that was the case, then she had no right to be angry.

And *that's* when the tears came.

After fifteen minutes of sobbing, she finally started to write a text to Jessica. Halfway through, she gave up and pushed the phone icon. Jessica answered after the first ring.

"I was just gonna text you," she said. "How was the rest of your day? I'm guessing the guys did a good job taking care of you since I didn't hear anything from you. Rachel? Ray? Are you there?"

Rachel started to sob again. "Barry is Moe."

"Hold up," Jessica said, and Rachel could almost see her holding up a hand like a stop signal. "What the hell are you talking about? Barry is Moe? What does that even mean?"

Rachel sobbed again.

"Never mind," Jessica said. "I'm grabbing my purse and jacket. I'll be there in twenty minutes."

Since Jessica was coming, Rachel gave in and found the half bottle of wine in her refrigerator, bypassing a glass. By the time she buzzed Jessica in, she was feeling a slight buzz herself.

Jessica came in the door and looked at her. "I've been thinking," she said. "Barry is Moe? Either you mean that you want to have someone in your life like Clarence's Moe, or you literally mean that Barry is Moe."

Rachel nodded her head vigorously. "Barry is Moe. Moe is Barry. And both of them are Jake Barrett."

Jessica took her hand and led her to the couch. She sat her down and took a seat next to her. She shook her head, opened her mouth to speak, and then stopped. She shook her head again.

"So you're saying that Barry and Moe *are the same person*? How is that even possible? Does Clarence know? Did Barry know? When did you find out?"

Rachel took a few cleansing breaths and tried to gather her wits. "It was like a soap opera," she said raggedly. "I walked into Clare's apartment, there were two pairs of shoes and his cheeks were pink. I told him to introduce me to Moe and he brought me in and it was Barry!"

"Christ," Jessica said. "But there's no way no one knew! I mean, there had to be clues!"

"You would think!" Rachel said, raising her hands. "But no. I mean, I talked about Clare, but he thought Clare was my best girlfriend. And I mean, there are millions of Rachels, but Clare calls me Ray. And I guess he never used pronouns when he talked about me, and maybe I didn't use them either. . . . Maybe both of us were feeling weird telling our dates that our best friends were the opposite gender. If anyone was going to figure it out, it should have been Barry." She paused and thought about that. "Or maybe not. Maybe Clare. Or maybe I should have—"

"Didn't Barry see the pictures of you and Clare on your fridge?"

"My landlord upgraded my fridge two months ago," Rachel explained. "I took all my pictures down. Then I was preoccupied and never put them back."

"Didn't Clare have pictures?"

"I think that was the first time Barry . . . I mean Moe, was at his place, and they were kind of preoccupied, too."

"Didn't you and Clare talk about your guys with each other?"

Rachel sighed. "We did. A little. It was kind of superficial. You have to remember, Jess, it's me and Clare. As we all know, we have a history. A recent history. I don't think either of us wanted to talk too much about our, uh, new love interests. It just felt weird."

"Oh." Jessica reached out and took the empty wine bottle from Rachel's hands. "So no one knew. Until tonight. And who's Jake Barrett?"

Rachel felt like she was going crazy. She started to laugh. "Barry. Moe. Jake. All the same person. Clare called him Moe because it's short for his full name, but I don't remember what it is. Something Italian. And I guess Jake must be another nickname for his name? And Barry is short for Barrett. And I think he really doesn't give a shit what people call him. He's kind of easygoing that way."

"Huh." Jessica got up and walked to the kitchen, coming back with a full bottle of red wine and a cork screw. After opening it, she took a swig and handed it to Rachel. "So what happens now?"

Rachel shook her head. "I have no idea. I mean, Barry broke up with me.

So he could be with Clare." Tears rolled down her cheeks, but her emotions were in such flux, she wasn't sure of the current precipitant.

"So Barry's gay?" Jessica asked.

"I don't know," Rachel said. She laughed again. "I mean, it never came up during all of our making out. The way I see it, Barry's straight, and Moe is gay. Or maybe together, Jake Barrett is bi."

Jessica curled her bottom lip and bobbed her head back and forth. "I can kind of see that." She moved closer to Rachel on the couch. "How do you feel about Barry right now? Do you . . . do you think you had a future?"

Rachel considered. "Well, he broke up with me. And apparently he broke up with me because he was having feelings for a man. He was confused. His sister wanted to fix him up, and he wasn't ready to tell her about his feelings. So, really, all that ever could have happened was that we became friends, or, well, he broke up with me. Looking at it like that, we had no future as a couple."

Jessica nodded. "Do you see Barry as someone you could be friends with, based on your time together? Or do you think that your attraction to him would make it too hard?"

Rachel put her face in her hands. "I don't know. I mean, I don't think that's a decision I could make right now. I mean, how could I? I'm humiliated, Jess. He dumped me."

"He gently told you that he didn't want to hurt you like other men hurt you before. He knew that if he didn't do that, history would just keep repeating itself for you, and he didn't want to do that to you."

Rachel wasn't ready to let go of the last vestiges of her anger. "But he shouldn't have—" She stopped talking. She knew better. Her best friend was a gay man. Even as an out gay man, it was hard to be gay in a world where people maintained certain assumptions.

"I'm not being fair," she said. "I mean, neither was he, but he was going through something, and I just happened to be there when it happened. He shouldn't have ever kissed me, but at the time, he was feeling like it was the right thing to do. I know he enjoyed it. It wasn't fake. But when I saw him standing next to Clare . . ." She sighed deeply. "He looked so relaxed, so at home. Even with everything that was going on."

"And what about Clare?" Jessica asked. "What do you think he's going through right now?"

Rachel slumped in her seat. "I hadn't even let myself think about it. I mean, I've been just thinking about what they did to me. But Clare . . ." She took another swig of wine. "When I went to his apartment to bring back his phone, which he had left at my place, he opened the door and I knew right away that something was different. He was different. His face, his eyes, Clare looked relaxed. He looked . . . happy. Like a kid on Christmas day. He told me that Moe had told him that he liked him, and his eyes just danced. I was excited for him. I demanded that he introduce us. And when Barry stood up and saw me, the look on Clare's face . . ." Rachel closed her eyes for several seconds. "Like the Grinch had just stolen his Christmas."

Jessica reached for her hand. "Clare has been into Moe for some time now," she said. "And Clare cares about you more than anyone. I think if Clare was forced to choose between you and anyone else in the world . . ."

"He would pick me. Every time." Rachel stood up and walked to the other side of the room. She turned around and looked at Jessica. "He's probably telling Barry right now that he can't see him anymore."

"How do you feel about that?" Jessica asked.

Rachel shook her head. Then she lowered herself to the floor and curled herself into a ball. "I can't do this right now, Jess. I can't let myself do the right thing right now. I'm too raw. My stomach hurts. I literally threw up when I got home. I need to wallow for a bit."

Jessica nodded. "That's fair enough. Do you want me to stay and wallow with you?"

Rachel looked up from her fetal position on the floor. She made sad puppy eyes and nodded.

Jessica got up off the couch. She reached for Rachel's hand. "C'mon. Let's go get ready for bed. I'll let you braid my hair while I read to you. That always makes you feel better."

Rachel let herself be dragged into the bedroom. "You know me so well," she told her friend.

Rachel rolled to the nightstand at seven o'clock the next morning, grabbed her phone, and texted her boss that she would be out sick that day. She wasn't ready to face the world, and she knew that even with a shower, she would still look red and puffy, like she had been crying all weekend. She had been. But she didn't want them to know, especially Becca. If Becca was going to find out about what happened, it would have to be from Barry. Or Moe. Or Jake. Whatever his name was. She rolled back over, curled up with Jessica, and went back to sleep.

At eleven, she and Jessica finally got out of bed. Rachel felt the slight pang of a red wine headache behind her eyes, but it wasn't bad enough to take ibuprofen. Jessica used the bathroom first and came out stating she was going to make pancakes. Her hair was still in a perfect French braid, and she was wearing a pair of Rachel's summer pajamas.

Rachel took off her pajamas, changed her underwear, and put on a pair of loose, comfortable sweatpants. She fished a clean Boston University T-shirt out of her drawer, and pulled on a pair of soft, fluffy socks. Then she joined Jessica in the kitchen.

"I have frozen fruit in the freezer if you want to add some to the batter," she suggested.

Jessica nodded. "I might." She finished mixing the batter and put the skillet on the stove. "What do you want to do today? Do you want to go somewhere, or just hang out here and watch movies, or something else? We can take a drive up to the beach at Hampton if you want."

"You have a class later, don't you?" Rachel asked. Jessica was working toward her master's degree in architecture, back at BU where it had all started.

Jessica shrugged. "I'm acing all of my classes, my professors love me, and I have an internship locked in for the summer. I think I can get away with one day off to be with my friend."

Rachel gave Jessica an appreciative smile and then hugged her. "I don't deserve you," she said into her neck.

"No, you don't." Jessica went back to the freezer and brought out a frozen banana. "This looks like a withered body part. Is it any good?"

Rachel laughed, and it felt good. "It's fine. That's just what frozen bananas look like." She sat down at the table. "I have to reach out to Clare, don't I?"

Jessica turned her head to her, made eye contact, and nodded. "I think you do," she said. "I think you guys need to talk this through, figure it out. You have things to tell each other. Things to work out."

Rachel sighed. "I know. I have to. I just don't feel ready."

"You don't have to do it right now. Let's have breakfast and then you can decide when you want to talk to him. Or you can wait until after lunch, or dinner. There's no rush."

There was a knock on the door. Rachel and Jessica looked at each other solemnly.

"That's him, isn't it?" Rachel asked.

Jessica's expression stayed static, but she nodded. "I'm pretty sure of it."

Rachel's heart was thumping. "Should I answer it?"

Jessica burst out laughing. "We both know you're gonna open it, Ray. Open the door. Let him in. You can talk, and then we can all eat pancakes."

Rachel nodded slowly and then stood up. She took her time approaching the door, and by the time she opened it, Clarence was raising his fist to knock again.

"Oh," he said. "I-I thought maybe you didn't hear me knock."

Rachel searched the hall behind him. He had come alone. Of course he had. "I heard you. I just had to decide if I wanted to open the door or not."

"Oh." Clarence looked down at his shoes. "That's okay. If you want me to go . . . I should have texted. I know you probably don't want to see me, but I had to—"

Rachel shook her head, took a step forward, and took Clarence into her arms. "Come in, you idiot. Just get in here. We have some pretty important things to talk about."

CHAPTER 21

RACHEL PULLED CLARENCE INTO HER bedroom and closed the door while Jess continued to cook in the kitchen. They sat side by side on the bed, facing each other.

"What happened with Barry? I mean—Moe? We need to figure out a common name when we talk about him."

"We could just call him Jake," Clarence said with a shrug. "It's his real nickname."

"Where is he?" Rachel asked.

Clarence shook the hair off of his face. "I don't know. I think he said he had to work today."

"Don't you have to work, too?"

Clarence shook his head. "I told my boss I have diarrhea."

Rachel laughed, despite herself. "You did not."

Clarence smiled mischievously. "Maybe not in those exact words. More like a stomach virus. But I'm off. I don't think I could function at work today. I take it you called in sick, too."

Rachel nodded. "I . . . there's no way I could work, let alone see Becca."

She shifted in her seat. "You didn't answer my question. What happened after I left?"

Clarence closed his eyes and sighed. When he opened his eyes, he stared at his shoelaces. "I don't really want to talk about that right now. I want to talk about us. I want to talk about what this all means for us. I mean, Ray, this is a really big deal. What's really important is making sure that we're okay, the two of us, as friends."

Rachel's forehead creased. "You didn't do anything wrong, Clare. You didn't know. There's no way you would have done something like this on purpose—"

"But I *should* have known," Clarence said forcefully. "I mean, we didn't talk. We were so superficial when we talked about them—him. I didn't know anything of substance about Barry. You never told me that he worked at Stop & Shop, or that he was from Michigan, or any other detail that would have given it away, and neither did I. That's what we need to talk about, why we didn't talk about it. Why we were so guarded about the details of our relationships. I think . . . I think we were trying not to hurt each other, but instead, we cut each other out. Maybe this whole thing was a message from the universe telling us to wake up and pay attention."

Rachel snorted. "So the universe needed to put that much effort into two little inconsequential people, to teach them a lesson? If that's the case, what was the universe trying to teach Ba—Jake? He was just there as a tool?"

Clarence lowered his head. "I didn't mean that literally, Ray. I just meant that maybe we need to think about this, why we felt like we had to be so reserved with each other. I mean, why couldn't I tell my best friend that the guy I like doesn't eat red meat? Or that he was born in Toronto and has dual citizenship?"

Rachel's eyes went wide. "He *does*? He never told me that!"

Clarence made an O with his mouth. "Well, I guess maybe we both heard some different things."

Rachel shook her head. "I didn't want to act too enthusiastic around you, or make you feel bad about yourself, like I was bragging about how great this guy was, like I was comparing him to you. I mean, you're such a great guy. I didn't want you to think—"

Clarence nodded. "I think I felt kind of the same. I think I didn't want to be all like . . . like being with a guy was so much better than you, even though for me, being with a guy is what I want. I could never get the same sort of thing from a woman, and therefore, you. I didn't want you to feel bad about yourself. I didn't want to rub it in your face"

"Oh, God," Rachel moaned. "We could have saved ourselves so much grief!" She leaned her forehead onto Clarence's chest. "I wish this could be easier. How did we get to this point? How do we get out of it?"

Clarence put his hand on the back of Rachel's head. "We forgive ourselves for the past five years and learn how to be best friends without being afraid of each other. We learn to open up to each other about things that might have been hard a year ago, or even a month ago. We take chances, and hope that we can accept who each of us is becoming on our own."

"That's very wise," Rachel said. "It sounds like something someone who has a BA in psych and is applying to grad school might have said."

Clarence couldn't help but chuckle. "Okay, so Moe helped me figure it all out. I told him everything, about our history, and my theories of why we fell into each other's arms five years ago."

"Really?" Rachel asked, sitting up. "And what would those theories be?"

"That we both have daddy issues we're working on. That we found each other at times in our lives when we were needing the kind of comfort we couldn't get the way we usually got comfort, and it felt so good, so warm, and so healing that neither of us wanted to let go of it."

Rachel's eyes filled up. "So then what do we do now?"

Clarence put a comforting arm around Rachel's shoulder. "We focus on the issues that got us there in the first place. We figure out what we need to do to come to terms with the shitty deal we got from our families. And we move on."

"We move on, together?"

Clarence nodded. "We move on together, and by ourselves. Maybe we ask for help from our friends, or maybe we go to therapy. But we'll be okay, both of us. And we'll be there for each other for the good times and the hard times."

Rachel curled up into the crook of Clarence's arm. "And where is Jake in all of this healing?"

Clarence's shoulders slumped. "Moe has a lot of work to do, too. He has some stuff to figure out. So he'll do that. And then someday, he'll find someone who he can love, who can love him back and give him everything he needs and deserves."

Rachel sat up, pulling herself from Clarence's arms. She looked at him with her brow furrowed. "Clare," she said. "What are you talking about? What about . . . what about the fact that I came to your place yesterday where the two of you had been on your couch, making out like teenagers right before I got there? What about the look I saw in your eyes, the one I'd never seen before? And I've looked in your eyes *a lot* over the years. Clare, you're crazy about that man. And from what you've told me, it sounds like he's been through a lot to get to be with you. You're just gonna let that go?"

Clarence sighed. "Ray, Moe is new in my life. I've known him for what, a month? But I've known you for five years. What we have is so important to me. I think this is what we need to do. Moe and I need to go our separate ways. It will hurt for a little bit, sure, but I know there are other guys out there, guys that I can fall for without the drama. It will happen for me, I promise."

Rachel stared at him. Then she shook her head. "No, Clare. No way. You will never find someone else that you'll look at in the same way you look at Moe. It might just be a month, but what you feel for him, what I've sensed you feel for him, I really think it's the real deal. Don't forget, I was hearing about at least some of the details about your dates this whole time, and I could tell you wanted him, badly. I wanted that for you. And Clare, I still want that for you."

"But it would be hard for you," Clarence argued, "to see us together, being happy. The two gays guys that couldn't give you what you wanted, being together and making each other happy? I couldn't do that to you. It feels cruel."

"But it's not," Rachel told him. "Remember? I get to decide what hurts me. I'm in charge of my feelings. And if I see you being happy, that makes me feel good. Yeah, I'm still sad about the way things ended with Jake. But I'll get over it. We were together about a month, too, and I'm pretty damn sure that what we had was nothing like what the two of you were experiencing. I think Jake and I were becoming friends. And he didn't do anything wrong. He was honest with me the whole time. And when he realized that I was getting too attached, he pulled back. Right away. He did the right thing." She looked at the floor in front of her. "You know, if you and Jake are together, then I get to be his friend. If not, I'll never see him again. So I guess I still get something out of it. Besides just you being happy. Does that make any sense?"

Clarence had to sit with this for a few moments. Was this Rachel's way of letting him have what he wanted and sacrificing her own feelings? He doubted that. Rachel was usually right up front with her feelings. "It makes sense," he said. "But maybe we should sit with it for a few days and then decide how we want to go forward. Wait, what are you doing?"

Rachel was staring at her phone, typing on her keyboard. "I'm ordering you an Uber," she said. "One Uber, from my building to the Stop & Shop in Weston. And you don't need to worry about the cost. It's on me. I've got the tip, too. You're going to Moe's work, Clarence Steiner, and you're going to tell him that we cleared things up, and you're taking him out tonight to celebrate."

Clarence looked at his best friend with gratitude and awe. "Can we not go out, though?" he asked. "Can we just stay in?" He recalled what he and Moe were doing the night before when Rachel had knocked on the door. He had been in the process of removing his shirt. . . . "We have some unfinished business."

Rachel rolled her eyes. "Clare, I don't need to hear the gory details. At least not now. You can call me tomorrow and fill me in. On everything." She grinned. "He's a good kisser, isn't he?"

Clarence felt a wave of longing go through his body. "Yes," he said. "He is a very, very good kisser."

Clarence thanked the Uber driver and got out of the car. As he walked across the parking lot toward the building, he marveled at its size. The Weston Stop & Shop wasn't a normal-sized Stop & Shop; it was a Super Stop & Shop, and it was huge. He watched as fine folks of Weston passed by him and through the doors to buy their groceries, snacks, cleaning supplies, or toilet paper, and wondered how he would ever find Moe among the aisles and aisles of groceries. He finally went through the automatic door and was immediately hit with the lights and sounds of the shopping mecca. Classic soft rock came across the intercom system. Employees rushed by helping customers. Others were ringing up items at the cash register. The dinging of the scanner was rhythmic and almost soothing in its familiarity.

Clarence started to walk up and down the aisles without a cart or basket, looking for Moe. He started in produce and had worked his way into the rice aisle when it all started to feel futile. He debated texting, but Moe might not have his phone on him at work, or he could decide to ignore him after the conversation they'd had last night. The conversation where Clarence had told Moe that he had to choose his best friend over their budding romance.

In the soup aisle, he finally gave up, approaching a young woman who was alphabetizing cans of Campbell's on a shelf. "Can I help you find something?" she asked with a smile. Her nametag proclaimed she was Tasha.

Clarence smiled back. "I'm looking for my friend who works here. He told me he stocks shelves, but I don't even know where to begin to look. His name is Jake."

The woman considered for a moment. "I'm not sure which Jake he is," she said. "Give me more."

"Um." Clarence glanced up at the warehouse-like ceiling. "He's twenty-four, six-one, brown hair, hazel eyes, really attractive . . ."

Tasha smirked. "Your 'friend,' huh?" She made air quotes.

Clarence felt his face start to get hot, but then he recalled what Moe had told him about his nametag. "Jake Barrett," he clarified. "Jake B.?"

The woman's eyes went wide with recognition. "Oh, Jake B. Yeah, attractive for sure. He's in the back checking in inventory. He switched with Tommy for the day. He said he didn't feel like he could face customers today. What happened? Did the two of you have a fight?" She smiled in anticipation of some good gossip coming her way.

Clarence tried to check his impatience. "Is there any way to see if he can come out here for a minute? I have to talk to him. It's important."

Tasha grinned and then removed a walkie-talkie from her belt. "Jake B., please come to the bakery for customer assistance. Jake B., get your ass out here. Please." She put the walkie-talkie back. "The bakery is by the door to the back warehouse. Go over there and wait for him. It's private enough." Realizing Clarence wasn't going to spill any interesting tea, she went back to working on the soup.

Clarence hustled to the back end of the aisle and spotted the bakery at the other end of the store by the bread aisle. He quickly made his way there, stopping in front of the cake display. Thirty seconds later, Moe came through the door. He spotted Clarence and started toward him. "You're the last person I expected to see here," he said, wiping his hands on the sides of his thighs. His face did not reveal his feelings on the matter.

Clarence took in the picture: Moe at work at the grocery store, his dark hair mussed, a black apron protecting his white polo shirt and his jeans. His face was scruffy from a one day of growth of beard. "I-I need to talk to you," Clarence said. "Can we go somewhere private?"

Moe looked around. "We can go out back behind the store if you want. I don't have much time. I didn't punch out for a break."

Clarence nodded and then followed Moe down a hallway to a freight door. They went outside and sat down on a low cement wall near the loading dock.

"Thanks for coming out to talk to me," Clarence said. It was all he could do not to grab Moe's hand and kiss his palm. Or grab him around the neck and kiss his mouth until they both lost their breath.

Moe nodded. "What's going on? Did you get a chance to talk to Rachel?"

Clarence nodded. "It went well. Really well. We're good. Really good. I mean, we need to work on our relationship, to redefine it, and learn to open up to each other about things that have been uncomfortable to us, but we're both willing to do it, so that's great."

Moe nodded. "I'm happy for the two of you. I really care about Rachel. I hope she knows that. I hope she knows that I didn't want to hurt her. I would never want to hurt her."

"She knows that," Clarence assured him. "Even before I got there, she had figured it all out. She doesn't blame anyone for what happened. It would have been different if we had talked to each other more about the people . . . *person* we were dating, but now we know."

"Yeah," Moe said sadly. "Next time if something like this comes up, you'll catch it much sooner."

Clarence tried to hold back, but he couldn't. He burst out laughing. "Oh my God, I'm so sorry, Moe. I don't mean to laugh. It's just that the thought of something exactly like this ever happening again, to us or to anyone else, is just too funny. I really think this was a one-off."

Moe smiled. "I guess you're right. I mean, it *is* pretty bizarre, right? That I ended up unknowingly dating best friends who had a history of fucking each other, when there are, like, millions of people in the Boston area to choose from. I wonder what the odds are."

"I could try to work them out for you if you want," Clarence offered, and then he laughed again. He looked Moe in the eyes. "So it feels like things are going to work out."

"Good," Moe said. "I want that for you. For both of you."

Clarence bit his bottom lip. "Moe, I want that for all three of us."

Moe shrugged. "I'll be okay, Clarence. I really will. I mean, you really helped me at a time when I needed that kind of help. I understand myself a lot better now, and I know that going forward things will only get better for me."

"I think you misunderstood me," Clarence said. He reached out for Moe's hand and lifted it to his face. He kissed his fingers. "I want things to work out for all of us. And I want things to work out for you and me."

Moe looked at him with confusion. "But just last night—"

"I know what I said last night," Clarence interrupted. "But that was last night. A lot can happen in a few hours."

Moe looked into his eyes hopefully. "Rachel gave us her blessing?"

Clarence smiled and then nodded. "Rachel paid for my Uber from Waltham to Weston. And kicked me out the door, telling me I couldn't come back until I found you and had at least kissed you one time." He held up a small bag in his hand. "And she sent me with some of our friend Jess's home-made banana pancakes for us to share."

Moe broke out into a huge grin. "Pancakes?" he asked. Then he put a hand on Clarence's cheek. "And one kiss. Just one kiss? I think I can give her that one kiss, and maybe change." He leaned in until his mouth was right in front of Clarence's, teasing him with his warm breath on his lips. "Permission to kiss you now?"

Clarence tried to catch his breath. He grabbed the back of Moe's head, and right before he pulled him in for the kiss, he whispered, "Permission granted."

CHAPTER 22

RACHEL WENT TO WORK THE next day. She was still feeling raw, and her appetite hadn't returned after she'd consumed fifteen of Jess's extra-large pancakes the day before. She knew she had black circles under her eyes, despite her efforts with the concealer that morning. But she didn't have enough sick time to justify taking another day off, so she decided to suck it up and just go in.

When she passed the front desk, she immediately saw Becca engaged in a deep conversation with Katya, the administrative assistant. Rachel tried to sneak by without being seen, but at the last second, Becca heard her foot-steps and looked up. She gave Rachel a smile that Rachel could only interpret as sympathetic. So Jake had talked to her about their breakup. She wondered what else Jake had told her.

She sat down at her desk and turned on her computer. While she waited for it to boot up, she sipped on her latte. She hoped the acid from the coffee didn't make her nauseous on an empty stomach. When the computer finally announced that she could enter her password, she steeled herself for a day of editing romance.

She was happy for Clarence. She really was. She wasn't just fooling herself. And she was happy for Jake. She wanted it to happen for them. After Clarence told her Jake's story on the phone the previous night, she knew that he deserved happiness. But that didn't take away the feeling of emptiness in her gut. Maybe destiny had already determined that everyone else got to have a happily ever after except for her. Jess had tried to reason with her, reminding her that she herself was not in a relationship and had no prospects, but she was still able to enjoy her life. But Jessica wasn't Rachel. Jessica was an extrovert, comfortable in her own body. She was satisfied with good friends, good food, and occasional good sex. She figured if love came for her, she would accept it. But Rachel felt that love was a huge abyss in her soul waiting to be filled, causing her heart to ache in anticipation.

"Rachel?" Rachel looked up and saw her manager, Debbie, standing in her doorway. "You got a sec?"

Rachel nodded. "Yeah, I was about to send you an email letting you know I need a faster computer, but I had to wait fifteen minutes for it to boot up. Now I'm waiting the ten minutes until my email opens."

Debbie laughed. "I know it's frustrating, but we have to wait for next year's budget to be released before we can make any big purchases. Hopefully you can hold out until July." She sat down on the chair next to Rachel's desk. "Are you feeling better?"

Rachel had a moment of panic. Had Becca told Debbie about what happened with Jake? But then she remembered that she had been out sick the day before. She gave Debbie a reassuring smile. "Much better," she said. "I think I might have picked up a stomach virus from one of my friends, but I'm good now."

Debbie nodded. "Good. God, stomach viruses. I hate those. Hey, listen, I need to talk to you about something."

Rachel felt anxiety rise up from her stomach. Nothing good ever came from "we need to talk" conversations. "Okay," she said tentatively.

Debbie laughed. "Relax," she said. "You're not in any trouble. It's just that you probably didn't hear that Sharmain had to go out on medical leave starting yesterday, and she's probably gonna be out for a few weeks. I'm trying to cover her projects, and I was wondering if you might be willing to take on one of them."

Rachel grimaced. "Historical fiction? Deb, you know I thrive on romance. Are you sure that you don't want to just have me proofread the final product?"

Debbie gave her a confident smile. "Rachel, if you tell anyone this, I'll deny it, but I think you're my strongest content editor, and I think if I put you on coffee table books, you'd make them into bestsellers. I think you can do historical fiction."

Rachel considered. That was an amazing show of confidence. "What's the project?"

"It's a standalone novel by an indie author named Dylan Roberts."

Rachel laughed. "So Bob comma Dylan?"

Debbie snickered. "It's not a pen name. He assured me. But it's a historical novel that takes place in the early twentieth century about a family that immigrates from Poland. Sharmain's worked on this guy's stuff before. It's good."

"Then why is he indie?" Rachel said.

Debbie gave her the side-eye. "Rachel, that's not fair and you know it. There are tons of amazing indie authors out there that choose not to go the traditional publishing route."

Rachel looked down shamefully. "Sorry," she said. "I think my brain is still out sick. Fine, I'll give it a try." She looked up as her email finally opened on her computer. "Is Sharmain okay?"

Debbie nodded. "Yeah. You know I can't tell you anything, but she'll be fine." She stood up. "Now that your email is on, I'll get that file to you shortly along with the timeline. Thanks, Rachel. I knew I could count on you." And then Debbie was gone, leaving Rachel to stare at her inbox.

She sighed. She knew she could probably edit an instruction book for changing oil in a car, but that didn't mean she would like it. But she knew if she had to go on emergency leave, her coworkers would have to cover her work, and she hoped they wouldn't gripe out loud about it. She opened her current project and got to work.

She was in the zone when a knock came on her door. She looked up to find Becca standing there. "Can I come in for a minute?" she asked.

Rachel was tempted to tell her that she was too busy at the moment, but the look on Becca's face softened her. She nodded. "Yeah, I think I'm at a good stopping point right now."

Becca came into the office, pulling the door shut behind her. She sat down on the extra chair. "Barry came over last night. He told me…everything?"

Rachel wasn't sure what Becca's definition of everything was, so she didn't want to take any chances. "Everything?" she asked.

Becca nodded. "He told me about Clarence. I have to admit, I was not really prepared for that. It's not that I have a problem with him being . . . well, he thinks he's bi, but I wasn't expecting it. And I'm kind of mad at myself about that. I mean, we're close. We've always been close. I'm really surprised that I didn't pick up on it. And that he didn't feel he could confide in me."

Rachel sighed. "From what Clarence tells me, I don't think that Barry was in any place to even confide in himself about it until very recently."

Becca looked down. "I should have known that the breakup with Karina broke him. I should have done something to get him away from her earlier. I knew it was bad, but I had no idea of the abuse she inflicted on him. I feel like such a bad sister."

Rachel sat quietly for a few moments. "I don't think that you could've done anything at the time," she said carefully. "I think that if you tried to get him out of the situation, he would've resisted, and maybe gotten mad at you. You know, I haven't been in an abusive relationship, but I have been in one that wasn't good for me in the long run, and if any of my friends had told me to get out of it, I would probably have doubled down and stayed longer, because it was *my* life, and I wouldn't have wanted anyone to tell me I was making a big mistake."

Becca looked into her eyes. "That makes sense," she said. "But maybe I should have known that something was off when he suddenly picked up and moved halfway across the country. And there I was, fixing him up with my coworker!"

Rachel reached out and put a hand over Becca's. "You were trying to help. And for what it's worth, I really liked him. A lot. Did . . ." She hesitated. "Did Barry tell you about me and Clarence?"

Becca winced and then nodded. "He wanted me to understand what was going on. I hope it's okay. Please don't be mad at him. It was really an important part of the story."

"I'm okay with it." Rachel had to swallow her embarrassment, but she wasn't mad at Jake. He had gotten the courage to come out to his sister, and that was huge. "Like I said, I really like Barry, and now that he and

Clarence are together, it means that we can stay friends. I'm okay with that." She noticed a tear making its way down Becca's face. "Are you okay? I mean, with all of this? I mean, I think that Barry's happy now. I'm happy for them. It might take me a bit to get over it not being me, but that's okay. The right people ended up together."

Becca gave her a grateful smile. "Thanks for saying that, Rachel. But I-I feel bad for putting you in this position. I was hoping we were going to be friends. We were starting to be."

"We *are* friends," Rachel assured her. "You did something really nice for me. Maybe misguided…" She noticed a slight smile on Becca's face. "But it came from your heart. I don't regret the time I spent with Barry. And I can see you and me, and Barry and me, becoming really good friends."

Becca nodded. "I think I can see that, too. I can't wait to meet Clarence. The look in Barry's eyes when he talks about him . . ."

Rachel grinned. "Yeah. I saw it too with Clarence. Listen, give me a few weeks just to pull myself together, and then we'll all get together and have dinner, or go to the movies or something. We can invite our other friends, Jess, Jerry, and Steve. I think you'd really like them."

Becca's smile was happy now. "I'd really like that." She stood up, came around the desk, and offered her arms up for a hug. Rachel fell into it. They stayed like that for several seconds, and then Becca pulled away, wiping at her eyes. "I have to get back to work. I'm on a deadline, you know."

Rachel laughed. "I'm familiar with the concept of deadlines!"

"I appreciate you coming early to talk to me," Jake said. He was gripping his glass of beer with both hands. Rachel thought it resembled a death grip. "I feel like we need to, you know, talk about what happened, just the two of us. To make sure we're both okay."

Rachel pulled at the label of her own bottle of beer. "No problem," she said. She was nervous. There was no getting around that. Talking to Jake was hard. She still felt the stirrings of attraction when she looked into his hazel eyes, so she did her best to look anywhere else. "I think it's a good idea for us to talk, to put everything out there."

"I wouldn't have wanted to go forward, with Clarence I mean, if it wasn't okay with you." Jake looked around the room. Maybe he was also worried about eye contact. "And I know for a fact he never would have. But I know your blessing doesn't mean that you're feeling great about all of this."

Rachel nodded absently. She had been rehearsing what she wanted to say to Jake ever since Clarence had called her earlier in the day requesting that they all meet at the pub. He had then texted later to ask Rachel to take this private meeting with Jake. She had been resistant at first, but she knew she couldn't avoid it forever. If she was going to have Clarence in her life, she had to work it all out, and the earlier the better.

"I'm not mad at you or anything," she said. "You never implied that we were going to have a relationship."

Jake closed his eyes briefly. "I mean, it's hard to date someone at all without having some sort of expectations of a future together. Otherwise, why even bother dating? When I met you, I was confused. I hadn't met Clarence yet. I had recently gotten out of a really long relationship with a really sick person." He paused. "I know that you know about narcissists. I don't know if Karina was a narcissist or if she had one of the many personality disorders I learned about in my psych major. I was too involved to spend any time diagnosing her. But as you know, people like that have a lot of charm and charisma. I got caught up in it. When it ended, I felt like nothing. I mean, like a void. Like my soul and body didn't even exist. I left home so I could have some space to figure out how to re-create myself, from the ground up. I have to admit, when I met you, I did entertain the idea for a few minutes that you might be the one to help me. But then there was the other thing."

Rachel nodded. "The thing about guys."

Jake sighed. "I had to find out. But I couldn't do it without letting you know that I was exploring. But I couldn't tell you the whole truth. Not even I knew what the whole truth was."

"And then you met Clare."

Jake looked into his glass of amber ale. "Then I met Clare." He laughed. "It sounds funny calling him that. The three of us and our nicknames. That's what got us into all of this trouble in the first place." He looked right at Rachel. "I felt it right away when I looked at Clarence. And the way he looked at me . . . it was a reflection of how I felt about him. All I could think about was seeing him again. I had to make that happen. But that didn't mean that I didn't still want to spend time with you."

"It sounds really confusing," Rachel conceded.

"It was." Jake took a sip of his beer. "I still didn't know if I wanted to take a chance on being with a man."

"What made you decide that you did?" Rachel asked.

Jake hesitated, then nodded with confidence. "I started to see a therapist. I had to. I had to have someone to talk to that wouldn't be shocked by my revelations, or judge me. I didn't want to come out to someone I knew just to get support. And I really made the right choice. Taking a dedicated hour once a week to talk things out helped me clarify a lot of things. And to recall a lot of things. It turns out that I didn't just suddenly start to be attracted to men. It was there all along. There were hints, small hints, all my life, but I never paid any attention to them. It's not like my family would have disowned me or anything. I have a great family. It's just that my awareness was . . . absent."

Rachel nodded. "Therapy, huh? I've been hearing a lot about that lately. So it really helped?"

"It did," Jake said. "A lot. I don't think I'm anywhere near out of the woods yet, though. I think I'll be working on things for a long time. I mean, there's still a lot I have to deal with. I have to talk to the rest of my family, to come out to them. Like I said, I know they'll accept it, especially when I tell them about Clarence, but it's still this whole manufactured thing that we do in our culture, having to come out to the people in our lives, to declare our sexuality to them . . . and sexuality is so fluid. It makes no sense. But still, we're at a place where we still have to do it. So I will. And then there's my friend Jayden." His face darkened. "I have to talk to him, make things right. I bought a plane ticket to go back to Greenway in two weeks so I can talk to my family and talk to Jayden. He won't answer any of my texts or calls, so I figure I'll just have to show up at his door and hope he doesn't slam it in my face." He smiled. "But I'm looking forward to it. As unnatural as it all feels, it will be a relief to have it all out there in the open." He laughed bitterly. "I wonder what Karina would say if she found out."

Rachel shrugged. "You get the last laugh," she said. "You're the one that ends up with someone wonderful, supportive, and gorgeous, who cares about you so much and would never hurt you."

Jake's face brightened. He nodded. "And don't forget that now that

Clarence and I are together, that also means that you're stuck with me." His jaw dropped. "Oh my God, I hope that wasn't insensitive. I didn't mean that—"

Rachel laughed. "Jake, don't worry about it," she said. "I might need some time to get my head on straight, but I'm happy now that we don't have to say goodbye forever. That we get to be friends. I liked you. I still like you. And I wasn't in love with you. I was just open to the possibility of love with you. And maybe I can still love you, but in a different way." She paused, looked at the table. "And I think that maybe I'll try out that therapy thing that everyone keeps talking about. Maybe it's time. Not just about the things that happened recently, but about the things that have been happening my whole life. My father."

Jake touched her hand for a moment and then pulled away. "I think that's a great idea." Suddenly, his eyes went wide. "Did Clarence tell you? During this whole fiasco in the last few days, I almost missed that the envelope came in the mail. I got into BU for graduate school! I'll be starting in the fall!"

"Oh my God!" Rachel jumped up and went to Jake for a hug. She held him tight. "I'm so happy for you! I know this is what you wanted! Congratulations!"

Jake beamed. "You know, I really feel this might be the first time in my life that everything's coming together for me. I don't want to jynx it by getting too excited, but . . . Hell, yes, I'm excited."

Rachel laughed, then sat down and lifted her beer bottle. "To new and happy things."

Jake raised his glass and touched it to Rachel's drink. "And to new friends." They both drank. Shortly after, Clarence arrived, ordered a beer at the bar, and sat down at the table.

EPILOGUE

Three Years Later

"TO DR. BARRETT!" SOMEONE CALLED OUT.

"To Dr. Barrett," everyone else yelled, and then there was the sound of champagne glasses clinking together.

"I can't believe you did it," Becca told Jake. "Your master's and doctorate in three years. And a great job lined up doing psychological testing!"

Jake beamed. "I'm living the dream." He reached out and took Clarence's hand. "And of course I could never have done it without—"

"Jack!" a man's voice called out, and then Jake's parents were in front of them, hugging their son. "Congratulations! The first person in our family to get a doctorate!"

His mother smiled. "Congratulations, Dr. Barrett," she said. She turned to Clarence. "And you, too, Dr. Barrett. Two doctors in the same family!"

Clarence's mother, Laurie, moved in closer. "Every Jewish mother's dream!" she crooned. Everyone laughed. Laurie hugged her son-in-law. "The other half of your family is very proud of you, Jake. We were so happy we could be here for your graduation."

"It's really incredible," Clarence's sister Tara said. "I always pictured

Clarence ending up as a clown in the circus, and probably marrying some acrobat—"

"That's only because that was what he told us he wanted," Jill said. "Remember when he used to smear his cheeks with mom's makeup and try to do magic tricks?"

Jake smiled and turned to his husband. "I think this might be a story you never told me," he teased. "I hope my lack of acrobatic skills wasn't a huge disappointment."

Clarence blushed and then leaned in closer. "Your acrobatic skills are just fine, thank you very much."

Rachel wandered over, holding the hand of a tall, thin man with short brown hair and scholarly glasses. "Congratulations, Jake!" she said with a grin. She pulled him in for a tight hug.

Once they pulled away, the man held out his hand, and Jake shook it. "Congratulations, Jake," he said. "Well done."

"Mom, Dad," Becca said. "Have you guys met Rachel's fiancé yet?"

Jake's mother's brows rose. "No, I don't think we have."

Rachel smiled brightly. "David and Melanie Barrett, this is my fiancé, Dylan Roberts. Dylan, these are Becca and Jake's parents."

"Nice to meet you," Melanie said, shaking Dylan's hand. David was next in line. "How did the two of you meet?"

Rachel blushed and then glanced at her fiancé. He gave her a nearly imperceptible nod. "Well, a few years ago, I was asked to edit this manuscript that was kind of not my genre, but I thought I'd give it a try anyway. It turned out I loved the book so much, I went back and read all of the author's previous work. I was so amazed. Probably the best writing I'd ever experienced, and I've read a lot of books. I mean a ton of books—"

"She was totally fangirling," Becca broke in. "She finally decided she had to reach out to the author and express how great she thought he was."

Rachel's face returned to pink. "I didn't hear back from him, so I just let it go. But when his book was published, I bought a copy and gave it a five-star review."

Dylan looked down and smiled at her. "The email she sent and the review got me thinking. I knew that Rachel was a professional editor, and that kind of praise is not given lightly. So based on the feedback, I felt confident enough to start querying for an agent. It took a while, but eventually

I found one that was willing to take a chance on me. It took even longer to find a publisher that was even willing to read my proposal for my next book. But eventually it happened, and I was given a contract. I wanted to share my excitement, and that's when it hit me that I needed to seek out this Rachel Morris and thank her for pushing me in the right direction. I emailed her, and she emailed back. And then I asked her to have dinner with me, to thank her properly."

"Dylan was living in Springfield at the time," Rachel said. "But it didn't take long for him to decide that Boston was really the place for him." She squeezed Dylan's hand.

"That's a really great story," Tara said. "Very romantic."

"It is," Clarence said. He took Rachel's free hand. "And Dylan's a great guy. He fit in with all of our friends so easily." He paused and then looked at Jake's parents. "Rachel asked me and Moe to walk her down the aisle at her wedding." He started to choke up a bit. "Of course we said yes."

"But we're not giving her away," Jake clarified, pointing his finger at his husband. "Just walking her down. There's a difference. Women don't belong to anyone, so they cannot be given away like possessions."

Rachel nodded. "That's right, Dr. Barrett. And don't you forget it. I belong to myself. It's just that I've made room in my life for other people who are special to me. But no one gives me away but me."

Jessica wandered over, carrying a small plate covered with finger foods. "The psych department puts on a pretty good reception," she said, shoving a small quiche in her mouth. She put the plate down on a table beside her. "Jake, Clare, come here. I want you to feel something." She took both of their hands and placed them flat on her extended stomach. "Both of them have been kicking up a storm all morning. I guess they figured out that it's a big day for one of their daddies."

Clarence felt a kick against his palm. He gasped. "Oh my God!" he exclaimed. "They're kicking now? When did that start?"

Jessica laughed. "They've been doing it for a couple months now, but not enough so you can feel it from the outside. Pretty cool, huh?"

"Can I try?" Melanie asked shyly.

Jessica smiled at her and then nodded. "You're the grandma. You have certain rights. But I don't want everyone pawing at my belly all afternoon, okay? Body autonomy and such."

While Jake's parents and Clarence's mother rushed to feel the movement in Jessica's belly, Clarence pulled Jake away from the crowd. He put hands on Jake's hips and closed the distance between them. "I'm so proud of you," he said softly. He gave him a gentle kiss on the lips. "You've worked so hard. You deserve everything you've earned."

Jake smiled happily. "I think the thing I'm most proud of is you," he said. "Working full time while getting your doctorate, and scoring a museum curator job, going on actual quests like a video game adventurer."

Clarence laughed. "It's not as dazzling as it sounds. I found a candy wrapper from 1984 the other day when looking for pottery shards."

"Mmm, ancient candy." Jake nestled his cheek against Clarence's shoulder. "We're more than halfway through the wait for our twins, and I think that's the most exciting thing I've ever anticipated." He pulled away and looked Clarence in the eyes. "I'm kind of scared. I've never been a dad before."

Clarence threw his head back and laughed. "Like I have? And you don't need to worry. Every dad has to start somewhere. And our kids will have two dads. They'll be so lucky. And they'll have Jess, their auntie-slash-tummy mummy. And Aunt Rachel. And all of the real aunts and uncles. There's nothing to be afraid of."

"But you're scared, too, aren't you?"

Clarence smiled. "Petrified. What if I do everything wrong, and screw them up? What if they hate me?"

"No one could hate you, Clare," Jake said. "You're amazing. I'll never forget how you helped me when we first met, and for the next year after that when I started grad school and tried to figure out what it meant to be a gay man. You comforted me, and you were so patient with me. You held me when I cried. And eventually I came out the other side, and now look at us. We're married, and we're expecting twins. We're both doctors, and we have our whole lives ahead of us. Things look really good for us."

Clarence nodded. "And Rachel's happy."

Jake nodded back. "And Rachel's happy."

Clarence grasped both of Jake's hands between them. "I'm still scared," he said. "But I know that with you beside me and our friends and family around us, we'll figure it out. I mean, we really have no choice now, do we?"

Jake laughed. "I'd reply that we always have a choice, but in this case, I think you're right. These babies are coming, and they're coming for us. And they're gonna double the size of our family. Clare, we knew what we were doing when we asked Jess to be our surrogate. Well, I mean after she had begged us to be our surrogate for two years and we were finally ready. We'll be great."

"We always are," Clarence agreed. He dropped one of Jake's hands. "Let's go back to the group and rescue Jessica from a thousand probing hands. And then let's get everyone together to leave for dinner. I was so far behind today that I forgot to eat lunch, and the tiny food here's just not cutting it." He squeezed Jake's hand.

Jake nodded. "Let's go do it," he replied. The two men headed back to their friend and family. It was time to begin spending the night in celebration of everything that they had all become and were still becoming.

THE END

ACKNOWLEDGMENTS

This is my first standalone book. Usually, I get so into my characters that I don't feel the whole story has been told. But this time, I have that one-and-done feeling.

Thank you to everyone who has supported me thus far—far too many to list right now. But I do thank my readers, and those who have encouraged me to keep up my passion projects.

Thank you to author Bobbie Isabel, who gave me a prompt to write about a character named Clarence. I had no idea where it would lead, and it led me right here. Thank you to both Bobbie and Chris, my sprinting pals, for listening to me reading all those long chapters out loud! Thank you to author Clint Chico for being the alpha beta, and brother Jonathan Meltzer, for begging for more chapters!

I want to encourage writers to write about LGBTQ+ characters, and readers to read their work. We all have a voice. We need to use it. Especially now. Thank you to everyone out there who takes the time to acknowledge and advocate.

Thanks as always to my editor Nicole Frail, cover designer Jai Design, and photographer Melana Gilligan. You are my entourage, and I would go nowhere without you!

And as always, thanks to Al and Tory. I couldn't do it without you.

ABOUT THE AUTHOR

Debby Meltzer Quick is a full-time social worker in Portland, Oregon. She has been writing for fun since age twelve. Growing up in Massachusetts, she became a huge fan of Boston sports, especially the Red Sox and the Patriots, and she aspired to be a sports reporter. She is an avid reader of fiction. She lives with her husband, daughter, two cats, and one rabbit. She has completed two series of seven books each that take place in the fictional city of Eastboro, Massachusetts, in the 1980s. Watch for more books in the McKinney High and Anomaly series coming soon!

ALSO AVAILABLE

May I Have Your Attention Please

McKinney High Class of 1986 Book 1

Do you believe in love at second sight?

James Newell never expected to fall hard for Sally Bachman. But that's exactly what he did on the first day of junior year. He and Sally had been acquaintances in junior high until Sally left for a year to go to private school. But now she's back, and something has changed. It only takes three days for this romance to start to blossom, and once it does, there's no turning back. Not that they would want to turn back. James and Sally follow their hearts and their hormones through a year of discovery while also having to navigate social disparities at school, addiction and mental health problems in their families, and difficulty with paying attention in their classes. They cling closely to their group of friends while they learn about the pleasures and surprises brought on by first love. But can first love really last forever?

Availabe in paperback and e-book.
ISBN: 979-8987187401

I Just Can't Say
I Love You

McKinney High Class of 1986 Book 2

How Do You Know if Love is Real?

Kim and Carl became fast friends in kindergarten, but they were struck by the cooties plague in second grade. For years, it was the boys versus the girls, but Kim has missed her first school friend. Now they are juniors, and Kim has a plan. She has gotten Carl to agree to go to the Junior Prom with her, and she has some ideas about how the evening will end. Carl won't know what hit him. But both of these teens have no idea that their childhood traumas will affect their ability to thrive in a romantic relationship. As Kim and Carl start down a road to love, they must learn to trust each other with their lives, and their hearts. Their journey takes them through high school and across the country, into a new life that neither of them could ever have expected.

Availabe in paperback and e-book.
ISBN: 979-8987187418

Absolutely and Totally Smitten

McKinney High Class of 1986 Book 3

Can you climb back up after you've fallen from the top of the world?

Chris Mahoney was born destined for greatness. He is a natural leader and rules a posse of junior high bad boys. But in high school, things start to change for Chris. He discovers first love, and he starts to mend his bad boy ways. When circumstances beyond his control lead to heartbreak and loneliness, Chris must find a way to get through, and humble himself enough to ask for help. Soon, he and his friends are off to college, and new experiences. Growth and more heartache follow him into his adult years, until something unexpected occurs. He encounters an old acquaintance from high school, and slowly becomes intrigued with her charm. But can he open himself up to possibly being hurt yet again?

Availabe in paperback and e-book.
ISBN: 979-8987187425

The Stories That Must Be Told

McKinney High Class of 1986 Book 4

Falling in love takes courage. Falling in love after trauma takes everything you have inside of you.

Stavros endured a horrendous loss at a very young age. He has to learn to adjust to go on with his life, but when he experiences another loss as a young adult, he has to learn how to cope.

Darlene has had her own traumas and coping is not her strength. She manages to get through the years with the help of her friends, but when the traumas start to pile up, Darlene must figure out a new plan, and fast.

When Stavros and Darlene meet for the first time as adults, they have been through more tragedies than the average person could bear. They must decide what information about their pasts is safe to share as well as whether they can help each other with their ongoing recovery.

Availabe in paperback and e-book.
ISBN: 979-8987187432

Don't Say
A Word

**Anomaly
Book 1**

The Reed children, Kaya and Graham, and their mother are devastated when their father suddenly decides to leave the family and go out into the world to find himself. But as time goes by, they must move on. What could be better than starting high school with your best friends, making the cheerleading team, and having everything you ever wanted? It's the best time of Kaya's life. But then something changes. At first, Kaya doesn't think the messages she's hearing are a big deal, and she's baffled by Graham's concern. But soon it becomes obvious that Kaya is hearing things that no one else can hear. This doesn't cause her too much distress, until one day she hears something so terrible, she can't ignore it, and neither can anyone else, including the authorities. Is Kaya really as ill as everyone thinks she is, or is something else going on? Graham makes it his life's goal to find out before it's too late for his sister.

Availabe in paperback and e-book.
ISBN: 979-8987187470

Blinding Justice

**Anomaly
Book 2**

Kaya Reed has survived her college ordeals and is finally marrying her longtime boyfriend, Grayson Pike, in Wisteria. But on her wedding day, she has an unexpected and uninvited guest: her father, Peter.

Alice Telman, a young woman who can sense when someone is lying, is working in the District Attorney's office in Florence, the next town over. She is dealing with her own issues. Among other things, Alice is trying to find out what is going on with local emancipated minor, Brad McHale, who has been panhandling in the park, and lying about why.

One day at the medical center, Kaya and Alice physically run into each other and sets off a chain of events that will lead the two women to a lifetime of friendship and adventure, as well as intrigue and danger, but they wouldn't want things any other way.

Availabe in paperback and e-book.
ISBN: 979-8987187487

www.ingramcontent.com/pod-product-compliance
Lightning Source LLC
Chambersburg PA
CBHW051952220626
47052CB00004B/916